LINDA SMOLKIN

LOVE THE WAY THEY LIE

A NOVEL

If you tell us that you've never lied in your life,
you'd be lying.
–*Anonymous*

I have a confession.
It turns out that we all lied.
But are some lies acceptable or forgivable?
Specifically, mine?
–Maggie Simmons

Chapter 1

The sound of his text annoys me—a rapid-firing ping he always promises to change. At first, I ignore it until the phone pings a second time.

"Babe, you forgot to put your phone on silent," I say and reach over, ready to fold my arm over Nate's chest. But my husband's side of the bed is empty.

I turn over and pull Nate's pillow closer, smelling the lingering scent of his aftershave. It's not only from the night before. It always lingers and takes me back to our honeymoon from three years ago.

We were heading home from Mexico and, with time to spare, hit up some stores in the airport. Nate wanted to buy some souvenirs for a few of his clients, although I thought Mezcal with the worm would be a better choice for his more demanding ones. After a few purchases, we stopped at another duty-free shop, where Nate tried various aftershaves. "This one," I said, with my nose against the nape of his neck. It was the third scent he'd tried. "You're right," he agreed after bending down to kiss me. He liked it so much that he bought an extra bottle.

The honeymoon thoughts linger as I roll onto my back, pulling the covers over my bare shoulders and rubbing my feet together to warm them. It's a Friday morning and I'm usually the one who gets up first on weekdays, but an evening out with friends and one too many mojitos the night before does a number on me. My head pounds and my throat feels like sandpaper. A glass of water sits on Nate's nightstand, and I inch my way toward it, gulping it down with record speed.

"Hey, gorgeous," Nate says as he opens the bathroom door. He has a blue striped towel around his waist and is using a smaller one to dry his hair. He walks toward the bed, bends down, and kisses my cheek a few times.

"I have to turn on the light, is that okay?" he says in a soft voice and pushes my hair back. His finger gets caught in a few strands, which isn't out of the ordinary. My hair always seems to be a tangled mess after my nights of tossing and turning.

He switches on the lamp and then removes the towel from his waist. I squint, watching him walk to the other side of the room after he hangs the towel on the closet door nearby. The light wrestles with my mini-hangover, but I can't look away. I don't want to. For a guy in his mid-forties, Nate's in great shape, fit and slim with long, lean muscles. He vows he'll never let himself go like a lot of his friends and makes it a priority to hit the gym several times a week.

With his back toward me, he's rummaging through a drawer. His tan lines are fading but still visible enough to tease me. They nudge me out of my sleepiness, having a similar effect as my morning coffee.

A lone polka-dotted sock sits on the floor next to the bed. I reach down and throw it playfully at him. "Is this what you're looking for?"

Nate turns around after it hits him on the ass. "Good aim." He picks up the sock and walks over to me, extending it with two fingers and away from his face, as if to pretend he took it out of the dirty wash basket.

"Don't you dare!" I yell and hide under the covers.

He sits on the edge of the bed and reaches over, trying to pull the covers down. I hold onto them for dear life until realizing Nate's no longer holding the sock. Instead, he's working his hands up my body, from my legs to my hips, stopping on my thighs as he caresses them.

It's always a warm welcome to feel his touch but my head throbs again. "Nate," I whisper.

"Maggie," he whispers back like he always does before we start fooling around.

"I really want to, but I have a nasty headache."

"Oldest excuse in the book," he jokes and props the pillow up to slide next to me.

"No, seriously, I do. Should've stopped at one mojito."

He motions for me to sit up and starts working his magic on my shoulders. "How many did you have?"

"Two. Maybe three and a half?" My words barely come out as he presses his thumb against the side of my neck and works his way up behind my ear.

"I have the perfect remedy." He leans closer, and I can feel his breath on me. "We get it on, then you call in sick, and go back to sleep."

His idea tempts me. I haven't taken a sick day in a couple of years, and Nate knows it. "Sounds so good. But we're having a going-away lunch for Tanya."

He pulls away slowly while clenching his jaw. It's his usual sign of disappointment. When he runs a hand through his light-brown waves, I have second thoughts.

The way his muscle flexes when he lifts his arm gets me every time.

I lean forward, kissing away a drop of water that has fallen down and onto his sideburn. "You know, I could be a little late for work."

Chapter 2

Thirty-two seconds—that's all it takes. Thirty-two seconds from the moment I push the button and wait for the "walk" sign to flash and allow me to cross. Sometimes it's shorter. This morning, though, the wait leaves me impatient. I'm already late for work after my morning romp with Nate, and my to-do list gets longer by the minute in my head as I watch the scene unfold in front of me.

Two policemen, wearing neon-yellow vests with whistles hanging from their necks, stand in the street, controlling traffic. A few raindrops usually send the traffic lights across from my office building into hibernation. This time, we can't blame the weather. It's something more serious affecting the lights, which seem to have more mood swings than my former adolescent self.

This morning, the police appear to unsuccessfully calm down a cyclist who's been sideswiped by a guy in a fancy SUV. The bike's a mess, tangled tires and all, and the cyclist's profanity turns out to be as nasty. I'm not opposed to profanity. But I'm selective, choosing my f-bombs wisely and for the occasional shit-storm.

My coworkers wave at me from across the street and stand there waiting. I wave them on and smile. It could be awhile. Even as the cyclist spews out his anger, the driver keeps his cool—perhaps attempting to stay out of trouble. He looks like he stayed up all night and is now nursing a hangover with his wrinkled suit and disheveled hair—at least what's left of it as his two bald spots almost meet in the middle.

Watching the scene brings back memories. We had an SUV once, an expensive one. Actually, it was Nate's. He traded it in before we got married for an affordable convertible, one that caught my eye that still had plenty of room. Sometimes he makes fun while driving it; apparently, he thinks jade green is a little too girly but appreciates all the fun that comes with it. When we bought it, the salesman mentioned its zippiness, which Nate discovered on the expressway when his kid got sick in the back as we zoomed around a few bends.

So, you've figured out that I have a husband, Nate. What else? Two stepkids, Max and Emily—nice ones, depending on their mood—or actually, mine. A decent job. A three-bedroom townhouse outside of Miami. And, yeah, I'm reminded how damn good my life is—compared with the guys in the accident and the homeless man sitting on a flattened cardboard box curbside. Crossing the street a few minutes later, I smile at him and enter the building, making my way up to the fourteenth floor.

Our large office bustles with its usual frenetic energy as colleagues have their heads down, camouflaged in paperwork or peering at their computer screens. Jillian waits for me at the end of the hallway by my cubicle, phone in one hand, pen in the other. "Hey, Maggie, I tried calling you."

"You did? When?" I lie, slipping the phone in my pocket.

"Marketing wants to know if we can increase the ad budget for the small-spaces line," she says, leaning against the cubicle wall.

I drop my purse and cardigan onto my desk, and push the space bar to wake up my laptop. "By how much?"

"Three percent. They're feeling the pressure to get sales up to make their quarterly numbers."

It's true. Sales have taken a hit, ever since research revealed that a ton of consumers are buying secondhand furniture and throwing on a slipcover for half-assed facelifts. As much as the marketing department worries, I worry more. As a senior buyer for Demora Furnishings, one of the largest home goods retailers on the East Coast, I have to figure out ways to get sales up. It's the career I've chosen, one that leads to some sleepless nights thinking about new business, existing lines, competition, and a bad fiscal year as young customers cut back on spending to pay off student loans.

I open my monthly spreadsheets, comparing two different lines. Jillian waits while I push the mouse around and make some calculations. "Tell them that's fine. I'll move some money around in the budget."

"Cool. Sounds good," she says, pulling down her pencil skirt as she straightens her back.

"And tell them we'll do a promo," I continue, looking up at her. "A two-day, twenty-five percent off deal. I'll put together the product brief with more info."

As Jillian nods in agreement and walks off, our intern's voice squeaks out from the intercom, reminding everyone about Tanya's last day and her lunch in the conference room at one.

We'll all miss Tanya, especially me after working with her for the past four years, sharing our stories and space across from one another. Tanya always teases me about the mess in my cubicle. This morning, papers overflow in hers, with two wastebaskets filled to the brim as she makes sense of what to ditch and keep for the new guy taking her place.

"What will I do without you, huh?" I joke and swivel around in my chair.

She stands up and lifts her arm to smell under it. "Damn, they need to make triple extra-strength for moments like these."

"You didn't answer my question."

She scrunches up a piece of paper and throws it at me, hitting her cubicle wall instead. "You could come with me. Then you wouldn't have to wonder."

"Yeah, right. Must be nice to have a career change and say screw it all."

Tanya's in her mid-fifties, almost twenty years older than me, with fewer responsibilities: no husband, no mortgage, no kids. Some might think she's sad not having to check off those expected life accomplishments. In Tanya's case, she's free and unburdened. And she mentions it more than once, as if she's rubbing it in or, perhaps, trying to convince herself.

"I've had about five screw-it-all moments already. You should try it," she says and sinks into her chair to sort through a pile on her desk.

"Hello? I need this job."

"Nothing has to last forever," she teases.

"Well, feels like I'm married to it, since we're short-staffed and the work keeps piling up." A ping comes through as an email notification, and I wait to check. "What do you mean by screw-it-all moments?"

"I change my life every four years, like when a driver's license expires. Started it while living in Jersey. Life's too short to be stagnant." She pauses and looks down. "Besides, it's not like I'm that amazing at any one thing to make a difference in someone's life."

I laugh. Not only at how ridiculous it sounds but also how sad, if you feel you're not making a difference. She doesn't dwell, though. It's a matter-of-fact statement with no hidden meaning because she lives her life to its fullest—at least every four years when she tries something new.

"Seems like a good plan," I say while thinking about how time flies, not remembering the last time I looked closely at my driver's license. "You know," I add, turning my chair, "can't remember the last time I renewed mine."

As I lean back to grab my purse, my wallet falls out and rolls in front of Tanya's cube. She grabs it and pulls out my license, placing it an inch from her nose to read what she calls the fine print. "Looks like you should've had your screw-it-all moment a couple of weeks ago."

I panic and jump out of my chair. "What the—let me see."

"How could you not notice?" She raises an eyebrow and gives me a look, the kind my mom gave when I was a kid and she'd catch me eating raw cookie dough.

How could I not notice? Because who looks at their own driver's license, especially with those photos from hell? Only bouncers and cops—or maybe a potential serial killer, pretending not to believe your age, hoping to track down your home address for their next bloodthirsty kill.

Tanya hands me back my wallet. "Looks like you'll be busy for the next few hours. Better bring a good book while you wait."

"Or do some serious people-watching," I say and, before leaving, grab my bag to head out to the Department of Motor Vehicles, hoping not to get pulled over along the way.

Chapter 3

Reading people's minds. Flying at lightning speed. Being invisible. If someone surveyed the most popular superpowers, these three would probably top the list. Not for me. Mine would be having instant knowledge of the wait time in a grocery store line, the bank, or any place, for that matter—and the DMV where I'm now waiting.

At this point, it's impossible to know how long before they get to me. I guess it wouldn't matter if my other superpower was napping peacefully until it was my turn. But naps aren't my strong point. Neither is checking when my license expires, obviously.

The atmosphere becomes thick with the stench of sweat and boredom as I fidget uncomfortably on the cheap plastic chair, crossing one leg, and then the other. On each side of me, two men fill out paperwork on a clipboard, and in front, a mother keeps her son occupied with crayons and coloring books featuring cars and trucks. She bends down to pick up a crayon and her polished nails in a deep red catch my attention. It makes me look down at my own chipped polish, wishing we could swap.

I turn around and see that the line now extends out the door. Neglecting Tanya's recommendation to bring a book, I check my email and social media until my phone's nearly out of juice.

A robotic voice throws out numbers in a sound similar to the one at the crosswalk near my office. They get called out until I hear "D92 at window seven" and jump up as if I'd won a game of bingo at my mom's community center on a Saturday afternoon.

Anxiety washes through me as I approach the counter, not knowing what to expect or if the clerk will reprimand me for my expired license. She takes my paperwork and, when she turns it over to check out the back, she frowns as the document slices her finger and blood drips onto the counter.

"Not again," she says, walking off. A minute later, the clerk returns with a bandage wrapped around her thumb and cleans up the mess in front of us. She puts on her glasses and types onto the computer keyboard. "Hmm," she mumbles as she looks up and down at the form, comparing its information with what's on her screen. "Did you know you have an outstanding ticket?"

I lean over for a better look. "Really?" I say in disbelief.

"Uh-huh, speeding."

"Speeding? I don't remember getting a notice for it," I shoot back.

She looks up and snickers. "That's what they all say."

"No, seriously, I don't. And I'm the one checking the mail."

"Let me get you a copy," she says and slides off the chair toward the printer on the opposite counter.

The clerk comes back over and hands me the printout, including a picture from the speed camera and, sure enough, it's our convertible. But it's not me driving. It's Nate. And he has a passenger, a woman I don't recognize with short hair and a denim jacket. She's leaning in close with her arm on his shoulder, her lips close to his ear as if she's whispering—or about to kiss him.

My heart beats out of control and my stomach drops. My hands begin to shake.

The picture has the date stamped on the top right corner: April 7, 2018—less than a month ago. Right away, I pull out my cell and check the day; it's a Saturday. From the note on my calendar, it was a girls' weekend in Key West with my best friend Rachel.

"Ma'am," the clerk blurts out, pulling me out from my trance. "We have people waiting. What would you like to do?"

My mind starts racing. "Shit, I wasn't even driving!" I snap. It's not her fault, but don't we wish we could all blame the DMV for something?

She looks at me above her glasses with a glint of impatience. "Ma'am," she says calmly. "If you own the car and it's registered to you, we can't renew your license." She pauses and we have a staring contest until she continues. "Do you want to check with whoever's driving and come back?"

"No, that's okay," I say and hand her my credit card to pay the fine, holding back the tears, thinking the worst.

She glances at me sympathetically, not requiring mind-reading skills to know what's going on. "Don't worry. If you can prove it was paid, we'll give you a refund."

I hold back the tears again when she asks me to look into the camera that's attached to the top of her monitor. The attendant at the window next to me tells her customer to smile. Mine doesn't ask. She knows I can't fake a smile to make a shitty DMV picture look even less shitty.

Who's the woman?

Where were they going?

Is he having an affair? Actually, another one?

How could I miss the warning signs?

Turns out trading in the SUV for the convertible saved me in more ways than one. No high payments. No worrying that somebody would hit our expensive car. And obviously, no need for a private investigator.

The clerk tells me to take a seat or step aside until they call my name. Numbers on monitors and long lines of people flood my vision. My head spins with thoughts of Nate laughing and sharing secrets with another woman, buying her dinner, having sex with her ... after having sex with me only hours ago.

I lean against the wall while waiting for my license and hold the printout close to my face, trying to make out the passenger. She has short, light-colored hair, possibly blonde, and one thing's for sure: this mystery woman is enjoying the hell out of my husband's company. I can't make out her face since the image is in black and white and shows her from the side. But sure as hell, I can pick out Nate anywhere. He loves his Georgia Tech baseball caps and often wears one to show off his alma mater pride.

A boy about five years old runs around in front of me, then stops, stares, and shoots me a smile. I smile back at this cute kid, all innocence, before he continues on his wild rampage until his dad asks him to calm down. The scene reminds me of how Nate's always telling his son, Max, to stop running around in stores. It makes me sad, thinking how I'll have to confront him, ask him about this stranger who's forced her way between us—and even sadder thinking about the worst-case scenario, that our marriage might be over, wondering how much I could lose by not seeing my stepkids, those sometimes bratty sweethearts of ten and thirteen.

It's not the time to let that sentimental crap fog my vision.

And it's not the time to let any of it be an excuse for Nate's bad behavior—especially when he told me before we got married that he'd never do it again and begged me to stay.

I snap out of it when they call my name from somewhere in the distance. As I go to the window, another attendant hands me the license. I take one look and realize that from this moment on, any time I see my ID, the thought of Nate with another woman would consume me.

She's so different from me, with my lifeless dark hair and large nose that's taken as one of those before shots from a plastic surgeon's website. After all these years, it seems that Nate does have a type—a type that looks nothing like me. Blondes with short hair. Maybe that's why he's always telling me not to chop mine off. Maybe he was trying to change the subject. Or hiding his wandering eye. Whatever the reason, I'm now confronted with his deceit again.

Is it the same woman he had an affair with before? She also had short, blonde hair, like the one in the DMV photo. Why didn't I learn my lesson the first time?

The little boy, who ran wild a minute ago, bumps into me and my license goes flying, landing on the filthy floor. The father apologizes and grabs his son by the arm, holding onto him while reaching down. He hands my license over as the boy wails, and I run toward the exit, throwing the door open and almost tripping over the metal DMV sign on the sidewalk.

As I dash into the lot, a driver slams on his horn and calls me an idiot for not looking. It startles me, and I move to the side as he speeds away while flipping me off. I want to match his gesture but instead dig for my keys, dumping everything out of my purse between two parking spaces before realizing I'm standing next to my car.

He promised me it wouldn't happen again. He promised! Once in the car, I yell a few f-bombs while banging on the steering wheel, wishing it was Nate's head.

CHAPTER 4

It's a little after noon and I'm still in the DMV parking lot, deciding where to go. They're expecting me back at the office. Deadlines loom. Creative briefs need to be written. Tanya's going-away luncheon is about to start. There's not an ounce of strength in me to put on a happy face and skip down the hall as if nothing happened. I charge my phone and then call Tanya and apologize, making up an excuse that it's still a long wait and then wish her well in her new adventure.

As I sit in my car, the details—or lack of them—begin to haunt me. Who knows what Nate has been hiding from me? I slam my fist into my leg over and over until my thigh starts to throb. I can't do this. Not again. I start the engine, pull out of the spot, and hightail it home while Nate's at work.

Chili, my Golden Lab named after her beautiful cinnamon coat and chilled-out demeanor, greets me at the door, all happy with her tail wagging. Normally, she goes out right away. This time, I'm on a mission and she follows me down the hall.

We live in Nate's house, although, technically, it's now ours after he put my name on the deed once we got married. Nate bought it right after we met, with some life insurance money he had stashed away after his mother died a few years back.

It's a stunning three-bed Mediterranean-style townhouse built in the early nineties with major renovations by the previous owner—a few walls blown out, creating an open plan, along with a modern kitchen with white marble counters, and a closet-turned-powder room at the front.

Nate says he'll never own another house made out of stucco since he's watched every other neighbor dip into their savings to fix cracks and crevices. Ours blends in nicely and matches the Mediterranean feel of our Floridian neighborhood filled with townhouses, condos, and single-family houses.

Chili continues to follow me into Nate's home office that's in the back on the first floor. He always keeps the room neat and orderly so I need to be careful, making sure nothing gets moved, checking the receipts on his desk, anything that might be from a hotel or a restaurant. Then I touch the keyboard to wake up the laptop.

All of Nate's passwords—from the computer to his email—are etched in my brain, and by accessing them from his laptop, there's no worrying about two-step verification. His email pops up and, at the same time, my phone vibrates with a message from him.

It was fun this morning. How's your headache?

His message makes me snicker and instead of responding, I throw my phone on the chair next to the desk.

A quick search in his already opened emails comes up empty. Then I try the same with his folders. An email exchange between him and a college friend catches my eye and the first line mentions his recommendation of a tax guy in Colorado. There's one more exchange between the two of them with a "more tax advice" subject line. It hasn't been opened yet so that one's left alone.

Next, I try logging in to the cloud to check out his texts, and it's not the same password. Various choices come to mind until my third attempt, Emily's birthday, works. And that's when it hits me: I shouldn't be snooping, no matter what he's done. But it's too late because my curiosity gets the better of me and overrides my moral compass.

The text icon taunts me. I hesitate for a minute then click. At the top, the text he sent me a minute ago. Then exchanges with Max and Emily, followed by a few from his college buddies. And then someone named Kira, someone Nate's never mentioned before. And even though the woman from the DMV photo has short, blonde hair, she's not the same woman from his first affair. Because I'll never forget that woman's name.

Next to Kira's text, there's a gray moon icon. I pull out my phone to do a quick search on what that means. Well, isn't that interesting? It allows you to mute alerts instead of getting them pushed to you in real-time.

My heart pounds. I'm scared to open it, fearful for what's there. I do it anyway, scrolling to the bottom, from the beginning of their texts in October 2017. I do some quick math in my head and realize it's a good six months before the DMV fiasco. Six months of not knowing about her, not even knowing if it's the same woman from the photo.

The first text is from Nate.

Hi, Kira, it's Nate. How was your weekend?

The next few exchanges make me nauseous. I want to look away but can't.

Had a great weekend, thanks. Yours?

Was nice. Took the kids to the beach. Thought about you.

She responds with a blushing smiley face.

Thought about you keeps replaying in my head. Was he thinking about their talks? About a flirty exchange? And was he fantasizing about her this morning when he was pounding away at me?

My heart beats faster with each new text, which happens about every other week. Saying good morning to each other with cute emojis. Talking about the places they've never been. Nate giving advice on how to deal with the ex-husband. Kira wishing him sweet dreams during a late-night exchange.

I scroll some more and that's when the photos start. Kira standing on a boardwalk in a tank top and shorts, giving the peace sign. Nate in front of his office wearing his favorite tie, the fun one with the flamingos … the one I bought him.

My fingers work at a record pace to find March 2018, a month or so before Nate's speeding ticket. Nothing exciting or different in the text exchange until, two weeks later, their outing comes together in front of me.

Hey gorgeous what are u doing next Saturday?

He called her gorgeous.

Wanna take a day trip somewhere?

I scroll down to see her response.

Sounds great! Let me see if my mom can watch Olivia.

Olivia. Is that her dog? Her daughter? Doesn't matter because, whether they've slept together or not, Nate knows all about this woman's life—and hasn't told me about her.

Their outing comes complete with more photos, one where they're standing next to our convertible taking a selfie. In the photo, she's leaning close to him with her face nuzzled into his neck and he's wearing his Georgia Tech baseball cap and a big smile. She's so different from me—tall, a couple of inches shy of Nate, who's five eleven, and so pretty, with a small nose and freckles sprinkled across her cheeks. They look happy, as if they enjoy spending time together with that cozy feeling you get when you're with someone you like—or love.

While still in his text messages, I scroll past more photos from their day trip and each day after that. Around ten in the morning, every day except for weekends, he texts her *good morning, gorgeous.* And every time, she texts him back, *hey, handsome.*

"Asshole!" I yell. Chili jumps up and her nails scratch across the floor as she runs out of the room. I log out, switch off the computer, and head to the foyer to find Chili curled up in a ball.

"Chili, you're not the asshole," I say in a sweet voice as she flops her tail back and forth. "You're a good girl, yes, you are!"

She gets up and sits in place, waiting until the leash is on, and we're ready to go. We make our way down the sidewalk as a woman approaches. My breath catches and my stomach tightens. She has blonde hair and my first thought is, *That's her. That's Kira.* Her tall, slender figure, unlike mine that's barely five foot three, makes me envious, because anything, even a potato sack, would look good on her.

She extends a manicured hand to shake mine after putting a casserole dish down on the grass. "Not sure if we've met. I'm Chloe."

Relief sets in. Of course it's not Kira. Although at this point, Nate could be sleeping with every woman on our block.

"My husband and I moved in a few weeks ago," she continues. "Emily made us some brownies. So sweet of her. And your husband, Nate, a great guy."

I stop short from laughing and a quick snort comes out. She fixes the bottom of her pants when it catches on the top of her lace-up sandals. Her long bangs fall across the bridge of her nose and she pushes them aside. "He offered to do our taxes for free since my hubby's in the military."

"That's so nice," I say and start walking away with Chili. "Sorry, gotta run. Was great meeting you!"

"What was your name again?" she asks.

"Maggie, and this is Chili."

She turns around before walking off. "Hope to see you again, Maggie. Maybe we can hang out sometime over a glass of wine?"

I nod, while thinking about confronting Nate and seeing what else he's been hiding from me. She waves good-bye and, after realizing it's close to three, I walk down to the bus stop with Chili to meet the kids while trying to hold it together.

Chapter 5

Nate has Max and Emily every other weekend to abide by the custody agreement with his ex-wife Heather. Sometimes when she's out of town, we'll get the kids during the week. The every-other-week visits, though, have been routine for these several years we've been together.

Since Nate's accounting workload can't accommodate the afterschool drop-offs, I'm the one who meets the kids at the bus stop every other Friday. The kids don't mind; they seem to like having me around since I'm the one who lets them watch TV and eat sugary snacks close to dinnertime. It's our little secret that Nate doesn't know about.

Now, it seems Nate has his own little secret, one that he'll lie about—confess to—or both by making up his own version. My mind continues to race. I keep cool for now, for the sake of my stepkids, the trust I've earned, and our little family.

Chili sits next to me and we wait for the bus. The day, overcast and gloomy, matches my mood. I dig in my purse and fish out my sunglasses to hide my red-rimmed eyes and then pull out my cell to search for a song, settling on "Summertime Sadness." My headphones become tangled into complicated knots, a challenging mission to unravel even for a Navy SEAL.

I place them back into my purse and play the song from my cell's speaker while sitting on the steps on the sidewalk, with Chili next to me. It's a song Nate loves, too, and I remember the first time we kissed and couldn't stop. How his stubble left a red rash on my chin. The way he brushed my hair away from my face and told me I was beautiful.

The song ends and goes into "I Fall Apart," another gloomy one. A moment later, the bus approaches and several kids pour out. As always, Max and Emily are the last ones off because they love to sit in the back. They even make it a priority to cut to the front of the line in the morning to make it to the back before other kids grab the spot.

Max throws his backpack to the ground and takes off his Nike hoodie to uncover wavy brown hair similar to Nate's, especially how it curls up at the ends when it gets too long. He bends down to pet Chili and starts humming to the lyrics. "That's a sad song. And why are you wearing sunglasses?" he says, looking down at me.

Emily, who's dressed in all black no matter how hot it is, rolls her eyes and kicks his bag with her combat boots. "Dude, don't pretend like you're all into the lyrics. That gummy bear song is more your speed."

"Shut up, jerk," Max says and pinches her arm.

"Ow!" Emily yells and pushes her brother until he crashes into a car.

"Maggie, Emily's being mean to me again," he says, as if he's keeping score.

I get up and brush off the back of my pants. "Emily, be nice to your brother. And Max, watch your language."

"She started it!" Max shouts and runs after Emily, who's already sprinting down the block toward our house.

"Loser, catch me," Emily teases, her auburn hair flying in the wind as her long, skinny legs take the lead. She continues up the path to our home, leaving us in the dust, and then turns around, arms folded, covering up her Ramones T-shirt. She stands there, sulking as if she's straight out of a punk fashion ad, minus the black liner and matching nail polish. "When's Dad gonna give me my own key? You don't need to keep meeting us."

I reach into my pocket and pull out my set. "When you're responsible with the stuff you already have. Do you even know where your watch is?"

Emily looks down at her bare wrist, then shrugs with a bored response. It's often her nonchalant approach to life that I blame Nate and his ex-wife Heather for, but decide it's best not to be too critical—after all, they're not my kids.

Max grabs the keys from my hand and opens the front door, both of them rushing in as they slip off their shoes and throw their backpacks onto the wooden bench in the hallway. Footsteps from the second floor make me nervous since Nate's never home this early from work. I'm reassured it's him when he calls out, "Hi, guys."

What the hell is he doing home? And God, I hope there's no evidence left behind from my snooping.

I pull out the keys, still in the lock, and throw them into a dish on the glass table next to the coatrack. "Homework before anything else," I say out of habit, forgetting that it's hit or miss with weekend assignments.

"We had subs, so no homework this time!" Emily sings out as she skips into the kitchen. Max follows her with a jump in the air to show his excitement.

Nate runs down the stairs, almost tripping as he ties the drawstring of his gray joggers, and comes toward me for a kiss as I pull away.

"What's wrong? Something happen at work?"

"Nothing's wrong. Just tired," I lie. "Why are you home so early?" I can hardly look at him. I'm afraid I'll cry again or scream at him in front of the kids as we make our way to the kitchen.

"A client canceled at the last minute, so I slipped out early to surprise you guys," he says and stares at me, scrunching his forehead.

My hands start shaking. "How long have you been home?"

He looks at his watch. "I don't know. Maybe fifteen minutes. Why?"

The doorbell rings, and Max and Emily run out.

"Check the peephole," I call out.

"He can't, even on his tippy toes; he's a shrimp," Emily says and we hear one of them pull the bench to the door.

"Be nice," Nate yells. He puts his glasses on the counter and rolls his eyes before whispering, "She can be such a little asshole."

Normally, I'd laugh, because the thought of calling your thirteen-year-old daughter an asshole seems funny and odd at the same time. This time, I don't laugh. Instead, I'm thinking: Nate, it's not Emily who's the asshole … it's you.

Max asks if his friend, Christopher, who's at the door, can stay for dinner and a movie. In unison, we say it's fine, and Emily comes back into the kitchen, rummaging through the fridge for a snack. She pulls out an apple and, between bites, turns to Nate. "Dad, Maggie was sitting on the sidewalk when we got off the bus."

"So, what's wrong with that?"

She shrugs. "Really? She's always telling me not to sit on the sidewalk because it's cold and germy. I mean, like, why would she tell me that then do it herself?" she continues, as if I'm not there. "Seems like bad advice."

"Hey now, don't be rude," Nate adds.

Quickly our attention turns to Max and Christopher, who battle with their pretend swords as their arms fly through the air. Christopher makes a quick turn and slides across the floor, banging against the kitchen table. He stops, taking off his socks for better traction, and gets up to resume his plan of attack.

Strands of light-brown hair, streaked with gray, fall over Nate's forehead. He brushes it away, continuing to watch the boys. I'm reminded how handsome he is with his square jaw, dimples that appear even with the smallest smile, and stubble that grows back after one shave. I imagine his lips lingering on this other woman's neck, his hands around her waist, his blue eyes gazing into hers—the way he looked at me this morning—and I feel a sting of jealousy.

His voice jolts me back to the present. "Remember the advice Maggie gave you about learning the state capitals?" He continues, "Worked, didn't it?"

"Yeah." Emily pauses to think and adds, "Except I put Albania instead of Albany for New York. My teacher said something about it being a test of capitals, not countries. I didn't get it. Where's Albania?"

"Eastern Europe," I add, slamming the cabinets, looking for something to ease the pain and satisfy my sweet tooth. I can tell Nate's looking at me, or at least I can feel it. He's a super-healthy eater and his slim build proves it. He often nags us for buying the occasional junk food, so the kids hide their treats on the bottom shelf.

I push aside pasta, oatmeal, and cans of tomato sauce and reach into the back to grab the chocolate chip cookies. Even though an entire chocolate cake is what I really need, the cookies will have to do.

"Maggie, come on," Nate says and tries to grab the bag from me. "That's poison. And we're having dinner soon."

I pull away and I'm about to tell him to worry about his new girlfriend's eating habits but hold back since the kids are nearby. Instead, I lie about needing to take a nap and rush up the stairs to sit on the toilet and sob.

Chili slides her muzzle into the crack of the door and looks at me from the other side. Her big, brown eyes kill me every time. She sidles in and presses her body against my leg.

After a good cry with Chili wrapped around me, I head to our bedroom and change out of my work clothes, hoping to calm down and get my act together. After tossing and turning for close to an hour, I get up and head back to the bathroom, throwing cold water on my face to reduce the puffiness. It doesn't work and part of me hopes my eye cream will—the one that should be renamed My Husband's Cheating … Again.

While smearing on some extra globs, I imagine the reworked description: *Our unique, patented formula helps improve the look of puffy eyes. Whether it's your first cry or your fiftieth, My Husband's Cheating ... Again makes you look more rested and feel like less of an idiot for staying with him.*

After one more glance in the mirror, I make my way down to the kitchen, where Nate's whipping up tomato sauce for pasta and Emily's setting the table. Max and Christopher are nowhere to be seen and the television blasts from the living room, almost making us yell in the kitchen to hear each other.

"Babe, how was your rest?" Nate asks, and I ignore him as he grabs the tongs to pull the chicken out of the oven.

He hardly ever cooks, which makes me even more suspicious. Nate screams for the boys to join us for dinner and we pass food around as everyone sits down around the table. The kids bicker again, like they'd done earlier, and it makes me realize that if we split up, I'd have a peaceful life, without the relentless arguing between them. My eyes well up, thinking if we did separate, I might not see my stepkids again. Not see them grow up and share in their experiences. I might not even recognize them as they walk down the block a year from now, considering how quickly they change.

"Maggie, why are you crying?" Max asks and everyone stops eating and stares at me.

"Sweetie, I'm fine. They're happy tears," I say and reach for a napkin. "Happy that your dad's home, and we can enjoy an early dinner with each other."

"How can you have happy tears?" Max asks, jutting his head forward as he peers at me.

"They're called tears of joy," adds Nate, not sure what's going on with me.

Silence takes over and Christopher looks puzzled before Nate adds, "Haven't you ever laughed so hard you're crying by the end?"

"Oh yeah," Christopher blurts out with a forkful of spaghetti raised in mid-air. "Remember when Mason sneezed and farted at the same time in Mrs. Talbot's class? I laughed so hard, I cried."

Max laughs while acting out the scene, interspersed with fart noises. "Oh yeah, yeah, yeah! That was so funny. *Achoo, pffft, achoo, pffft.*"

"You're disgusting." Emily rolls her eyes and knocks Max in the arm.

"Guys, not at the dinner table, okay?" Nate insists.

I can tell he wants to laugh about it when his voice cracks. But I can't. There's no way I can laugh about anything right now.

"Max," Nate continues, "how was your math test?"

"Pretty sure I got a hundred. Except…" He pauses to poke at the food on his plate. "I didn't have time to finish the last two questions."

"Sounds like you were sleeping when they went over percentages," Emily jokes and Max turns to her with a blank stare.

Nate puts his hand on mine. "What about you? How was your day?"

"Fine. Just long." I drift off for a moment, imagining the horror of Nate having sex with that blonde in every room of our house—on the wooden bench in the hallway, bent over the marble kitchen counter, doggie style in front of the TV, on the stairs leading up to the second floor, in our room, on our bed. God, what if they did fuck in our bed!

I feel my face flush red with anger as adrenaline rushes through me, making my heart pound. The anxiety I dealt with from his affair a few years ago—that made me so ill I couldn't get out of bed for a week—is back with a vengeance. How can I get my shit together now and act like a functioning human being?

Before being excused, the kids clear the dishes and take them over to the counter. Emily grabs the broom and sweeps under the table as Chili scoots in for leftover crumbs. Max and Christopher go at it again with their Mason imitation, pretending to sneeze and fart.

"Guys, what did I say?" Nate tries to grab Max by the arm. He's not fast enough as Max jumps back and slides to the opposite corner.

"You said it's not for the dinner table. We're not at the dinner table anymore," Max retorts, although it sounds more like an Emily comeback than one from her ten-year-old younger brother.

"Get out of here before I send you up to your room," Nate snaps and within seconds the two dash out of the kitchen, and we hear the volume on the TV get louder. Emily puts the broom back in its place, sneaks a few jelly beans from the pantry on the way out, and stomps up the stairs. And now, it's just Nate and me for the first time since my discovery.

CHAPTER 6

With the weight of fury, jealousy, and grief sitting heavy on my chest, I wonder if I'll be able to confront him. Will he tell me that it will never happen again, like the first time? I guess you could say, once a liar always a liar. Or rather, once a cheater always a cheater.

I forgave him and for years tried to forget about it. Now it rears its ugly head again—with the texts and pictures clearly showing some semblance of intimacy between them. It takes every ounce of me not to yell and call him every foul name I can think of.

Nate wanders around the kitchen counter to where I'm standing and puts his arm around me. I instantly back away. "Maggie, what's going on? Did I do something?"

I laugh hard and don't want to stop because I'm so close to crying again. Nate's staring at me with a puzzled look. Of course, he has no clue what's going on. How could he when he has Kira all wrapped up and tucked away in his text messages?

My bangs, which I've been trying to grow out for months, fall over my face. I keep pushing them off my forehead and then give up. "I saw you today. Well, sort of."

He forces out a hesitant smile, before adding, "Oh yeah, where?"

My voice cracks. "Right in front of me, in black and white!"

He stares at me, not sure what to say next. "Maggie, you're being cryptic. What's going on? You're clearly upset with me, and I have no clue why."

My story unfolds in a fast-forward rush, as if my brain can't keep up with the words that come out. And it's all over the place. How I was renewing my license, how it recently expired, why the DMV didn't do anything useful like send notices to people, or upgrade their lighting so the pictures on our licenses are at least halfway presentable.

Nate looks lost and confused. "And you saw me? I wasn't at the DMV."

"No! I didn't actually see you." My voice rises and it takes a few seconds to compose myself before continuing. "They wouldn't let me renew my license at first," I say and walk out to get my purse from the hallway.

"Go ahead, take a look," I continue, after returning to the kitchen.

Nate takes the printout from me. Still confused, he looks at it for a few seconds. "What's this?"

He places it on the counter and I pick it up and wave it in front of his face, almost clipping his nose in the process. "Seriously?" And I continue again, breathlessly, while pacing back and forth. "That's obviously you driving. The question is: who's with you? And don't tell me a friend, because friends don't cozy up to each other in a car. We don't even do that. And we're husband and wife!"

"This isn't for real," he adds, his face turning red. "I wasn't even stopped for speeding."

My heart pounds faster and sweat forms on my back and between my cleavage. I feel nauseous, breathing deeper to let it subside.

"Nate, don't lie to me. They got you on camera. Look, I don't care about the damn ticket. Who's the woman and where were you going? And I swear, if you—"

He interrupts and tries again to edge closer, trying to calm my nerves. "It's not what you think. You're over-reacting."

"Overreacting? Can you even hear yourself? Talk about a short memory!" I swallow hard, trying to keep my emotions in check, remembering the kids are nearby. "You promised me you'd never do it again. It's such a slap in the face. I guess I can thank the DMV for saving me money on a private eye."

"I'm serious," he says, studying me. "It's not what you think."

"Then, what is it? Is she an old friend? A client? Who is she?"

He stares at the floor and doesn't answer. The TV roars in the background and Emily comes into the kitchen a minute later for some more jelly beans. She stops and stares at us. I tilt my head, then look up and toward the direction of the foyer like those Monday mornings when the kids are running late for school. Emily quickly realizes we're having a serious conversation. She tiptoes out and stomps back up the stairs.

Nate doesn't look up or say a word, even after Emily leaves.

His silence speaks volumes.

Nate's phone sits face down on the counter, and I point at it. He'd flip out if he knew I've seen his texts and pictures with that woman.

"Go ahead," I say and stare him down.

"Go ahead with what?" he asks, finally looking at me.

Neither of us turns away as we study each other with sadness.

"Show me your texts."

"That's ridiculous. I don't ask to see yours," Nate says, his voice lowering in a defensive tone. He puts both hands in his pockets and leans against the back counter.

"Seriously? That's your response?" My jaw is clenched so tightly I can feel the pressure in my ears. "If you're not having an affair, show me your texts. Prove it." My anger takes over. I pick up the phone and with full force throw it at him. Nate tries to duck, and it hits him on the shoulder.

"What the hell, Maggie!"

I put the printout back into my purse and head to the hallway to slip on my shoes as Nate follows behind me.

"Maggie, please don't leave," he says softly.

"I asked you a simple question, Nate. Who is she?"

"It's hard for me to talk about. I swear nothing happened."

I open the door and glance back at him with raised eyebrows, responding like the DMV lady did to me. "That's what they all say."

CHAPTER 7

I walk slowly to my car, not giving a damn that it's pouring out. Water makes its way into my sneakers, turning them into soggy concrete blocks. It's dark out and even with the few streetlights glowing, my car seems invisible. I press the unlock button on my keychain until the orange lights flash from the front.

A few neighbors with large umbrellas take over the sidewalk. They greet me by name and scoot over to allow me to pass. Thank goodness it's dark to disguise my puffy eyes and red nose. I fake a smile, even if they can't see it, open the car door, and sink into the driver's seat. Driving while raining or crying isn't ideal and when you put the two together, it's the worst combination. No matter what it's like on the road, there's no way I'm going back to our house right now.

My Bluetooth, already synced up, defaults to my favorite playlist. The Killers' "Somebody Told Me" blares from the speakers. I've seen the band twice, once back in January with Nate, which was pretty much the best day ever when he surprised me beforehand with dinner. When we got to the restaurant, he handed me an envelope with the tickets inside and booked a night at a Miami Beach hotel.

We had pre- and post-concert sex with the Killers playing in the background, and morning and afternoon sex between our walks on the beach and tropical drinks by the pool. The memory makes me want to hit next on the playlist. Instead, I listen to the lyrics, feeling my chest tighten.

I keep blinking away the tears, thinking about our marriage. How did it get to this? How could I not see the warning signs? We spend time together. We have sex at least once a week—which he mostly initiates. We laugh at the same things. What could be missing? Something he's craving that I can't give him. Something he won't tell me he needs. Or did it happen spontaneously? You know, like the hundreds of excuses people give for cheating. Was it a client who came to his office and they clicked? Or someone he met during that once-a-year accounting conference where everyone gets shitfaced?

At this point, I'm clueless, but a separation seems like the only answer. I know that separation is hard as hell. And marriage? That's even harder if you live in denial.

It's a sad state of affairs, almost like a disease—that's denial for you. It creeps up on you and lingers, entangling you until you can't see clearly.

Facing reality takes strength. Who knows if I can be strong and walk away for good like I promised if he strayed again? I come out of my trance and find myself driving in circles through our neighborhood, putting the wipers on full force before heading onto the parkway.

I'm not sure where I'm going. Walking aimlessly through a shopping mall with bloodshot eyes and mascara staining my cheeks isn't a good look. Sitting at a bar making small talk, while knocking back mind-numbing vodka shots with strangers doesn't appeal to me, either. A hotel seems like the best option, where I can be alone, gather my thoughts, and not have to face Nate.

A guy behind me flashes his lights and honks, startling me, and I realize this whole time I'm driving in the left lane doing thirty where it's forty-five. He rides my bumper and before allowing me to move over, darts to the right and flies by. The closest decent hotel sits a couple of miles away, so I take the next exit.

Down the road, the hotel's art deco sign brightens up the avenue. It's a Friday night and the art galleries stay open later for art lovers and guys trying to impress their first dates. In between, loud and tipsy hipsters pour out of bars. Even though I'm only thirty-eight, to be twenty-five and single again without a care in the world sounds dreamy. I park in the hotel's lot at the back and, after turning on the light, look in the mirror and wipe away the tears from my cheeks and fix my mascara.

I climb out of the car and walk toward the hotel, shivering even though it's warm out, making my way through their rotating door into the brightly lit foyer. Two women at the front desk greet me with big smiles along with polished words straight from the hotel's manual. They're dressed in navy suits with a splash of magenta on their striped scarves that are tied around crisp white button-down shirts.

"Good evening, ma'am. Your name, please?" the attendant asks.

"Simmons. Maggie Simmons."

The bustle at the front of the lobby catches my attention as two cute-as-hell terriers bounce toward me. I bend down to pet them and then lift my head up when the attendant sounds confused.

"Hmmm," she says and looks at her computer. "I'm sorry, I don't see your reservation," she apologizes. "Your name again?"

"Oh, no, I should've said that I don't have a reservation. My bad."

Thankfully, they have a few rooms left and can accommodate me. I make small talk with the couple behind me, mostly about their two pups, while the clerk completes my reservation and sets me up in a room that's away from the noise. It's my usual request whenever traveling, even though I'm pretty sure I wouldn't be getting much sleep, no matter what.

She hands me the key and directs me to the elevators toward the back of the lobby. Paintings by local artists line the walls along with black-and-white photos of Miami with magenta paint as a dramatic backdrop.

I get off on the eighth floor and make my way down the hallway before seeing the number. It's big and bold in a brushed steel, almost taunting me. My room number—815—is the same as the day we got married: August 15.

I'm about to put the key in the slot. I can't seem to go through with this, staying in a room where I'll be thinking about our wedding day—a perfect day destroyed in minutes because Nate's too busy spending his free time calling another woman gorgeous and going on road trips with her while I'm away.

It's such a warped synchronicity, as if the universe wants me to discover his secrets. If my license hadn't expired, I wouldn't have seen his speeding ticket and be stuck in a hotel. I'd still be eating dinner happily with the kids, snuggling up on the sofa with Nate, making love without a care—while he deceived me, laughing in my face, like I was some dumbass fool.

I ride the elevator back down to the ground floor and walk to the front desk. There's a long line of people waiting to check in. I wait my turn and, instead of telling the two receptionists my reason for wanting another room, say that the toilet seems to be clogged.

"Ms. Simmons, I'm so sorry. We only have one other room and it's on the top floor. To be honest, we don't usually reserve it because the HVAC unit is on the roof right above and it's extremely loud so we don't put anyone there." She looks at the woman next to her, who nods before continuing. "I can't guarantee you'll get any sleep there. If you'd like to stay, we can offer you twenty-five percent off and complimentary breakfast."

Stay in the anniversary one or the noisy, low-expectation one? While deciding, I catch my reflection from a side mirror, gasping at my shitty appearance, unruly hair, and a coffee-stained T-shirt. I'd normally never go out in public like this, not even to check the mail.

"Sorry, think I'm gonna pass," I say and, after thanking them, walk out of the lobby and back through the pouring rain, digging into my purse for the car keys. As I head back home, anger takes over while recalling Nate's first affair.

CHAPTER 8

It was a few years ago, four months before we got married. I was on a business trip and came back the day before without letting Nate know, thinking he'd appreciate my surprise return. Before my trip, we talked about not spending enough time together and how great it would be to snuggle on the sofa while watching a good movie. Turns out, he didn't have snuggling on his mind. Or, at least, snuggling with me.

As I walk up our block that day, I spot a woman on our front porch. She looks like she's waiting for someone. At first, it seems innocent. A few seconds later, Nate comes out of the house and joins her. Something doesn't seem right. He smiles at her, a welcoming one as if he knows her well. She's standing a bit too close to him and, when he turns around to lock up, she runs her hand up and down his back. It makes me stop in my tracks and hide behind a palm tree while catching my breath.

I lean my back against the tree, then slouch down and peek around to get another look. Maybe I'm seeing things. Maybe she's just a friend. That's what I want to believe. My thighs burn from squatting and my hand takes the brunt of the spiky, overgrown grass. I push my hand down to flatten out the blades and hold onto the tree with my other hand.

They walk down the sidewalk and she presses the button on her keys as the lights of a white sedan flash. She's tall and slender, and it makes me envy the way her skinny jeans—white ones, no less—hug her hips and long legs. When they get to the car, Nate looks around before grabbing her ass. She doesn't jump or pull away and it makes me think: He's done this before. And she likes it.

I want to cry and scream at the same time. Instead, I dig my fingernails across the palm of my hand so deep until it feels like an angry cat has done a number on me.

Nate opens the door and gets into the passenger seat. I run back to my car and jump in fast. My hand burns from the dig marks when I grab the steering wheel and take off. There are a few cars in front of me and a red light gives me a chance to fish out a hat and sunglasses from my carry-on bag. Not that a disguise is needed. Out of the three of us, I should be the last one hiding.

They enter the parkway and damn if she doesn't have a lead foot. I weave between cars and switch lanes to keep up. A few miles down, she takes an exit. The sun is setting in front of me, casting a fiery pink glow, re-minding me of the times Nate sat next to me on the beach, holding my hand while we watched the sun set. I hold back the tears, wondering where his hands are right now. Mine are shaking, and I wrap them tighter around the wheel.

Up ahead, she pulls into a lot and, ignoring the no-parking sign, I stop to the side and watch from across the street. They walk down the block, and I lower the rim of my hat while keeping an eye on them. Nate smiles at her when she turns toward him to fix his collar.

I jump and look over when someone knocks on the passenger side. A policeman motions for me to roll down my window. He bends over and takes off his glasses. "Ma'am, you can't park here."

"Sorry, I'm waiting for my husband to get takeout from Lotus," I lie while glancing across the street.

"You know Lotus has parking, right?" He sounds perturbed before continuing. "It's up on the left. You'll need to wait for him there."

"Yes, Officer, thank you."

As I roll up my window and watch him walk off, the scent of cinnamon and curry from a nearby restaurant seeps into my car. I close my eyes for a second and breathe it in, hoping it will calm my nerves.

The officer stands a few feet ahead, with his arms folded, looking my way. He means business and waits for me to pull out of the spot. I pass Lotus on the left and see Nate and the woman standing outside with others. There must be a wait. New restaurant. Great reviews. It's the place we talked about last week. The place we'd planned to try once the crowds died down.

The car in front of me stops, and it makes me want to get out and run toward Nate with my arms flailing. Now's not the time to make a scene. Not here at least. While they wait outside, I take a quick picture and drive back home to see if they've left any evidence behind.

I unlock the door, not sure where to go first, with my eyes scanning the kitchen. A bottle of wine stands on the counter with two glasses next to it. My heart races as

I throw my purse and keys on the floor and run up the stairs to our bedroom.

The bed is unmade, with pillows scattered on the floor. By the ottoman, a floral duffel bag sits open that's not mine. I pick up the bag and turn it upside down. A magazine, lacy bra, and leggings spill out, with the label large and visible. Of course she's a size two, that tiny twig, something I'll never be. I flip the magazine over and read the name and address: Aubrey. From Pompano Beach. Her name gets repeated over and over until it's etched in my mind, annoying me like a scratched-up album that skips.

The light from the bathroom grabs my attention, and I walk over to find an open makeup bag and two damp towels laying on the counter. Did they fuck before or after their shower? Did he tell her, like he'd said to me many times, to turn around so he could wash her back?

I pick up the bag and start pulling it apart by the zipper until blood drips from a cut. My knees give way, bringing me to the floor, and I finally let out a scream so loud that my throat burns.

How could he do this? And for how long? Her floral duffel has "overnight stay" written all over it. Her cute, lacy bra and leggings make me wonder if, all this time, Nate has lied about loving my large boobs, wide hips, and shapely legs, his go-to descriptions for my never-gonna-be-slender body.

After rummaging through the bottom cabinet for a bandage, I grab a large plastic bag and start throwing all of her stuff in it. Every last piece—and the two used towels, ones we bought before moving in together. I open the window, tie up the bag, and throw it out, watching and waiting until it falls to the ground in our backyard. I'm expecting it to make a loud noise. Instead its dull thud leaves me unsatisfied and ruins the moment.

With my adrenaline in overdrive, I run down the stairs and into the kitchen, digging through a drawer, throwing sticky notes, pens, and a stapler on the floor until I find it—the pack of cigarettes hiding in the back. Nate hates my once-a-month cigarette and rags on me when I have one. Matches sit in the drawer next to the pack. It feels so good to light up and helps to calm me, even for a moment, until I take a closer look at the open bottle of wine and a glass with lipstick on the rim.

What else is he sharing besides our wine and bed? Does he talk about me? About the things that might annoy him? Do they compare the movies they love? Is he using a separate account to buy her dinner and gifts? And that's when I break down more, sobbing until it feels like I need to come up for air.

I pull it together, wipe away my tears with a rough napkin, and put the two glasses in the garbage—then sit quietly and wait.

Fifteen minutes pass. Then thirty. Then eighty. Finally, I hear footsteps and giggling by our front door. My shirt is covered in sweat, and I close my eyes and breathe in and out. I'm having second thoughts, but there's no turning back. I've rehearsed my words so many times while waiting, even Meryl Streep would be impressed.

It's gonna be okay. Whatever you do, don't cry. I bite the inside of my lip to hold back the tears.

"What's that smell?" Nate says after making a sniffing noise. He walks into the kitchen and jumps when he sees me. Aubrey screams and grabs onto Nate's arm.

"Maggie," Nate says and looks over at the counter, seeing that the glasses are gone, along with the bottle. He runs both hands through his hair, calculating his next move, his next words.

I cross my arms and tap my fingers. My chest pounds like the time we waited in line to ride my first roller coaster together. "How was dinner?" I add before lighting another cigarette and blowing smoke their way.

"I should go," she says and starts backing out.

"No, seriously, how was Lotus? We've been wanting to try it, right, Nate?"

"Maggie, let's wait," he whispers.

"From the looks of it, you and Aubrey worked up quite an appetite."

Nate tilts his head. "How'd you know her name?" he asks with a defensive tone, almost to prove to both of us that he's never mentioned her.

My voice cracks while my stare is solid. "*Vogue* magazine. Which, by the way, you'll find along with all her other shit out back."

"Maggie, I'm sorry," he says and walks toward me.

"You're such a piece of shit."

I start crying and bury my head in my hands, and I'm mad as hell for letting myself fall apart in front of them. A moment later, I look up and she's gone.

"How could you do this?" I ask and can't believe how calm I am. It's as if there's nothing left in me, only numbness. "Let me guess," I say, staring him down. "You had to get it out of your system before we got married."

Nate sits on the kitchen floor in front of me, with his arms wrapped around his legs. He's rocking back and forth and mumbling that he's sorry over and over again.

And then he opens up, telling me about Aubrey and how they met at his first job after college.

I can barely look at him now. Disgust runs through me. "Who reached out first?"

He gets up and goes to the fridge to pull out a beer. His hands shake as he takes the opener that's hugging the panel. "She did."

"Oh yeah?" I question him, because who knows what to believe. "She called you?"

"No, she sent me a message through Facebook."

"Figures."

"What do you mean, figures?" he asks and pulls out a chair next to me. His knee touches mine, and it makes me scoot back.

I play with my engagement ring, twisting it around, deciding whether to leave it on or take it off and throw it at him. "What do you want me to say, Nate? Congratulations? That you got the attention you wanted? I guess I wasn't enough, huh?"

"It has nothing to do with you," he says.

"It has everything to do with me!"

Nate leans back in the chair and sighs. We stare at each other and his eyes well up. My throat still hurts from my screaming earlier as I break down. We both break down. He inches the chair closer to me, and this time I don't back away.

He holds me and, after a few minutes of silence, tells me more.

How it just happened and was only twice.

How he made a big mistake and it'll never happen again.

How he loves me and, more than anything in the world, wants to marry me.

And like an idiot, I believe him. Because I can't imagine my life without him. And because I love him way too much.

Chapter 9

His first affair eats at me as I park and walk up to our townhouse. Those thoughts get pushed away for safekeeping, for now, so Nate's current infidelity can be faced head on, even as my stomach twists in knots. The porch light glows, as if he's expected me to return. Not wanting to attract gnats and mosquitos, we never leave it on. Tonight it acts as a beacon. Maybe Nate hopes it will navigate me home.

The curtains are pulled back in the kitchen and Nate's profile appears in the window. He must be reading the paper; that's his morning spot, not usually in the evening. He's waiting for me, and I imagine him in the same place, a few years from now for Emily's first date as he awaits her return home.

I stop to wipe the rain from my forehead and push away my hair that's dripping wet. I'm completely soaked through, with my rolled-up jeans sticking to my legs, making it hard to walk. Why didn't I take that hotel room? So what if it gave me a sleepless night? It's not like I'll get any sleep here, either.

Nate pulls the curtains back some more and sees me. He jumps up and a moment later opens the door.

"Hey," he whispers.

I don't say a word, brushing past him, and then lean on the bench in the hallway to take off my wet sneakers. Bending down in soggy jeans presents a challenge, and I continue up the stairs toward our bedroom as Nate and Chili follow behind. It's hard for me to be upset with Chili around, with her tail wagging and big brown eyes. I compose myself and remember why I'm here, why I came back.

The clock on the wall says 9:47 p.m., which tells me the kids are in their rooms, most likely awake. I need to keep cool, keep my emotions in check. Man, it's so hard not to yell, not to throw something at him, not to say, Why again? Or, Why me?

"Maggie," Nate whispers and stands by the bed, watching me wriggle out of my wet clothes. "I'm glad you're home."

I slump down on the mattress and he sits next to me, reaching for my hand. He probably thinks, because I've changed into my sweats and a different T-shirt, that I'm staying—willing to give it a shot and work through this, whatever *this* is.

Hell no, that's not going to happen. I swore to myself, and to him, that there wouldn't be a next time. Gone are the days that I let myself get taken advantage of. That I give my trust to someone when they don't return it. That I'm with someone who doesn't want to be with me. Only me.

"Nate," I whisper, so the kids can't hear. "Don't make me keep asking you what's going on. We can't do this again."

Chili walks up to me and puts her head on my lap, begging for a solid behind-the-ear petting.

"I know." He reaches down to rub Chili's back. "I owe you an explanation. That obviously was me in the car."

My heart sinks. "Who is she?"

"We met at that coffee shop near my office," he adds and then buries his head in Chili's face before looking up again. "I kept bumping into her, and we started spending some mornings together at the café. Maggie, I swear, nothing's happened physically between us."

I want to call his bluff, to say the texts and photos tell me otherwise and instead ask him point-blank, "Where were you going with her? Was it spontaneous or planned?"

He doesn't answer. Instead, he sighs and gets choked up, like the first time. This time, I'm not falling for it.

"Come on, Nate, tell me. We're both adults. You owe me that. Was it spontaneous or did you plan it, knowing I'd be out of town?"

"We planned it."

I'm about to get choked up as well. *We planned it.* He used the word *we* so freely. As if they're a team. They planned the day, what time he'd pick her up, what they'd do together, where they'd stop for lunch on their merry-ole-way to wherever. They planned something that we, as husband and wife, haven't done in a while because my accountant husband always says he's too busy to arrange anything at this time of the year.

"It's like a bad dream. What the hell was I thinking, giving you a second chance?" My voice carries, the words linger, and in my mind, I'm thinking, *How could I have been so stupid?*

"Look." He gets up from the bed and stands in front of me, lifting his arms like he's playing a game of charades. "It's not what you think. You're totally overreacting. It was an outing with a friend, that's all."

"An outing with a friend, huh?" I walk past him and roll my eyes while laughing because he's turning out to be the biggest bullshit artist. Chili jumps up and barks, thinking that it's time for her walk. "Shhh, beautiful girl," I say. "It's not time yet."

The closet door stands open and our navy-and-green plaid luggage sits on the floor next to a filing cabinet. It's a beautiful bag, one that we bought right before our honeymoon that has collected dust for a while now.

"Maggie, please, don't go."

I throw the bag on the bed. It hits his arm, and without an apology, I add, "I'm not the one who's going. You are."

"Are you serious?" Nate says and when he sees my stern expression, he knows not to expect a response. He sits and stares at me, playing with his wedding band. It's the first time in a long time I see him full-on cry. The other time was at his mother's funeral—and when he cheated that first time. "What about the kids? Have you even given them a thought?"

"Oh please, you see them twice a month. Don't start acting like you're father of the year."

It hurts him, but his feelings don't matter to me right now. I go to the dresser and throw his underwear, socks, gym shorts, and T-shirts into a disarrayed pile on the bed. He sighs as if he's frustrated, but resigned. I watch with my arms folded as he stands up and starts packing.

That piece of luggage has always put a smile on my face, often reminding me of our honeymoon in Cancun. This time, my smile has completely flatlined and has been replaced by a scowl and a splitting headache from clenching my jaw so much it hurts.

"I can't believe you're so quick in your decision. We can work through this. I swear, nothing happened." He stands in front of me and anytime I try to move out of the way, he gets in front of me.

As he grabs for my hands, I pull away and shake my head, looking straight at him.

"Quick in my decision? That's funny. It's taken me three years to make one. This isn't the first time, remember?"

He remains silent and then mutters, "You're always going to remind me of that."

"Because it's obvious you're a repeat offender. I'm tired of not being enough for you."

He doesn't say a word, making me feel worse. I grab my phone from the nightstand. It takes several minutes to find the photo from his first affair. My thumb starts to ache from the scrolling. When my finger stops on the right one, I hold the phone up to show him. "Remember her? What was her name? Oh yeah, Aubrey, right?"

He turns away. "I can't believe you followed me."

"And I can't believe you betrayed me."

I don't look away while waiting for a comeback. Nate doesn't say a word as he continues to pack the last few items.

"You're actually throwing me out while my kids are here? No way I'm leaving without them," he says as he puts the luggage in front of the bed and comes toward me.

Light shines through the crack of Emily's door. She might still be awake. I need to respond quietly, even though it takes every effort not to scream at him and have the entire neighborhood hear.

"Please, Nate, let them be. I'll take them to the bus stop Monday morning like normal. It should give you enough time to settle in somewhere by the time you have them again."

"Wow. How long have you been thinking about throwing me out?"

He's trying to play games, and this time it's not working. Chili knows something's going on. Her tail lowers between her legs and she starts to shake. I pet her head and lean down to rub her tummy as she rolls over onto her back.

"What about Chili? The kids will miss her," Nate says.

How dare he bring her up. There's no way he's getting my dog.

It's not my style to be bitter. After he mentions Chili, though, I can't help it. I want to keep slicing him into little pieces.

"They can visit her anytime," I say softly. "Or if you want," I add, "just adopt one … like you adopted a new friend who was all cozy with you while you were driving."

Nate picks up the bags and heads out. Both Chili and I follow him downstairs. When he gets to the foyer, he stops. "Think about what you're doing, Maggie. There's a lot at stake here."

His words eat at me and mess with my head, making me think about Emily and Max again. How they'll take it and what they'll think, having to go through another breakup. "Maybe you should've thought about that before you got caught."

He throws one of the bags over his shoulder and picks up the keys from the table. "Let's try to stay civil, for the kids' sake."

"Absolutely," I say, not sure if I can keep my word.

CHAPTER 10

It's Monday morning, a few days after kicking Nate out, and I'm weeping in the shower. With the kids still here, it's the only place where I can let it out. So the bathroom, the one that's on the first floor and farthest from their rooms, has been my refuge, my twice-a-day habit for the past three days.

My shoulders feel the weight of my sadness, and I lean my head back and let the water run over my face and wash away the tears. They need to disappear, for now, for the sake of the kids. I need to smile in front of them and be strong. And even though Emily and Max will find out soon enough, it's not my job to tell them the news. I'll leave it up to Nate, who will make up a story, no doubt, about why we've broken up. And that's okay. They don't need to know their father betrayed me.

Confronting Nate comes at a price. And saying good-bye to him doesn't come without repercussions. It means I might not see the kids for a while—or ever. It means being single, having to tighten my belt and start over. It wouldn't be the first time someone has started over. My mom did it twice and survived.

Knowing that I'll eventually be okay comforts me until the anger takes over—at Nate for cheating on me.

At myself for not leaving him the first time. And then the tears flow once again, this time harder than before. I bang on the tile with my fist until my hand throbs and, as quickly as my grief starts, it stops because I need to get my act together. At least for the time being because it's a school day, and we always have a special Monday breakfast that the kids love.

Chili is waiting in the hallway by the bathroom door and follows me upstairs to my bedroom. I throw the towel on the counter and look in the mirror. My face is all patchy like my college roommate's during allergy season. I dig in my makeup bag for some bronzer and put on an extra layer to hide the redness in case it doesn't subside by the time the kids wake up.

It's almost seven and, after getting dressed, I head into the kitchen and start the batter. Flour. Eggs. Salt. Sugar. What am I missing? The recipe should be etched in my mind by now, after all these years. I open the pantry, get on my tippy toes, and reach for the book. The page is already flagged for me to find the forgotten ingredient: baking powder, that's it.

I wrap the apron around my sundress and pull out an extra bowl to divide the batter once it has been mixed. Blueberries go into one batch and bananas and walnuts in the other.

As soon as she hears the clicking noise from the gas stove, Chili scurries out of the kitchen. She sits curled up in the foyer, with one eye open, ready and watching. She knows that once the oil starts cracking and the pancakes get cooking, it's almost time to run upstairs and wake up the kids.

"Chili, go on, get them up," I say while flipping the last one and pulling out the plates.

She stands up, tail wagging, and looks at me once more. She's waiting for me to egg her on with the second go-ahead.

"Come on, Chili, it's time for school," I sing.

She bolts up the stairs, with her nails scratching the wooden steps along the way. With her low, continuous bark, she becomes the kids' alarm clock, even though I'm certain Emily is already up and getting ready. Max, on the other hand, isn't much of an early riser and Chili's morning wakeup call makes sure he's only half asleep at this point.

A few minutes later, Emily slides into the kitchen and pulls an apple from the fridge. She's dressed in all black again and, this time for a change, has her hair pulled up high in a ponytail. It swings to the side when she pulls a stool out and sits at the counter.

"Your hair looks pretty."

"I tried braiding," she says and wipes the apple with a napkin. "It was a total fail."

"Let me do it for you. First, can you get your brother to come down? You guys will be late for school."

Emily goes to the stairs and yells, "Max! Breakfast!"

"You know that's not what I meant."

She looks at me and shrugs. "Come on, Chili, let's get Max up. Okay? Okay!" They run up the stairs and, minutes later, all three come down, with Max stumbling into the kitchen. He sits down and puts his head down on the table. I don't even bother asking. It's like this every Monday morning.

"Who wants hot chocolate?"

"Wait," Max says and lifts his head. "You guys never let us have that before school."

"Seems like a good day for it. With marshmallows. How's that sound?"

I take the kettle from the stove and pour hot water into three mugs and ask the kids to help me take the plates and pancakes to the table.

"When will Dad be back?" he asks.

"Dude, she already told us. Tomorrow. It's like you never listen."

"So?" Max says and stabs a pancake, plopping it and one more onto his plate.

"Your sister's right. He'll be back tomorrow. Your mom will get you after school, and you'll see him in a couple of weeks, like usual."

I take a sip of hot chocolate and then move my chair behind Emily's to braid her hair. It's halfway down her back and, when the last part gets twisted, she gets up to look sideways in the mirror that's hanging on the opposite wall.

"Thanks, Maggie."

"Looks nice," I say and bite the inside of my lip, holding back the tears. She's only thirteen but seems all grown up. And when she stands sideways, I see the bump in her nose reminding me of the first time Nate introduced me to the kids. Emily was eight at the time, shy as could be. She'd always stand sideways and try to hide behind her dad's legs. It took awhile for her to warm up. Once she did, her bubbly, snarky personality came out.

"What if I drive you guys to school today for a change?" It's out of character for me to offer. They don't know I'm trying to buy some extra time with them.

"For real?" Max says with a full mouth.

"That's okay. We can ride the bus," Emily adds and tightens the band on the end of her braid.

"Just because you got a new boyfriend doesn't mean we can't get a ride."

"Max, shut up! Just shut it!" She walks over to the table and pinches his arm, and he laughs it off.

"Emily, come on," I say, really wanting to ask if it's true about the boyfriend and add that she's too young to have one, even though my first kiss was at the same age in, of all places, the back of a movie theatre while watching *Sleepless in Seattle*.

"Oh crap!" Max yells, pushing the chair back and jumping up. "Forgot it's Pajama Day for Spirit Week."

Emily tugs on the drawstrings of her black hoodie. "Not me. I'll wait until Thursday for Crazy Hair Day."

Max flies out of the kitchen and runs up the stairs. We can hear him stomping back and forth above us, and we're imagining how he's trying to remember where he took off his pajamas.

Emily goes to the edge of the kitchen and yells for Max to hurry up so they don't miss the bus. She walks over to the table and takes the dishes to the sink, as she always does. I rinse them off and hand them back to her to place in the dishwasher. After she puts a few in the lower bin, she stops and looks at me.

"Don't tell Dad."

"About what?"

"The boyfriend."

"What boyfriend?" I tease and she gives me a nervous grin. "Not a word, promise. Do you like him?"

She nods and tells me how they met in history class. That he's really not her boyfriend. They happen to sit next to each other on the bus and have lunch together. He's new, moved recently from Atlanta, to be closer to his grandparents.

I don't want to pry but want her to know I care. "What's his name?"

"Dylan."

"Cool name. What do you like about him?"

Emily pauses and looks at the ceiling. "He's cute. And he likes the Ramones."

I'm about to tell her to keep me posted when Max runs down the stairs. He's wearing red pajama pants with reindeer on them and a Marlins T-shirt that's wrinkled beyond repair.

Emily laughs when she sees him. "Are you sure you wanna go out in that? You're like the neighbor's Shar Pei."

Max lowers his chin and pulls his shirt down, trying to flatten out the creases. It doesn't seem to help and, when he lets go, the shirt is the same crumbled mess, along with a couple of thumbprints.

"He looks great, doesn't he, Chili?" I say, and she prances over to Max when he reaches out to pet her.

"Come on, we're gonna miss the bus!" Emily yells, and we leave the last dish in the sink and walk into the foyer to grab our bags.

Chili follows us to the door and sits while Max puts on her leash. As we start down the block, we hear the school bus from around the corner and the kids take off. Chili and I run behind and, by the time we get to the stop, the bus is already there. The driver waits an extra minute for the kids to jump aboard.

I'm about to get choked up, thinking this might be the last time with the kids and the last time saying good-bye to them at the bus stop. Emily goes in first and when Max steps up, I'm tempted to yell, "I love you." Instead, as the driver closes the door, I mouth the words and, at the same time, Chili barks twice as if she's saying good-bye to both of them—and for both of us.

Chapter 11

Three weeks later, Chili knows what's in store when she sees me grab her special leash and service-dog vest. She's been trained not to jump on people, so she wiggles her hips and dances as if to say, *I've been waiting all month for this.* And me, too, if I'm honest. Having Chili around helps distract me from thinking too much about Nate, his moving out, being single again, and my overwhelming thoughts of not being able to trust those closest to me.

I throw the vest in my backpack, along with some doggie treats and gossip magazines. Chili stays by my side as we walk down the block to my car. The backseat is overflowing with dog hair, which is a small price to pay for unconditional love.

Chili hops in the back and as I drive off, she throws her head out the window, letting the sun beat down on her face. Kids in the car next to us point and grin as they watch her lips flap in the wind. They wave as we pass, continuing our way downtown, a quick twenty-minute drive from home. It's the first Saturday of the month and, when we reach Longwood Retirement House, it's late morning, our usual time.

The lobby doors open, and the smell of disinfectant mixed with mothballs hits me in the face. I hold my wrist under my nose for a whiff of lavender oil I'd dabbed on earlier and head to the check-in desk. George, my favorite attendant, smiles and hands me the clipboard with a pen tied securely with a rubber band at the edge.

"Maybe I should get Chili to start signing instead," I joke.

"I'm sure she'd do it for a few treats."

"She'd probably do it for one," I add and bend down to put on her vest, the red one with the big white letters that reads THERAPY DOG in all caps. It's a little snug, even though Chili doesn't mind. She knows she's about to get endless tummy rubs and ear tickles when she sees her two favorite residents.

"Are Betty and Al in the sunroom?"

George nods and reaches for the phone to answer a call. "And probably napping, since they just came back from their walk not long ago."

Retirement homes always seem to have the best architects with their beautiful designs, spotless exteriors, and landscaped grounds. I wonder if it's planned that way so families have a clear conscience about sending their loved ones there.

Longwood isn't any different, with its lemon swirl stucco exterior, large fountain by the circular driveway, and spruced-up gardens with shrubs and colorful flowers. Inside the first-floor hallway, the light shines through the large windows and skylights as we head to the sunroom, a comfortable space with several lounging areas and flower arrangements set atop glass end tables. The residents sit throughout, some playing cards while others look out the windows or nap in their chairs.

Chili spots Betty and Al at the back of the sunroom and starts chatting away—a mix between a bark and a friendly growl—and the regulars turn around to greet her. We stop along the way and Chili's in her element, standing calmly as she lets them pour love on her. Most of them make conversation about how much they miss their pets, sprinkled with stories about how their kids talked them into getting dogs, and then never walked them. I nod in agreement, remembering when my sister begged our parents to get our terrier we named Razor, before realizing the responsibility that comes with owning a dog.

Betty, who has a cozy spot near the window, wakes up from her nap and waves when she sees us. A joyful light radiates from her that makes me smile. Chili and I have been coming to Longwood for the past couple of years. We seem to spend the most time with Betty and Al because their energy is infectious, their stories full of life.

"It's the dynamic duo," Al calls out while fixing his cardigan sweater. He's standing next to Betty and extends his arm when Chili approaches. He rubs her belly and reaches into his cardigan pocket, pulling out a piece of bacon wrapped in a napkin.

"Hey, now," I tease. "Remember what I said about giving her scraps?"

"Yeah, yeah, I heard you the last time," he teases back as he takes the bacon out of the greasy napkin and hands a small piece over to Chili, who gobbles it down in record speed. "What's the harm? She doesn't keep kosher, right?"

"No, she's watching her figure," I say before realizing I'm not winning this battle and, besides, who doesn't like a little bacon every now and then.

Betty chuckles and rubs Al's arm. "Darling, remember our first dog, Duke? He used to run around in circles when he smelled bacon frying in the pan."

"He was a hoot. I miss that guy." Al looks out the window as a squirrel stops for a few moments on a branch, and Chili approaches the glass, thinking that, if she's slow and steady, she'll outsmart her wannabe-prey.

While they watch Chili as she lifts her front leg, I pull out the gossip magazines from my bag and set them on the table. Betty reaches for one and flips through the pages. She stops in the middle and skims over it, underlining the print with her finger. "These Hollywood couples never make it, do they? It's always the nanny, which makes me wonder: Why have a nanny?"

Al chimes in. "Betty, plenty of folks have nannies and nothing happens." He looks at the magazine when Betty holds up the front cover. "Those Hollywood men think they're the center of the universe. They want more and more, and keep taking!"

I should have read through the magazine before buying it. Even so, both Betty and Al are wrong. It's not only Hollywood couples. And it's not always the nanny.

Betty puts down the magazine and sits up straighter in her chair. "Sweetie, you seem distracted. Is everything okay?"

I've spent a lot of time with them. They can feel it; they know something's not right. It's hard for me to put on a happy face, to hold it together, day in and day out. Nate's actions still consume me. I lie awake most nights thinking about this new woman and the one from three years ago. My weariness overcomes me and now my dark circles have bred dark circles of their own.

At first, I don't want to tell them. I'm here to offer company but Betty becomes relentless in her questioning and so my story unfolds about what happened at the DMV and later that night at home.

She pauses and pets Chili, who wanders back over and sits in front of her. "Maybe he's being honest. Maybe she is just a friend and, if that's the case, it's not the be-all and end-all."

My smile toward Betty hides my pain. Because I don't want to share my snooping or the details of Nate's first affair—and I can't bear the thought of being judged for staying with him.

Betty continues as she shoots Al a loving glance. "Better to make a change than be unhappy with the situation you're in. Trust is essential between a couple."

"I wasn't unhappy," I say, fidgeting with the leash. Chili turns around and puts her muzzle on my leg to calm me down. After all, she's a therapy dog, and who knew it would be me who needed therapy the most? "I was blindsided. Like a hit-and-run with an SUV. Bam!"

Chili jumps, feeling startled, and moves to sit in front of Al.

"Well, I'm glad you threw the bastard out," Al says and crosses his arms. His look is stern, protective, like the one my granddad would give to the neighbor who parked a little too close to his Chevy.

"I miss him, but I'll never, ever take him back."

"Are you sure?" Betty asks. "Maybe you need to talk to someone, an outsider to help figure out why he did this."

"Don't need anyone's help figuring this one out. I'll never take him back," I repeat and think about Nate's first screw-up.

"Sounds like divorce vows to me, which he deserves no less," Al quips. "You should take him for all he's got."

Betty and Al only hear my side of the story, believing I did nothing to bring this on—in fact, I'm having a hard time believing it myself. I watch them interact with Chili and can tell they truly love and respect one another.

They tell me their story again, as if it's the first time. Both eighty-three years old and married for fifty-five of them. How they grew up two blocks from each other and never met until they worked together at a publishing house in Manhattan. How he'd ride the bus but couldn't sit next to her because the women's skirts were so full back then that they'd take up all the space on the adjoining seat. How she saw him for the first time and remembers his gray tailored suit and slicked-back, dirty-blond hair.

After he shares more about their many decades together, I can't help but ask, "So, what's your secret?"

"What do you mean?" Betty responds.

"What's your secret to a long marriage?"

"Oh, that's easy," she says. "Talking."

I know exactly what she means without having to elaborate. They openly communicate and maybe that helps them trust each other.

"And we do just about everything together," Al adds.

Betty nods. "Even our naps."

The two of them smile at each other and as I zip my backpack to get ready to leave, Al calls out my name and pauses, making me think he's about to give some words of advice. "Remember," he says, "life's too long. Make it matter."

I throw my backpack on and twirl the car keys in one hand. "Don't you mean life's too short?"

He shakes his head and gives Chili one final belly rub. "People say that all the time. That life's too short. And here we are. Eighty-three and still going strong. So make it matter, because you don't want to look back fifty years from now with regret."

As I wave good-bye and head toward the door, Betty calls out my name, making me turn around. "Al's right," she says. "Make it matter."

CHAPTER 12

Chili's hanging out on my bed, surrounded by a mound of sundresses, jeans, sandals, boots, sneakers, light sweaters, and bathing suits. You name it—it's on there. That's what happens when you plan a trip to California. The temperature's gorgeous and warm during the day, chilly at night. Great for living there; difficult for packing. I've been to California twice but this time will be my first one to San Diego and the first time for work.

Every year in June, my company sends me to the American Textiles Summit, where buyers get to hear about new trends, what consumers are snapping up, what they're longing for, and what might be dead in the water in three to six months. Actually, it's the buyers who forecast the hits and the misses. The worst is when something's all the rage and we don't see it coming. That's when we want to kick ourselves for not selling it soon enough to reap the rewards. It's almost like the one that got away. We joke about it each time we meet for a recap upon my return to the office.

It's the same conference every year and they switch it up to get people to attend based on the location. Last year, it was New York, the year before, New Orleans. They could've gone with Nashville to keep up with the list of places beginning with N. Or maybe they figured you don't need a hard sell when it's in San Diego, with its beautiful beaches, great weather, and friendly people. Just mention the name and they drool, practically give up their first-born to attend and make a vacation out of it. Lucky for me, there's no need to convince my boss, since they send me every year, and I hand over my company credit card to register and pay the expensive conference fee.

The doorbell rings, followed by three quick knocks. I run downstairs, already knowing who's there before opening the door. Chili growls at first and when she sees my best friend, Rachel, standing on the porch, her tail wags uncontrollably. Rachel wears her brown hair in a high ponytail, and she's dressed in yoga pants with a loose-fitting tank that shows off her toned arms from years of competitive swimming. Rachel has looked like this—beautiful and muscular—since we met in college. She loves the sun, and it loves her back—in a good way—with her olive complexion hiding a sliver of crow's-feet that shows up briefly when she smiles.

After kicking off her flip-flops, she hands me some chocolate and a bottle of red wine. Chili sniffs the truffles, and I have to remind her that they're bad for doggies, but oh so great for me.

"You'll have to watch me pack," I say as Rachel follows me upstairs. "I'm leaving bright and early and still haven't figured out what to take."

She walks into my room and glances at my bed. "Looks that way. Pack a toothbrush and buy everything else when you get there."

"That could work. I keep forgetting I'm only there for four days."

Rachel goes to my closet and starts looking through it, moving the hangers to the left one by one and then stops. She holds up my sundress with yellow and pink flowers on it. "Bring this one."

I snicker, both at the remark and at the dress. "Definitely not. I'm planning to get rid of that one. Might even burn it."

"Seriously?" Rachel asks, raising her voice as she sings out the question. Chili opens one eye before going back to sleep on my bed. "It's gorgeous. And you'd look so pretty in it."

I walk toward the closet and take the dress from Rachel. Even with the horrible light that we always complain about on the second floor, the pattern looks beautiful as it catches the light from the closet. Instead, it should look washed out and tattered because it's the one I wore on my first date with Nate, on our first anniversary, and every anniversary after that. It's a favorite of his, mostly because of the memories.

I take the dress off the hanger, ball it up, and throw it toward the wall with full force. It smacks the wall and falls down into a sad, crumpled mess onto the floor. I shriek and Chili shoots out of the room and down the stairs with fright.

I don't know how to control what's happening to me now. I've always been the more even-tempered one— or rather, the one to keep my emotions in check. Rachel picks up the dress and I grab it from her hands, ripping it apart, first by the bottom seam, and then, all the way up to the top. The strap doesn't budge, and my fingers start burning as I tug on the edge.

Rachel comes closer, takes the dress, and hugs me tight.

"Why did I give him a second chance? I'm such an idiot." I cry onto her shoulder.

"Because you trusted him. That's what we do when we love someone."

"Well, I fucking hate him now," I manage to blurt out between sobs.

Rachel grabs some tissues from my nightstand and hands me a few. "You don't have to hate him. I mean, you can, but it won't do you any good." She pauses, being cautious with her words. "You need to move on. I know, easier said than done."

"What did I do wrong?"

She moves back and puts her hands on my arms. "What the hell are you talking about? Why are you blaming yourself? You did nothing wrong!"

We stand by the bed, and I rummage through my pile of clothes, partially to stay busy so my mind doesn't continue with crazy thoughts. I decide on the bathing suits and throw two into the luggage, thinking some sun might do me good.

Suddenly, my brain switches into full throttle. Rachel's right: I did nothing wrong—and still it eats at me. Was I working too much? Spending too much time with my friends? Not stroking his ego or laughing at his jokes enough? Did he need more attention? Then I realize the warning sign and, man, it was a big one: He started dating me quickly after his separation—within two months.

I remember how we met, at the gym, and how he looked over my way while I fumbled with buttons on a treadmill. Nate walked over to me, with a smile that could put a sleep-deprived teenager in a good mood, and started walking me through the touch screen. He asked for my number almost too fast and told me he was separated and not for long. Maybe I should've run the other way. My short and failed attempt to figure out the treadmill and get in shape snagged me a husband instead—one who wasn't ready for a second go-around. Seems I was a rebound for Nate, and he remarried too soon.

Rachel knows me so well. We've been friends since college. She knows what's going on in my head, a series of violent waves crashing over and over during a horrible storm. And it's hard to make it stop. "Hey you," she says and takes the sweater from my hand and places it on the bed. "I'm concerned you think it's your fault. It's not. It's all on Nate."

"You're right," I say, wanting to believe her. "The overthinking's driving me crazy."

"Go to San Diego, soak up some rays, talk to strangers."

"Talk to strangers? Great advice, Mom," I joke.

She smiles and throws a bathing suit in my bag, the one she likes best. "You know what I mean. Be open to whatever comes your way. And when you get back, we'll go out and have some fun. It'll all be okay."

CHAPTER 13

The American Textiles Summit might be the largest since inception. As I check in, they tell me I'm one of two thousand attendees, give or take. I've been going for the past five years and sometimes, I try to get my company to send somebody else. Every year, they want me there; they think I have some uncanny ability to foresee the future on what sells and what doesn't.

I've done pretty well so far with deciding what to buy. There have been a few duds along the way, like the blanket with a built-in foot massager. Somehow, it made a few customers want to pee during the night, which got bad publicity and, frankly, I didn't see that one coming. We got our money back from the manufacturer for the returns. Still, it required a lot of work, like getting it off the shelves and replacing upcoming promotions with another product.

This year in San Diego, the conference staff all wear matching shirts: turquoise with a purple band around the sleeves and collar. A guy with dark hair, long on one side and shaved on the other, hands me the hefty program guide. I step aside and flip through it. On the inside cover, the keynote presenters make their appearance, along with a quick snapshot of the daily events.

First up this afternoon is a guy who got his furniture line into Modness, a fancy retail chain, after starting his business in his parents' garage after being evicted from his apartment. The write-up says he'd been rejected seven times by the retailer before earning a spot in their show-room—I guess his keynote title, "From the Garage with Grit," created intrigue. We all could use some encouragement, and I adore his supportive parents without even knowing them.

The elevator door opens, and I flip through the rest of the program guide on the way up to my room, making a mental note of the sessions and networking opportunities. A woman in her twenties rides the elevator with me. We make small talk and she mentions the Rooftop Meet and Greet at seven after introducing herself. Free drinks and appetizers? I'm so there, she adds, and before getting off on her floor, says she'll see me later. I'm not shy or introverted—you can't be in this business—but it's nice to have a familiar face at a huge event, even if it's someone you don't know.

After getting to my room, I throw my bag onto the desk and pull out my phone to take a picture. The old married-and-in-love version of Maggie would've texted Nate pictures nonstop. This time, I slide my phone into the back pocket of my faded jeans and enjoy the moment, just for me, because none of that matters anymore. The sharing of moments with Nate is a thing of the past.

I open the sliding-glass door to my balcony and hear hip-hop blasting while watching tanned waitresses carry trays of drinks to guests lounging poolside. Palm trees surround the area and, if that isn't enough, the calm bay reflects the sunlight, and I imagine the view at night with the pool lit up.

My phone vibrates and a text comes through from Rachel.

Talk to any strangers yet?;-)

I reply:

No because my mamma taught me better.

She pings back:

Come on, have some fun. For me, at least!

At that moment, Al's words haunt me: *Life's too long. Make it matter.* Making life matter involves living in the moment. I should live in the moment and forget, even for a second, about what Nate did. About how I trusted him. And the ways he betrayed me.

Forgetting doesn't have to mean forgiving. I'm not one of those people, so in touch with my feelings that I can forgive a second betrayal, but living in the moment might turn out to be as hard. The bed catches my attention, inviting me to lie down. Instead, I ease into the cushiony chaise lounge on the balcony and let the sun beat down on my bare and pasty legs. I wake up to a chill and jump up, realizing that it's way past the first keynote and time for rooftop networking.

***

A thirty-something hipster with a flannel shirt and a long beard hits R in the elevator as we make our way to the rooftop. He's dressed way more casually than me, and I instantly regret choosing a wrap dress over my comfy jeans and a tee. On the way up, we stop at a few more floors, and a flock of conference attendees fill up the space. They're all chatting as if they know each other, and I smile and nod as if I'm in on the joke while reaching in my bag to reapply my lip gloss.

I'll get a little tipsy, I think, and it'll make me comfier with these strangers. I'll probably get so tipsy that we'll be best friends by the end of the evening, and I'll forget what Nate did to me twice or more times. Who knows? Maybe he would have confessed or given more details if he were drunk. There's something about being shitfaced that breaks down barriers and exposes secrets. Some call it truth serum. I like to call it cocktail confessionals.

There's a spot at the end of the counter and the bartender takes one of my two drink tickets that come with the networking event. A few more attendees join me, and we make small talk, asking each other about where we're from, what we do at our jobs, and what companies we work for. I glance at their hands and see they're all either wearing wedding bands or engagement rings.

Without me asking, one of them talks about her impending nuptials and how she wants something big and fancy, and that her fiancé, who's been married before, wants something small. I bite my tongue, holding back on what I really want to ask her, like how long he's been divorced and how long before he started dating her. I wrestle with my thoughts, pin them down so they can't move, because I know, deep down, not every guy is like Nate. So I wish her well and don't mention that I'm divorcing. Just that I'm single and loving it. A bit of a lie, of course.

I've already gulped down a glass of white wine and taken another to keep handy for more questions. Tipsy may or may not be a good look for me as it eases the pain and the personal questions thrown at me.

About an hour in, the hipsters leave for a bar in the Gaslamp District. The sun has started to set, and appetizers balance my alcohol intake. I pick up the plate and make my way to the outdoor seating area. Small lights, strung from one end to the other, give off a glow and make it hard to see where there's an empty spot.

A few folks gesture for me to join them and one of the guys drags a tall bar chair over for me to squeeze in. After a few laughs, two of them get up to leave, saying they're early risers who like to get in a few miles before breakfast. I joke about my record-breaking ability to hit the snooze button, to make me seem like less of a loser that I don't run in the morning, or at any time for that matter.

"You look familiar," I say to the only one who's left at the table. It's not a pick-up line, honestly. He looks a little like Chris Martin from Coldplay with his tall, lanky build, dirty-blond hair, and strong jawline.

"I'm Drew," he says and puts his hand out to shake mine.

"Oh, now I know! You're the keynote guy. 'From Garage with Grit.' Good title," I add and pull my hair back into a ponytail.

"You're close, but I won't hold it against you." He smiles and picks up his beer and stops before taking a chug. "This year, they had mini-keynotes before the main keynote. Guess you could say I was the grit guy's opening act."

"Sorry—was probably confused when I saw your photo next to his in the program guide."

"No worries. So, what did you think?" Drew asks.

"Well ... actually—"

"Uh-oh, that doesn't sound good," he says and inches his chair closer to hear me better.

"I'm embarrassed to say, I fell asleep on my balcony and completely missed it."

We both laugh and turn around when a loud group from the conference pours out onto the rooftop. "Don't blame you," he continues after they pass our table. "And it's better than falling asleep in the audience. Especially if you're snoring."

"So, is Drew short for Andrew?"

"Nope, just Drew."

"Just Drew. Has a nice ring to it."

"Yeah, maybe I'll add that to my business card. Just Drew. Or maybe Just Drew It."

After some small talk about San Diego, Just Drew asks about my life, and I don't want to share much, because I'm tired of rehashing everything. In no time, we discover that we're practically neighbors, living less than an hour from each other in Florida. When he finally asks if I'm married, I tell him not really and when he asks what that means, I share that I'm separated, and there's no way in hell I'm ever getting back with my husband. For some reason, saying this over and over helps me move closer to closure.

Drew doesn't ask for the nitty-gritty details and instead asks for my number. He takes my card and grabs a picture of it before handing it back. It could be the alcohol talking when he mentions there's a connection between the two of us. I nod in agreement then wonder if it's me being tipsy and so desperately wanting to get back at Nate—and all the things he probably hasn't told me.

Before long, Drew offers to buy me another drink, since I've reached my free networking limit. I politely decline, as my bed is calling, and he teases me about sleeping through the morning's keynote. He doesn't offer to walk me back to my room. Or try anything at the table. I love that he leaves it right there, on the rooftop, with a goodnight and a smile, and the mystery still intact.

Chapter 14

Just Drew doesn't call.

I keep staring at the phone during the day.

Can't concentrate during meetings.

I wake up in the middle of the night and check for texts.

Get up in the morning and check for missed calls.

I do this every day for five days after returning home. I can't stop thinking about Drew, who told me we had a connection. That should've been a red flag. Who tells someone right away, within an hour, that they have a connection?

Why'd he take my number if he wasn't planning to call? Was he trying to be polite? Was it all about business and nothing about me?

Two weeks go by and still no call or text. Rachel calms me down after I think about my losses and tell her how much I miss seeing Emily and Max.

She says everything will be okay.

I tell her that maybe it was the wine.

Or the great rooftop view that romanticized the moment.

Or maybe Drew's with someone and enjoys flirting while on the road.

Or he's married like the rest of them. Like Nate.
Rachel keeps telling me not every guy is like Nate.
And, I want to believe her.

CHAPTER 15

In the three months since being separated, Nate has called several times, begging me to take him back. It sounds a little pathetic when he calls, to be honest, and I imagine that's how it must sound when I'm falling apart in front of Rachel, and even Betty and Al.

I'm falling apart not only because I trusted and loved him but I'm letting my mind play tricks on me. I'm doing all the "what-ifs" to see how one of them could have kept Nate from reaching out to this other woman in the first place. What if I complimented him more or cooked better? What if I wore sexy lingerie instead of my support bras and mismatched panties? What if I didn't always wait for him to initiate sex?

Nate tries to convince me again that I'm making a big deal out of nothing—trying to make me think I'm overreacting because he doesn't know about my snooping. For my own sanity and peace of mind, even if I still love him, I could never take him back. Because his track record—even without my snooping and the DMV photo—says it all.

I sit at Stella's, my favorite hangout, and wait for Rachel to arrive as these thoughts consume me. A few minutes later, she walks up and plops her bag on the counter. She fixes her hair and takes the ponytail holder from her wrist to create a loose braid that always looks good.

"Outro drivers don't get it," she says, hugging me. "We don't want the windows down while we're in the back. Totally messes up our hair. And, get this, I lucked out being his very first customer."

"First of the day or first ever?" I ask.

"First ever, and it might have been his first day driving in general."

"And maybe your first time praying?"

She nods and laughs, which catches the bartender's attention. He walks over and places two cocktail napkins in front of us. Rachel orders her usual dirty martini with extra olives and, figuring we'd be out for a while, I stay away from the hard liquor and choose red wine.

"So, am I allowed to ask about Just Drew?"

"You just did."

"Good one. Maybe we should drop the Just?"

At this point, Rachel can choose whatever she wants to call him. I lower my head and don't answer because my defensive side is about to come out.

"Did he ever wind up texting?" she continues.

"Nope. And it's been a month. He would've by now."

"You intimidated him with your beauty."

I laugh. "Yeah, flabby arms are all the rage now, haven't you heard?"

We pick through the trail mix, and Rachel tells me the best way to get out of my funk is to move on and then she brings up a whole slew of motivational crap—that it's Drew's loss and he'll regret it. I want to say easier said than done, and bite my tongue because she's also been through a short marriage, an even quicker divorce, and is now perfectly happy playing the field. When it all happened, she never cried in front of me or maybe never cried at all. Maybe she's stronger. Maybe she's more realistic. Maybe she moves on faster.

Not sure which is better—to move on or let it work its way through me. These days I'm crying at the stupidest things, like at the grocery store when I pass the apples and remember how Nate would put little drawings on our shopping list next to each item. Or when the line's too long at a coffee shop, and how I can't bear to stand in it, because it makes me think that's how it all started with Nate and this woman in the DMV photo.

As we're chatting, a seat empties up next to us and a guy sits down. He looks over and smiles and I look away at Rachel. She leans in and raises her eyebrows as if to say, "looks like your type." It's not like I have a type but Drew, the Chris Martin lookalike from the conference, is the kind I used to go for in my twenties. The guy next to me looks more like Nate with dark, wavy hair and long sideburns, and he isn't wearing a wedding band.

Rachel leans in and whispers, "He's super cute. You should talk to him."

I whisper back. "He probably wants one thing."

She picks up her drink. "Just stop already with that thinking."

"I thought we were done with the 'justs'?"

We both laugh and the guy looks over. "Let me guess," he says, leaning a little closer as the music blares over our conversation.

My red wine has kicked in, making me a little more relaxed at small talk. "Let me guess, what…?" I ask.

"You'd say 'no' if I offered to buy you a drink, right?"

He is right. I don't let strangers buy me drinks, but I smile while considering it because I've never heard that line before. I'm wondering if he's using some reverse psychology bullshit on me. "Nope, you're wrong," I reply. "I'd say 'yes' but you'd have to buy one for my friend, too."

He nods and calls over the bartender, who pours us another round. Rachel takes a few sips and anytime I turn around to talk to her, she winks as if to say she doesn't feel left out.

She goes to the bathroom and my nerves get the better of me. I play with the napkin, folding it a few times into smaller squares.

"You've got some mad skills there," he says and points to my hand, almost brushing against it and making me feel flushed.

"You should see my paper airplanes," I say as a quick comeback.

"I'd like to see them."

"See what?" I say, quickly distracted and forgetting our conversation.

"Your paper airplanes."

"Oh." I giggle and turn around when Rachel touches my back. Rather than sitting back down, she leans in and asks if I mind if she leaves.

I mouth *Don't go*, because I'm not sure if I'm ready to leave, and I don't want to stay alone.

"Stay," she whispers. "I'll text to see if you're all right, or you text me. He's really cute and into you. And you seem to be enjoying his company."

I nod in agreement and tell her this is my last drink before heading home. We hug good-bye and she waves as she heads through the exit.

"So, back to your paper airplanes," he says. "How long can they fly?"

"At least thirty-eight seconds," I blurt out with an air of confidence. The number means nothing, really, other than my age.

The cute guy calls over the bartender and asks if he has some paper. The bartender nods and, after looking in a few drawers, returns a minute later with two sheets. He hands me one sheet and keeps the other for himself. "I'm not that great at it; been a few decades since making one," he says and starts folding his, making a crease in the middle.

He finishes his airplane and leans in to pick up a pen at the edge of the bar. "What's your name?" he asks.

"Maggie."

He writes my name in all caps and draws circles and stars around the plane for an added touch. I'm about to finish the last fold on my sheet when he says, "I'm Ryan."

"Mine won't look nearly as good as yours, Ryan," I say to remember his name and do my best to make the thing presentable, having to refold it in a few spots. "Let me guess…"

"I don't know, what?" he says back and shows me the cutest damn smile I've seen in a long time. Part of his front tooth is chipped and I want to ask what happened, and make up a story in my head instead—one where he played hockey in high school or was riding his skateboard around when his long, floppy hair got in the way and caused him to hit the curb.

"Are you an artist?"

"Sort of. I'm a creative director," he answers and, out of nowhere, touches my arm and asks, "Are you hungry? Wanna grab a bite? There's a great Italian restaurant down the block."

Ryan's probably talking about Little Joe's, a place I know well. Nate and I went there often. Part of me wants to tell him that it's out of character for me to leave with a stranger. That it's too soon and he's wasting his time. That my situation is complicated. That *I'm* complicated.

"Sure," I wind up saying, which surprises even me. I'm trying to live one day at a time and in this moment, it feels right. And, besides, I'm craving pizza.

Ryan pays the check and before standing up, says, "Don't forget your airplane."

We leave the bar and slide through the circular door and onto the sidewalk. My eyes wander over his broad shoulders and tall, muscular build. I still can't believe I'm leaving with this stranger who sat down next to me and showed off his crooked smile, one that made me find comfort in the unknown and unexpected.

Ryan turns around and waits for me. He lifts his arm to hold up the plane. "Should we give them a try?"

"Don't know; it's busy here. And I don't want to hit anyone."

We wait for a few older couples to pass. They smile at us, probably thinking it's our first date.

"You ready? On three, okay?" He pushes one leg back for balance. "One, two, three!" On three, he throws his plane into the air and I wait a second or two so mine will stay up longer. It doesn't work, crashing lifelessly to the ground.

"Thirty-eight seconds, huh," he teases.

"On a good day. The wind has to be oh-so-right. You know, the velocity or whatever it's called," I joke and bend down to pick them up and hand one over.

We walk down the block and stop across the street from Little Joe's. While waiting for the light to change, Ryan reaches for my hand and my heart beats faster. It catches me off guard and the thought of being with someone new—and this cute—makes me nervous. I don't pull away because the attention is such a warm welcome after Nate's betrayal. Even if it's fleeting.

"Damn, you have the prettiest smile," he says.

His words make me blush. "You know nothing about me." I instantly regret saying and ruin the moment by adding, "I'm separated and getting a divorce."

"That's good. I mean, not good. Shit, that totally came out the wrong way," he says and puts his hand on my arm. "What I meant to say is: I'm sorry about your divorce, but I'm glad you're single."

We wind up missing the light and wait at the edge of the street. "It's okay. Most people don't know what to say."

As the cars go by, Ryan faces me and says, "I am sorry. Maybe I should've said congratulations? Maybe it's a good thing?"

I have no response, only a nod, because both seem fitting. It is a good thing that I'm no longer with Nate; it's also a shame our marriage didn't work out. The thought makes me teary-eyed and as Ryan brushes a strand of hair away from my face, he says, "I really want to kiss you right now."

My chest tightens thinking about kissing someone else, someone new for the first time in more than six years. Thoughts of being wanted, especially after what Nate has done, makes me want to say yes, to feel the newness of this stranger's lips on mine. "I want you to kiss me, too."

Ryan drops his plane on the sidewalk and leans in. Our lips meet, and for that moment, I forget about Nate. I forget that I'm supposed to text Rachel. I forget everything and enjoy the moment as my body warms to his touch.

We stop when a horn startles us. Ryan smiles and takes my hand. "Little Joe's has the best pizza."

"The best," I say, and we cross the street, still holding hands.

We share a few kisses at our table, and we leave it at that—a touch of the lips, a hint of garlic. And it's more than okay and enough.

CHAPTER 16

Over the next few weeks, Ryan texts a few times a day. We talk on the phone for hours. He makes me rediscover my smile, the one that needed resuscitation. Ryan doesn't seem to care that I'm separated and not divorced yet. I care, though, and Rachel reminds me that I don't owe Nate a damn thing. He's moved out and I need to move on.

I'd be lying if I said there was no looking back and falling prey to my insecurities, a twisted version of myself that warps when staring at it too long, like one of those funhouse mirrors that makes you look like a freak. Why wasn't I enough for Nate? When did our marriage suddenly collapse? Complacency never even had a chance to set in. It's as if our marriage certificate became an exam that came back with a big, fat F written in red ink.

I need to stop dwelling on what can't be changed—that Nate's a liar and a cheater who needs attention from women besides me. And Ryan seems to be a perfect distraction. Along with his morning texts and cute emojis. His compliments and sense of humor. And thinking about our upcoming date.

For our next one, we meet in a dive bar about twenty miles northwest of Miami, because, there's still an uneasy feeling about being seen with another guy, and I know Nate wouldn't be caught dead in this part of town. He's always hated its grittiness, its quirkiness, its dive-bar-on-every-corner and tattoo-on-every-body-part reputation. I don't mind it, considering I have two tattoos of my own and miss that nobody-gives-a-shit mentality of my college town instead of our fancy-schmancy art districts where everyone is comparing themselves and being overly judgmental.

The Outro driver drops me off in front of Halloway's, known for its cheap beer, fried pickles, live music, and occasional fights between drunken college students with fake IDs. Ryan stands outside, waiting. He grins when he sees me, walks over, and gives me a long hug. My nerves are calm but his warmth, his presence, make my heart race.

We show our IDs and the bouncer opens the door, letting us pass. It's not packed yet and as we enter, as if on cue, the overhead lights dim. There's a small stage in the corner with a drum set and a few guitars leaning against a stand. I grab a table in the corner near the stage, and Ryan talks to the DJ and then gets two beers at the bar.

A few young couples stumble in and look at us before hitting the dance floor as the DJ starts playing Lady Gaga. A young woman points to me and asks, "You gonna join us?" when she sees me dancing in my chair.

Ryan stands up and works his way toward the floor, gesturing with his hands for me to join him. I usually wait for a bar to fill up, because I hate the idea of being watched while dancing, but I've already downed half a beer and my inhibitions disappear with every sip. We dance to what's left of Lady Gaga and stop on the floor when Imagine Dragons' "Whatever It Takes" comes on.

"I love this song, requested it from the DJ," Ryan yells in my ear over the music.

"Me, too!" I say and take off my watch to show him the apostrophe tattoo on my wrist.

"No shit. I was thinking about getting the same one." He takes a closer look and adds, "So, there's more to see, huh?" referring to the lyrics.

I smile and realize he's not making up his love for the song. "Got it last year after it came out."

"They're my favorite band," he says and sings along to another verse from the song.

We continue to stand on the floor and, at this point, we're doing more singing than dancing. While it plays, we don't take our eyes off each other—as if the song has deeply rooted us, connected us with its chorus. We sing along until the end, not missing a word.

After a new song starts, Ryan fetches us two more beers from the bar. My first one has become lukewarm when we make it back to our table. He moves the glass to the edge and puts the cold and frothy one in front of me.

"Are you trying to get me drunk?" I tease.

"Some say it's truth serum," he teases back, as if he's read my mind.

"Then you'd better start downing yours," I tell him. "That way, you can tell me some juicy stories."

He leans in for a kiss and stops short. "There's nothing to hide. I'm sure you already know what I'm thinking—and how I feel about you."

My heart races. Is that an invitation to ask? And am I ready for it? He doesn't tell me about his dating life, and I don't want to know. Are we both rebounds for each other? Should I be cautious with a guy who seems so into me after only knowing me for a month?

We dance some more when the band starts playing and it fills up fast. By midnight, we realize we can't compete with the twenty-somethings and the nightlife demands, so we head outside for a walk. Dozens more, mostly drunk and loud, pour out of various bars as we walk down the block to a hotel that was recently renovated to its former glory.

"We did an amazing shoot here last year when it re-opened. Let me show you some cool stuff," Ryan says as he tells me more about his job as a creative director for a hotel chain. As we walk hand in hand through the lobby, we discover a patio with ivy trailing along the walls and a fountain in the middle surrounded by sofas and over-sized chairs. All the tables are taken, so we stand and look around. He talks about the history of the hotel, how gangsters used to hang out here in the Roaring Twenties, and the ad executives who lured clients away from other agencies in the sixties over martinis.

We head back inside and stop in front of a panel with intricate linking circles made out of steel. It's dimly lit, and as we take in the artwork, a young man passes by, holding a sleeping toddler in his arms.

"Wonder what the circles stand for?" I say. "Maybe it represents the universe or planets lining up?"

"Or maybe family? Man, woman, and child linked together as one." He brushes my hair behind my ear and then bends down and kisses my neck, stops for a moment to look at me, before making his way to my lips.

As his lips follow the outline of my face, he makes his way back to my ear and whispers, "It's pretty late. Let me call you an Outro."

CHAPTER 17

After the evening with Ryan and for the rest of the week, I think about my new life and a new beginning. My mind races as I'm constantly reminded of endings—and there are so many. Like the last time I had dinner with the kids; the last time we'd vacationed together during their spring break; the last time Chili wagged her tail when Nate came home from work. They're all endings, and I still haven't completely said good-bye to them, to grieve and make room for the newness I so desperately want and deserve.

Nate doesn't escape so easily from my thoughts with his indiscretions, and I have to force myself to flip the switch. And that makes me think of my beginnings with Ryan. The first time he smiles at me at the bar. The first time he kisses me on the street corner. The first time he reaches for my hand and touches my leg.

But should someone be allowed into my life so quickly and for the distraction? A distraction to override the pain that Nate left? I can't replace the emptiness with someone to keep from hurting, even if there's chemistry. And I can't live in denial and not think about what happened with my marriage. Do I need to face the hurt head on and allow myself to be vulnerable—and to be alone for a while to get over it?

Maybe it's me being angry with Nate for his betrayal that tells me it's okay to move on, to have some newness, a connection, some laughter and light, something that's easy. Things that almost make you hurt from the joy they bring.

The doorbell rings and when Chili growls, we both look out the bedroom window. An email from the furniture company clearly states delivery between noon and four and it's only eleven. Honestly, I'm glad to get this over with.

I take one more look at my empty bedroom. There's not one piece of furniture in this space. All of it—my bed, the nightstands, the dresser, even the little table in the corner—all gone, given to a home that needs it. There won't be any old reminders of my life with Nate and the intimacy we once shared. New furniture helps me start over again and what better place than to begin in the bedroom, especially when it involves a lying, soon-to-be ex-husband?

I rush downstairs and open the front door. Two burly guys with tanned biceps and dark hair pulled back in ponytails stand by the truck and jump into the back. They pull out a few boxes and prop them on the sidewalk before grabbing a few more. The guy at the door hands me the paperwork to check the items: a box spring, headboard, mattress, and two nightstands.

"Looks good. Is there a mattress in there somewhere?" I ask, knowing that out of all of these items, it's the most important.

"In one of those boxes." He points. "We'll let it inflate in the room while we're putting the bed together. Takes about thirty minutes."

"Yeah, I watched the video on their website," I add. "The whole bed-in-a-box concept. It's pretty cool—and the reviews were awesome."

With the front door already open, the biggest guy heads up to the bedroom with a couple of boxes on his back as the other lifts a nightstand in front of him. I call out for them to be careful because it's hard for me to break an old habit, the one where I'd remind Emily and Max to watch it on the stairs.

As promised, the mattress starts to inflate once they take it out of the box. Within the hour, they're done assembling the foundation, nightstands, and headboard—something that would've taken me forever. It reminds me of the time I gave up putting together a desk years ago and paid a hundred bucks to a neighbor to do it for me—more than the actual desk cost.

Once they're done assembling, they slide the mattress onto the bed and pick up the cardboard and leftover screws. "You want these?"

"Sure, you never know when you need a screw," I say before realizing how wrong it sounds.

They laugh, even though they've probably heard it a thousand times, and I let my hair hang over my face to hide my embarrassment. One of them bends down to pet Chili and it gives me an easy way out to change the subject.

I follow them downstairs, reach into my pocket, and hand each guy a tip before heading back up to put on the new sheets, comforter, and fluff some pillows.

And that's when it hits me: The old is gone. All of it. Every single piece. And the new is a big fucking adjustment.

Setting up my bed gives me such mixed emotions. It's a great new start to a room. And at the same time makes me wonder: How long has it really been empty? And without me even knowing it?

For a moment, I remember Nate sleeping next to me. When he said goodnight, was he thinking about her? Was he planning their getaway in his head when the lights went out? Was our marriage something he rushed into after his first one became a façade? And that's when I realize my bedroom has been missing real, honest intimacy for longer than I want to admit. And like books that tumble down when you remove one of the bookends—it all comes crashing down on me.

How could a relationship come to a sudden halt? In reality, it probably ends up happening gradually, like oil from an engine dripping out bit by bit. You don't notice, or you realize something's barely broken—and maybe if it's ignored, it will go away. Instead it continues to fall apart. Or it's when nothing happens. Simple complacency. Maybe that's what happened to Nate and me. Maybe the complacency of our relationship was all his wandering eye needed.

I sit down on my new bed, look out the window, and listen to the birds making their home on a tree outside. A ping from a text gets my attention.

> *Hey there. Any plans for the weekend of July 14?*

How's it possible that Ryan knows more than ever that I need a distraction? I check my calendar and text him back.

Nope, no plans, whatcha thinking?

Ever been to Savannah?

I contemplate my answer, wondering where this is going. Before texting back, he continues.

Going for work. Meet me? My treat. And don't worry, we'll get separate rooms.

Savannah's a city I have always wanted to explore and quickly check the flights—a quick nonstop from Miami.

Can I let you know by the end of the week?

I wait for his reply and seconds later he gives my text a thumbs-up.

It would be a nice getaway and needed distraction, but it's kind of full-on, intimate with Ryan—someone I'm just getting to know. Are we jumping in too fast? It could be romantic or a complete disaster. I fluff my pillow and lie back, imagining the trip, allowing myself to fantasize about romantic walks along cobblestone streets while deciding whether or not to go.

CHAPTER 18

It never crossed my mind that an airport could be called charming. Savannah's walkway feels like a mix of an outdoor promenade and a train station, with its large hanging clock and benches alongside lush plants resembling a park scene. The glass roof adds to the charm as the moonlight shines through. I stop and stare at the sky, trying to count the stars, imagining the times my family stopped on the side of the road to look at them—just because. It's those moments, the just-because spontaneous moments that we remember, where we stop what we're doing and enjoy what life brings us.

I pull the hotel information out of my bag and plug it into my Outro app. We're staying in what Ryan calls the riverfront district and within twenty minutes, my driver stops in front of the hotel and pops the trunk. I get out of his car and walk to the back, grabbing my bag, and then look over at the lights on the bridge and their reflection on the river.

The lobby staff greet me as I wander into the hotel and, after giving them my name at the front desk, they say my credit card isn't needed, that one's already on file. They hand me the key and direct me to the elevators. It reminds me of the night I drove to the hotel near home … the night I confronted Nate. The thoughts still consume me and when I check the room number, I'm relieved that it has no meaning to me, no resemblance to a happier time that's been clouded with deceit. My phone pings and it's a text from Ryan. Perfect timing.

Hey there, have you arrived?

Before texting back, I open the door and take in the spacious interior, with its calming cream walls, king-size bed, and plush accent pillows in orange and white stripes.

Literally just walked in. Room is beautiful, thank you!

Great! I'll be done by late morning. Let's meet in the lobby at noon. Sweet dreams, Maggie.

His text makes me smile and I text him back before throwing my jacket on the desk and running my hand along the pillow. You can tell the quality of a hotel by two things: toilet paper and thread count. My years as a home goods buyer gives me the ability to touch a pillowcase and know the count in a second. It's not quite a superpower, knowing what will have you sleeping like a baby, although a six-hundred count will have you snoozing in no time with its soft and luxurious fabric against your skin—if you can sleep through the hallway noise, slamming doors, or the ding of an elevator.

A magazine on the coffee table tells me the background story of Savannah—a charming Southern city with trendy stores and great restaurants mixed with an eerie atmosphere, commercial fishermen, and mythical ghost stories. Its breathtaking views along cobblestone streets seem to keep travelers coming back for more.

***

The floor-to-ceiling curtains stay open overnight, so the morning light seeps into the room along with a view of the Talmadge Bridge and steamboats in the distance. Fun and adventure await me, in a city that's earned top marks as a great place to visit. I stretch and roll out of bed, making my way to the closet to choose an outfit, changing three times before settling on my tan jeans, a dark gray v-neck, and ballet flats.

As the natural light streams across the room and onto the mirror, it shows off honey-colored highlights my hairdresser added around the front, adding some warmth to my light complexion. I reach for my concealer and put it aside after taking a closer look. It could be more than the highlights making me look rested. Maybe the new bed is doing the trick. Or having Nate out of my life. After putting on some blush, I work product through my hair, dab on pink lip gloss, and add navy liner to the outer edges of my brown eyes to make them look bigger.

At noon, Ryan is waiting for me in the lobby and when I see him, like every other time, my imagination gets the better of me. It's a mix of nervousness and excitement, of freedom and guilt.

As he pulls me close, his damp hair brushes against my cheek and smells like the same citrusy shampoo from my room. He's wearing a blue T-shirt, faded jeans, and flip-flops. When he walks ahead of me to ask a question at the front desk, his broad shoulders and slender waist get my attention.

I imagine him lying in bed and, at the same time, wonder if what we have is only a physical attraction or something deeper. Do I like him enough? Can I imagine him as a friend, someone to turn to when needed? Would he be a hero when challenges came up, or would he run the other way and not look back?

Ryan comes toward me and takes my hand. "Are you up for a walk?"

"Sure, I'm up for anything."

"Anything?" he teases as he holds the door for me. "What about some raw oysters and a shot of vodka?"

"Vodka, yes. Oysters, not so much."

"Not a fan, huh? To me, anything chased with vodka makes it worthwhile."

"You're on," I say as my competitiveness kicks in. "Let's see who looks like they're gonna puke first."

Ryan pulls out his phone and checks the map. He pinpoints a seafood restaurant known for its raw bar, and we stroll there along the waterfront. In front of us, the cobblestone street has its way with a woman in heels and it's not long before her date helps chisel out her shoe from between the cracks. They continue down the street, arm in arm, as she calculates her steps.

Along the historic street, we pass art galleries, ice cream shops, and souvenir stores. The hustle and bustle of the waterfront, the ships and boats docking, and dads chasing behind their kids as they rush into candy stores: It all reveals a charming chaos in this picturesque Southern city.

"There it is." Ryan points.

As we approach the restaurant, we walk down a few narrow steps and through a dark hallway before going up another set of stairs. It feels like an old-timey tavern, one from a movie with soldiers sloshing their beers in tin mugs and stumbling out to find their horses. It makes me giggle and when I share my thoughts with Ryan, he wonders how they'd find their horses while drunk. "I bet they would've loved a Find My Horse app."

"If you're too drunk to find your horse," I add, "you're probably too drunk to use the Find My Horse app."

He chuckles as we walk into the restaurant. "True, and you shouldn't be riding while drunk anyways. You could hurt someone."

"Like yourself?"

"Or the horse you rode in on," Ryan jokes when the hostess approaches and mentions there's an hour wait for a table.

As we're deciding whether to add our name to the waiting list, two seats open at the bar and we grab them before it's too late. The bartender hands us menus, and Ryan checks out the cocktails while I see which appetizers look good. Crab-stuffed mushrooms, mussels with white wine sauce, and of course shrimp cocktail and a variety of raw oysters.

"Okay, I know you're adventurous, right?" he says with authority.

"Depends. Where's this going?"

"I want to order something without you knowing what it is, and you have to agree to drink it." He moves away when I try to grab the cocktail menu from him. "Come on, it'll be fun."

"Famous last words," I say, and go in for a kiss while trying to grab the menu again.

"Who's last words?" he asks. "Mine, yours, or the drunk guy on the horse?"

"Okay," I say, giving in to Ryan's persuasiveness. "I'm up for some adventure. Go ahead and order."

The bartender comes over and leans toward us. Ryan points to the drink, says we'll have four, and hands him the menu to keep it away from me.

"Four! What have I gotten myself into?"

"Two's not enough. And six will make us wish we had a Find Our Hotel app."

"And what about eight?" I ask.

"Don't want to find out. At least on an empty stomach. Speaking of which," Ryan says and puts his hand on my leg, "see anything that looks good?"

"Depends on what we're drinking," I tease, hoping for a clue, and moments later the bartender approaches with four shot glasses filled with a red concoction.

He sets them down and separates the glasses equally in front of us. Mini celery sticks stand upright and lemon wedges sit on the rims of each glass.

Ryan rubs his hands together and lifts a glass in a toast. "Bloody Mary oyster shots. You ready?" he asks.

"Oh, hell no."

"What do you mean, hell no? You promised!"

We go back and forth teasing each other until we agree that he'll get a taste of his own medicine at the next bar. Our glasses come together with a toast, and we down the shots faster than you can say, *What the hell were we thinking?*

Ryan's about to gag, and it makes me want to gag and laugh at the same time, which could be a disaster considering there's a woman wearing a white silk blouse sitting next to me. I'm trying desperately to get the oyster down without upchucking, and at this point, Ryan's done with his and pats himself on the shoulder in victory.

I squirm and push my second shot toward him. "That's downright torture. There's no way in hell I can get another one down."

He pushes it back my way. "Pretend you're stranded on a deserted island and it's the only food you have to survive."

"I'd rather be eaten by sharks when I try to swim to the next island."

"Where there's a McDonald's drive-thru?"

I laugh and imagine the impossibility of fighting off sharks with my bare hands while dreaming of a Big Mac. Ryan picks up our last shots and hands me mine.

The first one has kicked in fast. We clink again and wait for the other to make the first move. I down mine in seconds and raise my eyebrows in victory. He raises his arm in a cheers motion and throws the shot back.

Suddenly, I'm very tipsy. His T-shirt hugs his chest and biceps perfectly and makes me wonder how he'd look naked. Was this his plan? Do a search how to make a girl horny? Top results: Bloody Mary oyster shots for the win.

Our bar food arrives, and we stuff our faces with calamari and spinach dip, pay the bill, and say good-bye to the hostess. Feeling the breeze, we stroll along the waterfront in the early afternoon and pass by several shops, making our way down the cobblestone street. There's one shop that catches my attention and we stop in front of the window that's filled with funny T-shirts, kitchen gadgets, retro posters, and other tchotchkes.

"I've been here before," he says. "Lots of unique stuff."

A woman with bright-pink hair, a nose ring, and a scorpion tattoo on her arm greets us from behind the counter. We split up and wander throughout the racks of mugs, novelty gifts, and calendars. Every few minutes, we call out for the other and hold up an item that makes us laugh. The salesgirl, who's wearing a Joy Division T-shirt, has great taste in music with her 80s playlist blasting in the background. Ryan makes his way to the greeting cards and I join him, swiveling the rack around to find a few for friends back home.

"Ooh, Simon Le Bon," he says as "Save a Prayer" comes on in the background before adding, "My mom had the biggest crush on him."

First our connection with Imagine Dragons, now this. How could I not fall even more for this guy? Duran Duran brings me back to my youth, also reminding me of my mom and all the times she danced to this song. It's my childhood at its finest, like the smell of my mom's homemade lasagna, eating mint chocolate chip ice cream in front of the TV, and the Jennifer Aniston haircut she insisted would look good on me.

"My mom played 'Hungry Like the Wolf' on repeat," he says as he stops to listen. "It's amazing how much I still love it despite hearing it a thousand times."

"I've always imagined dancing to this song," I blurt out and instantly regret saying it and letting my guard down. Being vulnerable has consequences. Will he pretend he didn't hear me? Will he be too embarrassed to dance in public? Or will I be too embarrassed, pulling away if he asks—too scared of what strangers will think?

He takes the cards out of my hand and places them on the display. "Let's make it happen."

In a second, his arms are wrapped around my waist and we're dancing to "Save a Prayer" in this cute, quirky store on the Savannah waterfront. The clerk smiles and reaches over to turn up the volume enough for me to notice, and when we get to the middle of the song, Ryan looks at me, and I get teary-eyed and turn away. He's killing me. Not because we don't give a shit who's watching—because I'm remembering my mom, our family vacations, my childhood. And because I'm sharing this rare moment with someone who was a stranger a month ago.

CHAPTER 19

I haven't forgotten my plan: to get Ryan back for the oyster shots. We continue down the street, arms entwined, following the crowd that floods the streets with life and energy.

As we stand in front of another bar, we hear whistling and cheering, even though the singer sounds off-key and tries to hit notes that are way out of her reach. We look through the window. It's dark inside, so we keep listening outside near the bouncer, who sits on a wooden stool with his arms folded.

"Sounds like she played hooky during her choir class," Ryan says.

"Or slept through it," I add.

"Oh, that explains it." Ryan points up to the neon karaoke sign.

He walks toward the door and the bouncer stops him, asking for ID and ten bucks for the cover. After Ryan hands over the money, we walk in. Dimly lit, the bar has a mixed crowd: some older, some college students, and a bunch of young rowdy guys throwing back their beers.

Ryan grabs my hand and leads me toward the back as my ballet flats stick to the beer-covered floor. "Have you ever done karaoke?" he asks.

"Once."

"Oh yeah? What song?"

"Not saying. Way too embarrassing."

"I'll get it out of you, sooner or later," he says and points to a high-top table across from the bar.

"What about you?"

"No way," he says. "And it's never gonna happen."

I grab one of the chairs. "Never say never."

"I'm saying never. Now, and anytime you ask."

I pull out my phone and read some reviews. "Best karaoke bar in town, it says here." Another reviewer calls it "My go-to place for fun, great beer selection." Another adds, "Somebody, hold my drink, going up for another drunken attempt at 'Walk This Way.'"

Ryan listens as I read them and tells me for a third time that there's no way he's going on stage. He makes me promise I won't push him. I agree, of course with fingers crossed behind my back.

It's loud as hell and entertaining as we watch several wannabe rockers take the stage and butcher every great song chosen. We try not to laugh and agree that we couldn't have done any better.

Ryan pulls me close and we start kissing. He tightens his hand around my waist. It's dark and who knows if anyone notices because nothing matters except his touch and lips on mine. He has no idea how horny I'm getting but I don't feel comfortable telling him yet. I pull away and reach for my beer.

"Nobody's watching, nobody cares," Ryan teases and starts playing with my hair.

"If nobody's watching or cares," I scream over the music, "why don't you go pick out your karaoke song?"

"Good try," he yells back over the host, who calls up the next singer.

By now, we're tipsy after our two oyster shots and part of a beer. I gaze at him for several seconds.

"Stop it," he says and bites his lower lip.

"Stop what?"

"Stop looking at me like that."

"Come on, it'll be fun," I beg. "You'll love it. And besides, nobody will remember. We'll never see any of these people again."

"Except you. I hope I'll see you again."

"Only if you do karaoke."

He laughs and contemplates my request, rubbing his chin, giving me a smile that kills me every time with his chipped tooth that reminds me of the day we met.

"I'm horrible at singing," he says.

"No worse than anyone here."

"You should consider motivational speaking; you'd be great at it."

A couple starts singing at the bar, catching my attention, making me wonder how they met, what they do for a living, and how long they've known each other. Ryan and I haven't known each other long at all but the connection feels so real and the urge to get my hands on him no matter where we are, no matter who's watching, is undeniable.

"So, what will you give me if I do it?" Ryan says with a wink.

"I'll let you download the Find My Horse app."

"Oh, so I need permission?"

"Yeah, you do. For the premier version where you get to skip the ads and choose an upgraded saddle."

Ryan downs his beer and heads over to the DJ booth. He bends over to look at the guy's laptop and spends a few minutes searching through the song list.

"Well?" I ask when he returns.

"I'm seventh in line." He shakes his head and looks around the crowd. "Can't believe I'm doing this."

The bar gets busier by the minute and each time the host calls up another singer, Ryan feels relieved it's not him. He's trying to talk himself out of it, then bites his nails while waiting for his turn. I tell him he'll be great and to have another beer to calm his nerves. He won't tell me the song he's chosen no matter how I try to get it out of him. Maybe it's "Whatever It Takes" or "Save a Prayer." He shakes his head with each attempted guess.

Ryan downs his beer and sets the glass down when he realizes they've called his name. He heads his way to the stage, and I weave my way through the crowd and follow him up to videotape it.

Ryan picks up the mic and looks over at the DJ, who projects the lyrics from his laptop onto a screen on the wall. The crowd screams as "Hungry Like the Wolf" blasts through the speakers propped on the walls.

He starts singing—and it's so off-key that I'm cringing while loving every second. As the lyrics keep moving up on the screen, Ryan doesn't look over—it's as if they're etched in a childhood memory from when his mom played it on repeat.

I don't let on how much I'm basking in this moment, how I'm desperately trying to keep it together. He's looking straight at me and coming closer and closer while singing, his brown eyes fixated on me with a look that says there's no other person in the room.

He jumps off the stage when he's done and gets a crazy round of applause from the crowd. His face and the front of his shirt are covered in sweat and when he makes his way toward me, he tries to grab my phone. I turn around and walk back to our table.

"I can't believe you recorded me! Don't you dare show that to anyone."

"You were amazing. Wanna see?"

"Not sure." He squints. "Does it belong in the comedy or horror section?"

I hand him my phone, and Ryan watches the recording without the sound. He grimaces and decides the catastrophe should be deleted immediately for the good of the universe and all humanity.

He hands the phone back. "Surprised I didn't break something with that jump."

"Or your other moves. You had several."

"Mick Jagger's got nothing on me."

"Who's that?"

Ryan lets go of my hand and looks at me with disbelief. "Seriously? You don't know?"

I hit him on the elbow. "Who doesn't like the Beatles?" I joke again and he grabs me by the waist as we walk to the front.

We leave the karaoke bar behind and neither of us can stop smiling, stopping on every corner to kiss. What's going on? How can I be into someone so soon and be thinking about him all the time? Could I have a future with this guy who showed up next to me with his crooked smile, challenged me to a paper airplane contest, made me drink oyster shots, and danced and sang to my favorite Duran Duran songs?

But why does it matter? I shouldn't be worried about the future when I'm still waiting for my divorce to be finalized.

We make it back to the hotel, still tipsy, and Ryan walks me to my room. We stop in front of the door and kiss some more. It takes so much willpower to say goodnight in the hallway. I close the door behind me and look out through the peephole. Ryan's still standing there with a smile. He walks off, and I lean back on the wall.

Part of me wants to open the door, to call his name as he's halfway down the hall, to see him run back and into my arms. I don't tempt myself. I'm doing this on purpose, the waiting game that is, because it seems right to wait even though my body aches for him. I lie on the bed and think about him while touching myself, hoping it leads to dreams where we're ripping each other's clothes off.

CHAPTER 20

It's Monday morning and I'm back home. I jump out of bed after hitting the snooze button three times, reminiscing about the weekend in Savannah. The walk by the waterfront. Our dancing in the store. Ryan's butchering of "Hungry Like the Wolf." It's easy to get distracted and caught up in the memories.

My phone pings with a notification. Our Monday morning meeting gets pushed back to ten, and it allows me time for a shot of caffeine at my favorite spot. The idea of going to the coffee shop gets a little easier now, even though Nate and the other woman are still on my mind.

It's ridiculous to swear off coffee shops because they met at one. The passing of time helps and my addiction to caffeine makes it easier. Nate getting caught red-handed doesn't consume me as much anymore during the day; it's at night when I can't sleep, or whenever I see a woman with short, blonde hair wearing a denim jacket.

This morning, the shop by my office has an unusually long line. The cashier and baristas take care of the customers as a guy behind the counter pulls muffins out of the oven and slides them onto a cooling rack next to the showcase.

"Medium-dark roast," I say when it's my turn.

"Room for whiskey?" the cashier says, beating me to my usual follow-up line.

"You know it," I respond and hand over a few bucks in exchange for a jolt of liquid fuel and a smile.

I pick up the cup, grab a cookie sample from the plate, and head toward the crosswalk, the same one I cross every morning. Usually, it's less than a minute for the wait. This morning, I want the light to take forever when Nate waves and grabs my attention from across the street.

He's standing in front of my building, wearing the jacket he bought on our trip to New York the year after we got married. We haven't seen each other for several months and damn if the separation doesn't agree with him. He's got a slight tan and the gray around his temples has become more pronounced. It's a good look, I want to tell him, and hold back for fear that it'll go to his head, or that he'll take the compliment the wrong way.

"What are you doing here?" I ask instead while approaching.

"Nice seeing you, too. You look good, by the way. Changed your hair color."

"Seriously, Nate," I say and switch my bag to my other side. "It's been awhile since they invented the telephone. Last I checked, it still works."

"How are you?" he asks and grins, to perhaps offset my blank stare.

I still don't know why he's here beating around the bush. After some uncomfortable silence, he continues, "Wanted to talk to you about this in person and figured you didn't want me coming around to the house."

My shoulders get tense. I wonder if there's something wrong with the kids. He says they're fine and stares at me, making me feel uneasy.

"I want you back," he blurts out. "Would you consider giving me a second chance?"

"You mean third chance." I can tell it stings him and doesn't faze me one bit.

He has some nerve showing up like this, unannounced and at my office. There's no way I'll take him back and give him another chance. He must be lonely or already bored with the blonde. Or maybe the blonde threw him to the curb like he deserves. It's hard to believe that my feelings could go from love to hate so quickly. Since we're in public, I stay civil and keep calm.

"Look, it's hard for both of us, but it's not going to happen. I promised myself last time. There's no way I'm going back on my word—or back to our pretend-happy life when it was a pack of lies."

I want to say how the memories of his actions still hurt and make me break down but keep it to myself. He needs to think of me as independent and strong as shit.

Nate steps closer and it makes me move back. He stops when realizing the awkwardness. "I've been trying to work up the courage. It took a lot to come here. I swear nothing happened. Can't you forgive me for not telling you about my friendship with her?"

"Do you think I'm stupid? You must be forgetting what you did the first time around. You're clearly a serial cheater or whatever you call it." I fold my arms and wait for his response, until he looks down at the ground.

"Okay," I continue, looking through him. "If she's just a friend, then why didn't you tell me about her? What would've been the big deal?"

"For this exact reason. I knew you wouldn't believe me. You'd flip out."

My temper is calm, my voice even. "This is flipping out? Far from it." My coworker waves as she passes, and it distracts me before focusing again on Nate. He can't know about my snooping, so I play stupid. "I get it. You were scared to tell me. Now, it's too late to make it go away."

"I wish I could, wish I'd told you from the start," he says. He's trying to rewind, to get sympathy.

My patience is dwindling—and at this point, there's none left. "Look, why don't you admit you got caught? I'd have more respect for you if you were honest with me. And to come here after the fact? You didn't appreciate me when you had me."

"Funny that you bring up appreciation," he says with a sarcastic tone. "You didn't appreciate my relationship with Emily and Max. Or how they'd feel."

"What the hell are you talking about?" It's hard for me not to scream.

"Throwing me out while the kids were there. You should be ashamed of yourself."

He's trying to make me feel guilty. His words hurt, and he knows he's gotten to me. I move closer. "Do you know how hard it was for me to ask you to leave, knowing that I'd be giving up my relationship with the kids? I love spending time with them. Waiting for them at the bus stop on Fridays, hanging out with them, making pancakes."

I choke back the tears and barely get the words out. "Are you forgetting how I stood up for you when your ex wanted them to come home early on Sundays instead of Mondays? I care deeply about the relationship you have with them. How could you stoop so low?" I say, running my nail against the inside of my wrist to ease the painful memories and hurtful words Nate continues to drown me in.

It's quiet between us for a moment and as the traffic goes by, I think about a fight we once had. How he blew up and was hurtful out of spite, telling me that I was never happy, and never knew how to be. On the street, in front of my building, I remind him of that time because words like those always leave a scar. "You know, Nate, you were so wrong about my happiness. I am happy—"

"Good," he interrupts.

"Let me finish, will you?"

He waits and puts his arms behind his back in a defensive mode.

"I'm happy and I realized it has everything to do with me. I'm happy at work, happy with my friends, happy out and about. I'm happy. Period."

"I get it, you're happy!" he interrupts, the boldness of his words played out in sarcasm. He's trying to dismiss me, trying to make me second-guess my feelings. This second time around, it's not going to work.

I sigh, patiently waiting for him to finish. And as I continue, he's not listening when I say that when the bottom fell out of our relationship and when he moved out, my life was better without him. I repeat the last part twice and it hurts, but he needs to hear it.

"You're missing the point," I continue.

"And what's that?"

"You need to let me go."

Nate's blue eyes are bloodshot and glassy. He turns away when a car's horn startles him.

"Isn't it better than holding on, only for me to get even more resentful? I'm already pissed enough and finally getting over it."

Nate nods and looks away. "The last thing I ever wanted was to let you down. It eats at me every day."

"Don't worry." I force a smile and continue. "You're not letting me down. Not anymore at least."

He comes in for a hug, and it's awkward. We pat each other on the back as if we're long-lost relatives saying good-bye at a reunion, knowing we may never see each other again. Before heading into my office building, I watch him walk down the block and disappear around the corner.

CHAPTER 21

"Would you like to come over tonight?" I say to Ryan over the phone the weekend after running into Nate in front of my office. He hasn't asked me to invite him. It's simply because I haven't been ready to bring him home, to a home that not long ago Nate was part of, along with Emily and Max. At the time, I hadn't realized we were a family of incompletes, like a puzzle with missing pieces.

It's hard not to have Max and Emily in my life like before. I miss them so much. Now they feel like friends who live far away who you don't see often. The memories are what comfort you. And even though you miss them, you make yourself believe the mental images you have of them are enough. But it's not enough, and I'll always worry about how they're doing.

The doorbell rings and Chili goes berserk. Once she hears me say "friend," Chili calms down when she sees Ryan for the first time. He bends down to pet her behind the ear and suddenly she has a new best pal.

"Hey," Ryan says and gives me a long hug before passing me a bottle of red wine as we make our way to the kitchen. "Better than oyster shots?" he jokes.

I'm nervous as hell, because it might happen tonight. And Ryan can sense it by asking if we should go out for a bit or take a walk in the neighborhood. He laughs when I tell him that I'm recreating the oyster shots—in the blender to go on top of omelets.

"Sounds pretty good. Put some extra cheese in them for me," he adds.

"I do make a mean omelet."

Chili begs for a snack when she eyes the cheese platter on the counter. Ryan opens the wine and fills our glasses.

I drink slowly, afraid to get tipsy, to let my vulnerabilities show, to let the truth serum seep into my veins. When Ryan mentions Savannah again and calls it our river-walk rendezvous, it stops me in my tracks. Do we share the same brain? How does he know I've used that exact phrase to describe our adventure more than once?

"Rendezvous? You speak French now, huh?"

He nods. "My grandmother was from France and we spent all our summers with her. We were really close."

"Seriously? And I was messing with you about knowing French."

"She died a few years ago and I got a tattoo in her honor." He lifts the sleeve of his shirt to show me a line of numbers. "Coordinates. Exact spot of her house."

He pushes his sleeve down and pours some more wine. "So, when did you get the apostrophe?"

"Last year," I tell him, a little irritated that he didn't remember from one of our dates.

"You think you'll get any more?"

"Two are enough," I say, not realizing until afterward where my answer might lead us.

"Oh yeah, what's the second one?"

"A butterfly. Got it in New York on one of my extended business trips."

"That's cool. Where is it?"

I point at my left side near my bra.

"I'd like to see it someday. Maybe when we go to the beach?"

"Why wait?" I whisper, having to push out the words because I'm anxious about being intimate with someone new.

Ryan puts his glass down. He comes closer, and we start kissing. I can feel Chili's eyes on me and, sure enough, she's standing in front of us, trying to get attention. I snap my fingers, and she prances over to her bed near the kitchen door.

"Uh-oh, is she in trouble?" Ryan asks before kissing my neck.

"She was staring like nobody's business."

"You don't like being watched?" he teases.

"Definitely not by Chili. Though Zac Efron wouldn't be so bad," I tease back and kiss his neck as he tries to reach up my shirt.

"Wait a second," I say, sliding across my kitchen floor to dim the overhead lights.

My nerves get the better of me and, for a minute, I have second thoughts and lean back against the counter.

"You're beautiful in any light," Ryan says and walks closer. He bends down to kiss me and unfastens the top button of my blouse. "Is this okay?" he asks and, since I don't stop him or say no, he unbuttons the remaining ones and pushes my shirt back until it falls to the ground. He kisses my shoulder and reaches behind me with one hand.

I laugh after he unsnaps my bra with one try. "You're good at that."

"A trick I've seen in the movies, by what's his name?" He gets distracted and takes my bra off as I fold my arms in front of me. I'm still so nervous. Other than Nate, no other guy has seen me naked for years. As I stand, still with folded arms, he moves to my side. "There it is," he says when he finds my tattoo and brushes his hand against it.

"Love how the pink blends into the charcoal, and it's the perfect location." Ryan makes his way down my body, kissing me gently beginning at the tattoo and down to my hip. I moan and tell him to keep at it until he reaches my belly button.

"Stop," I whisper and take his hand in mine, leading him upstairs to my bedroom. Chili follows us and looks at me with her big brown eyes before I shut the door to keep her out.

Ryan's standing by the window, looking out. "It's nice and quiet here," he says and turns around and walks toward me.

A picture on my desk catches his eye. It's the one of Max and Emily from our Orlando trip. Even though Nate isn't in the photo, it makes me think of him as I walk toward the picture to turn it around. "Sorry," I say, right before standing on my toes to reach him when he comes in for a kiss. Excitement and nervousness continue to work their way through me like the first time on the way to Little Joe's.

"Let's put on some music," he whispers in my ear.

"Sure. What would you like?"

"Let's use my playlist," Ryan says and hooks his phone up to my Bluetooth speaker. He fiddles with his Spotify app and puts on Muse, another band I love.

After putting his phone down, he comes back over.

Am I really ready for this? Or am I trying to fill a void? These thoughts go through my head, clouding my mind, making it difficult to enjoy the moment. We stop kissing, and he moves his hand down to unzip my jeans.

"Wait," I ask.

"Okay, sure," he says and readjusts his pants.

"Are you seeing anyone else?"

"You're direct, aren't you?" he says and adds, "No, of course not."

"Not even dating?"

He shakes his head.

"Sleeping with anyone?"

"Nope."

I start regretting my words. I'm ruining the moment. But I need to know. "Were you dating anyone seriously before we met?"

He nods and sits on the bed.

"For how long?" I ask and join him on the edge.

"Six months."

We sit for a minute and it gives me time to think. That's not long for someone to be serious. Seems like nothing. It almost takes that long to figure out where to go on your second or third date.

"I can't date more than one woman at a time," he says, breaking the silence.

"Why not?"

"Because when I like someone, I like someone. One's all I need."

Is he bullshitting to get me in the sack? Can he be trusted or will he be like Nate?

I don't want to be Ryan's rebound. And I don't want him to be mine for fear of being alone or substituting what's been lost. There's no way of knowing if I don't let my guard down.

"Starlight," my favorite Muse song, comes on and the light shines from the bathroom, cascading onto the bed. We stare at each other and he looks at the door when Chili belts out a low bark.

"Should I check on her?" he asks.

"She's fine. Probably dreaming about squirrels."

This time I'm the one who leans in for the kiss. He kisses me back and lowers me onto the bed before taking off his shirt. We get under the covers, where we take off the rest of our clothes.

He kisses me again, his lips making their way to one of my breasts, then the other. I know what's next as he inches his way down my body and to my stomach, but I don't want that right now. I want to feel his breath on my neck. To feel him inside me. To hear him moan. To feel like he'll never leave me.

***

We lie naked, and Ryan props up the pillow as I lay my head on his chest. He plays with my hair and massages the back of my neck.

"My ex and I never had this." It's the first time I've brought up Nate in conversation.

"What's that?" Ryan asks.

"The intimacy, and the talking," I continue. "He used to roll over after, and in minutes, he'd be snoring."

There's silence between us, and my regret settles in. I'm about to apologize for bringing up Nate until Ryan makes a joke about snoring and then gets serious when he says that looking at relationships helps us realize what's important.

"Don't worry," he adds, after pulling the comforter up and over my back. "I'll always communicate with you. Maybe a little too much sometimes."

"It's never too much. And the fact you listen, that's key. You know," I say, "you rarely talk about your job. Is that on purpose?"

"You're onto me," he says after a good laugh. "It's pretty stressful right now. I love it, even with the crazy deadlines. Trying to keep it out of my mind at the moment."

"Okay, how about this." I quickly change the subject. "What haven't you done in your life that you still want to do?"

"Sounds like something I need to answer when I'm fifty."

"That's next year, right?"

He tickles me, and I twist away and sit up. "Seriously, what's on your bucket list?"

He pauses. "I can think of two things off the bat. Jumping out of an airplane."

"And the other?" I ask and turn on my side to face him.

He pauses. "You go first."

"Okay. A cross-country drive. And to fall hopelessly in love."

"That's ambitious," he adds.

"I know, right? It takes about three days."

"That's pretty quick to fall in love."

We laugh before he continues to nudge. "Weren't you in love with your ex-husband?"

His question surprises me. It's the kind that could require thought, and some carefulness. For me, the answer comes to me naturally, so easily, because it's something I still yearn for. "Yes, of course, I'm talking about something different. That crazy, passionate kind you see in the movies."

"Ahhh, a hopeless romantic. I love it."

Of course, the word "hopeless" sticks out. Is it hopeless to fall madly, can't-help-myself, forget-to-eat-and-drink in love one of these days? Or at least once in my life?

Ryan continues. "I've had that feeling of being crazy in love, only to realize it was lust the whole time."

"Maybe you should stick to the jumping out of airplanes part—it might be less risky."

"Maybe," he says. "Wanna jump with me?"

"No thanks. Think I'll keep my feet on the ground."

"Are you sure about that?" he teases and flips me onto my back, kissing me, making me beg him not to stop.

Chapter 22

Monday morning comes too soon and the snooze button keeps getting hit. I'm still thinking about my first time with Ryan. His morning texts are racier since Friday night. Instead of "good morning" or "have an awesome day," they say, "thinking about tearing your clothes off" or "when can I see you again and kiss my favorite spot."

It's not long before my alarm goes off again. We have two long Monday meetings and to get anything done between them, an early start is a must. The shower awakens me and beats down my back as I wring out the excess water from my hair. After drying off and throwing on a floral-print dress and strappy sandals, I head off to work and the parkway cooperates without too much traffic.

During our two Monday meetings, deals are decided, discounts are worked out, sales numbers are projected. Decisions are made about whether we should keep certain brands on life support or cut them off and let the reps know. We hate making those calls, but we have to stay competitive. And since most people shop online now, we have to come up with creative ideas to keep people coming back. The new assistant buyer who's right out of college blows us away with her ideas. And our art director and copywriter, who we call the dynamic duo, make the magic happen with their ads and ideas for social media, along with videos that include celebrity influencers.

By the time lunch rolls around, I work up an appetite from all the talking and head over to BeeBar24, where a woman named Bee whips up twenty-four-hour breakfasts, hence the name and my crazy addiction to it. Bragging to Ryan about my great omelet skills would make Bee laugh as she shows me how it's done, keeping one ingredient a secret she claims she'll take to her grave. My thoughts about Ryan get pushed away when I finally walk out of there feeling sated, and notice Nate standing in front of the restaurant.

He's leaning against a parking sign. When he sees me, he places his satchel over his shoulder and approaches with an awkward hug. I want to make another half-assed joke about him forgetting there's such a thing as a phone but bite my tongue and wait for him to speak.

"Sorry for showing up like this. I know it's your Monday lunch spot."

"I'm a creature of habit," I add and switch my purse to the other arm. "What's up?" I ask. "You keep materializing like something out of *Star Trek*."

"Good one." Nate grins and squints as the sun beats down on his face. He puts his hand over his forehead as a makeshift visor. "I promise, I'm not stalking you."

"Sure feels like it. A phone call would be best at this point. You can't keep showing up like this."

"I know. Felt I had to see you in person again … this last time," he adds. "And figured the house is off limits."

Nate doesn't continue and silence takes over before I ask, "So, what couldn't you tell me over the phone?"

"We're in the final countdown," he says. "The lawyer sent me the divorce waiver and I've signed it."

My stomach drops. The divorce is what I need, the only thing that will help keep me sane—who needs a serial liar in their lives? But it still hurts. And it stings, thinking about writing "divorced" on paperwork and telling strangers and friends who shoot back sad looks when they feel sorry for me. "Couldn't you mail it?" I say, holding back the tears.

"I was about to. In all honesty, I wanted to give us one last try. And to say I'm really sorry about what happened."

"So, you came here for that? An omelet with some extra remorse on the side?"

"Ouch." He clenches his hands together as his eyes tear up. "I still love you. And Emily and Max miss you."

"Really? Then why, every time I reach out to talk to them, you make up a lame excuse that they're busy? Or they're doing homework. Now, all of a sudden, you bring them up."

He knows how much I miss the kids, and he's dangling them as if getting back together is the only way I'll get to see them. My head starts to throb, wondering what kind of bullshit he's already pulling with his emotional-support girlfriend, if she's still in the picture. Thinking about it makes me snicker, which comes out more like a laugh.

"You think it's funny that the kids miss you?"

"No, of course not. I just don't like to be manipulated."

"That's not what I'm trying to do," he says and folds his arms. "You're reading too much into it."

"I'm not reading shit into it. Look, I want a divorce, and nothing will change my mind. So please stop showing up without warning. It's beneath you."

Nate takes his bag off his shoulder and dumps it on the ground before opening the front pocket. He pulls out a folder and hands it to me.

"Here you go. You can give it to your lawyer." Then he adds, "Maggie, you know I want you to be happy, right? Those things I said when we were fighting, I didn't mean them."

"Thanks," I say and don't tell him to be happy back, because I'm not sure what happiness means to Nate—or if I can find the strength or maturity to want that for him. "Say hi to the kids for me," I wind up adding. "Tell them I miss them back."

CHAPTER 23

Just because you're getting what you want out of life doesn't mean it's easy, or that it doesn't involve a whole slew of emotions, like when you ask someone to be brutally honest with you. It's hard to take sometimes, hearing those jarring words to help you move on or make a change. That's how my separation feels. I couldn't stay and give him another chance. Sure, after my discovery at the DMV, it would've been easier to look the other way. Pretend I didn't see the picture. Pretend it didn't happen. That it was all a dream.

We overlook so many things in relationships to play it safe. This time, I can't do that. I can't allow myself to forgive and forget a repeat offender who begs to stay—only when he gets caught. And it would only get worse—the resentment, that is—wondering when he was coming home late, was he really with someone rather than at the office finishing up all those tax returns?

Not long after Nate hands over the signed waiver, I walk to my mailbox, reach in, and pull out an envelope from our courthouse. My heart races and my palms get sweaty as I flip the envelope from one side to the other. Is it a stamped copy of the waiver? Do they need more information? It taunts me and, at the same time, makes me hesitant like the days we waited for decisions from college admissions offices. Once I rip it open, "Final Judgment and Decree of Divorce" sits in big letters at the top of the document with an official stamp.

Our neighbor, Cynthia, the one with the two cute terriers, walks toward me with her broad smile, polished nails, and perfect chin-length bob that shows off the right amount of blonde highlights. Before I can speak, there's a volley of words that fly at me, one after the other. She talks about her son who's starting college, her daughter who's setting state records as a sprinter in high school, and her husband who recently launched a travel business. She's so self-absorbed, always has been. At this moment, I'm relishing in it, because it's a distraction from my old life that's flimsily wrapped up and finalized in an official court document.

After several stories, Cynthia mentions how she hasn't seen the kids or Nate in a while and makes a joke about tax season being every season. I go along with it because I haven't told her my news. I know she'll bring up how Max used to love petting her dog … that'll make me break down, and I don't want to be sad. Not anymore.

I want to remember this day, the day the decree comes, as a time to move forward and say good-bye to the lies, the deception, the cover-ups. Instead the what-ifs keep surfacing. And I've had so many what-ifs that it gives me headaches, leaves me achy, and feeling needy.

What if I stayed?

What if I didn't go to the DMV that day?

What if I thought of Emily and Max more when it came to my decision?

What if Nate told me, instead of me discovering it?

What if I'd left Nate the first time this happened?

So, Cynthia doesn't get to hear a thing from me. Sooner or later, she'll find out and I'll feel different. A day when I won't feel like crying, when nobody has to feel sorry for me. Because no matter how many times people hear from me that "it's all good" and "don't worry about me" or "it's better this way," they still want to feel for me—even though they don't know the whole story. I don't blame them; it's human nature to think that divorce is a bad thing.

We say our good-byes after she tells me to join her for the next book club, and I go back to my house as it starts sinking in. I'm officially divorced. But I was married a minute ago—or at least before checking the mail—and the grieving process doesn't stop with a snap of a finger or a letter from the court. We've lost something that was once so dear to us.

Even with its permanence and Nate's mishaps, it makes me wonder if I've given myself enough time to understand what really went wrong. It's never one-sided. It's never only someone else's fault. Or maybe in this case it is. Or maybe it's as simple as being with the wrong person and not knowing it at the time.

Reality sinks in, even more, when I think about how Emily and Max aren't part of my life anymore. And that kills me. All of these lost loves kill me, little by little. Thinking about it makes me want to call Ryan, have him distract me with smiles, and laughs, and long kisses that make me yearn for him. Instead, I text Rachel a picture of my divorce decree.

She texts me back right away with plans to meet. Rachel's been through it so she's a pro. I need her to distract me. To tell me that Emily or Max still think about me—even if she lies.

CHAPTER 24

We sit at the bar and play with our wine glasses. The evening calls for an entire bottle rather than a glass because we're toasting to a few things. It's almost like that bittersweet moment close to midnight on New Year's Eve when you say good-bye to the old and ring in what's to come. Those familiar moments become the past as the exciting and unknown take their place.

The bottle is open and waiting for us to give it some attention. Rachel leans in to fill up our glasses rather than call for the bartender.

"Here we are," Rachel says. She lifts her glass and leans toward mine, her smile offering me some comfort.

"Yep, here we are." A smile and a sigh make their way out of me. "I can't believe we're toasting to my divorce."

"Why not?" She clanks my glass against hers. "It's a good thing. You're moving on. You've moved on, I should say."

Rachel has always been so positive and tough as nails, not showing her emotion, letting me think she's the stronger one. Holding it all together doesn't make someone tougher, necessarily, but not losing it paints a picture of strength, something admired by many who've met her.

I've only seen her break down once, when her grandmother died. It's an odd feeling to be grateful for that kind of moment. Not because she cried. Because, when someone crumbles in front of you, it means they feel comfortable enough to show their truth.

I need to be more like everyday Rachel, and hold it all together. It seems these days I'll lose it in front of just about anyone, even the guy who works in the deli department at Trader Joe's, or Victor, who owns the gas station near my house.

Rachel polishes off her wine and fills her glass. "It's hard, I know. I also know it's gonna be a great time for you."

"I can't help think the ink has barely dried."

"It's a good thing," she reminds me. After all…" Rachel pauses and looks over her shoulder at the table behind us.

"After all, what?"

She tries changing the subject. It's not working on me.

"Just say it already!"

"Nate could've asked you to leave, considering he originally bought the house. He could've been even more of a shit."

"So, is it possible to be an asshole and a nice guy at the same time?" I ask, and we both laugh because we realize how ridiculous it sounds.

"Totally, and it's best to spot that behavior and snap out of it—and fast. Especially when the asshole part is the dominant feature."

Rachel's right. And direct. I need to focus on moving forward.

"Now that you've gotten the divorce, can I tell you something? I've held back because I didn't want my thoughts to weigh in on your decision. It was a big deal to you, what Nate did. Maybe he had shit going on at work and didn't want to talk to you about it."

"Are you serious? Hiding that relationship from me and—"

"Maggie, let me finish. Is it so terrible to have someone to lean on, other than your wife?"

I'm about to get defensive, and stare down at my wine instead as if it's the enemy before downing what's left. Nobody, not even Rachel, knows about my snooping and finding Nate's texts and photos. I'm too embarrassed to say it aloud and ashamed that he fooled me all this time.

She reaches over and pours me some more.

"Rachel," I say calmly. "You're forgetting he had an affair before we got married, remember? He promised me it wouldn't happen again."

"I know," she whispers. "It doesn't mean he had sex this time around."

"Seriously? Then why wouldn't he show me his texts when I confronted him? And how do we even know it was only twice? Maybe he wasn't caught." I grab my purse and dig into it, moving my gum, phone charger, and sunglasses out of the way, as anger builds.

Rachel puts her hand on mine. "What are you doing?"

"Looking for that photo, the one the DMV gave me with that woman nuzzling up to him. I'm sure it's in here somewhere. I'm so done with him. How could I be married to someone I don't trust?"

She pulls my purse away from me and places it on the bar. "You lost complete trust and that's why you couldn't stay. I want you to remember that when the going gets tough, or you're thinking about the what-ifs." She leans in. "Maggie, it was never your fault. You did nothing wrong." She lifts her glass to mine. "Let's make a toast. Here's to your new life and new adventures. Forget about the past."

I give her the side-eye. "So that was your plan all along? To make me realize that divorce was the right thing to do?"

She nods. "You have to be true to yourself. And you have to stand by it. You're stronger than you think."

You're stronger than you think. Hearing those words from Rachel, a friend I admire so much, someone who's so strong, brings me comfort because it's more than a compliment. It's validation.

"Can you promise me one thing? That you'll be open to whatever life brings you."

"I'm trying my best."

"Speaking of which, have you heard from Ryan?"

I smile and look down, almost embarrassed to feel like I'm falling for him. "He calls me about every night. We're planning to see each other in a few days."

"Are you going to tell him about your divorce being final?"

"Yeah, gonna wait until I get back from the spa."

She nudges my elbow. "I'm glad you're doing that. You need it."

It's more than an escape. It's a necessity, and I thank her for the gift and making the appointment because she knows too well that I might never get around to it.

She can't help but ask about Ryan again. She wants some juicy details and it makes me blush. I want to tell her about the connection we have. How he says the same phrases, likes the same songs, wants the same tattoo—how he's always in my head. After opening up and telling her about our similarities, she tells me to stop overthinking.

"Maybe Nate planted him to spy on me," I say and gesture to the bartender for the check.

"Do you even hear yourself?" Rachel bumps me on the arm again and knocks the bag off my shoulder. "Next you'll be saying your house is bugged."

"Hmm, I didn't think of that. Maybe Nate bugged it and is listening in on every conversation. Or maybe Ryan has?"

"Or maybe Ryan's an alien," Rachel jokes. "Or maybe aliens put a chip in Chili and they're feeding Ryan lines while he's on a date with you."

We both laugh, and while I'm paying the check, all this ridiculous banter makes me wonder: Can somebody be so connected and have so much in common that it seems like you've met before? Or that it's too good to be true?

CHAPTER 25

Ryan texts me the next morning with a cute and clever message.

What are you wearing...

I see the three dots and wait to respond.

...for our next date?

It makes me smile, and I try to come up with something. Mine isn't as clever.

Depends where we're going. If it's to church, I'd better buy a dress—for my repentance.

Are you free on Friday night? And not for church. Who needs to repent when there's nothing to feel guilty about?

We go back and forth with texting and choose the place and time.

On Friday, we meet in front of Verbs & Verve, a local bookstore that's been around for decades, passed down from one book-loving relative to the next. It sits on a busy corner where the quaint cafés, antique stores, and independent shops line the street.

Families play Frisbee in the small park across the way. Dog owners stroll down the block, allowing their companions time to sniff the grass and waddle along.

Before getting out of my car, I put on lip gloss and pin one side of my hair back. I step out, tie my navy cardigan sweater around my leggings, and walk toward the shop, where Ryan waits for me. He's wearing a light-blue button-down with a white T-shirt poking through and jeans rolled up above his brown canvas sneakers. He looks up from his phone and smiles as I approach.

"What is it about the way you smile that makes me so damn happy?" he says and comes in for a long hug. "I'm one lucky guy."

I want to tell him the same, but hold back, cautious with my words, fearful that I might say and feel too much, too soon. He steps back, keeping his arms around my waist. It makes me think about our first night together, the way his lips lingered on my stomach, a moment that makes me yearn for him now.

Ryan moves a few steps behind me, and we enter the bookstore. "So, how does this work again?" he asks and allows a few women to pass in front of us.

I explain the rules of a game called PageTurner, one that my mom played with us when we were young: We pick three books and after reading the first page of each book out loud, the other person chooses which one sounds most interesting without seeing the cover.

We look at the different sections within the bookstore. I point to the Biography sign. "Let's meet over there in fifteen minutes. That should give us enough time."

He nods and gets into a sprint position. "What if I can't decide and choose four?"

"Then that would be a different game."

We look at our watches, synchronize our meeting time, and go our separate ways. Ryan, who's a few feet away, sifts through the thriller section and I settle on the classics.

A few kids run past me on their way to grab some picture books and their parents scream for them to slow down. It reminds me of Emily and Max, and my heart aches, reminding me of the times we'd read together before bedtime. I want to reach out to them again, and instead, talk to the kids in the store and acknowledge their great book choices. For a brief moment, it fills a void.

Ryan taps me on the shoulder and asks for extra time and scoots off before my response to continue his search. He inches his way up to me after a few minutes and whispers in my ear. "I've got a few good ones."

"Me too," I say in return, and hide the choices behind my back.

We don't spot any chairs so instead sit in the corner with our backs against the wall. Ryan closes his eyes, and I read the first page of the three books. It's hard for him to choose which one sounds the most interesting.

"Remind me again what happens next in the game?"

"I can see right through you," I tease. "You're trying to buy time to make a decision."

He smiles and opens one eye. I throw the books quickly behind me. "Hey, stop!"

"I can't choose!" he belts out and closes his eyes.

He asks me to read them once again, so I pick up one of the contenders and reread the first page to him.

"They're all so good."

"Okay, I'm giving you one more minute to decide on the page-turner. Which one makes you want to read more?"

Ryan peeks again, so I slap him on the knee and then bend over to kiss him when he doesn't expect it. "That was nice, do it again," he says, and we kiss for a minute. As we're kissing, he tries to reach for one of the books.

"You're relentless," I say.

"Thanks for the compliment. Okay, drum roll." He pounds on the floor for sound effects. "I'm going with the first one."

"What made you choose?"

"The whole mother dying bit was intriguing and how they didn't know which day she died. And someone knocking on the door? I have to know what happens next." He tries to peek again, as my hand hides the cover. "So, what is it? The anticipation is killing me!"

I hold up *The Stranger* by Albert Camus. "I thought for sure you'd pick the other."

He reaches behind me and grabs the book. "That's because I knew it was *White Fang*. I was a big Jack London fan. Read them all when I was a kid … Now it's your turn."

We go through the same exercise. It's hard to choose and once I do, Ryan holds up a book by Dostoevsky.

We purchase both and find a coffee shop nearby, taking turns reading a chapter from each. The place is noisy with customers chatting and we don't get very far when he puts the book down and places his hand on my leg. He keeps looking at me with that smile, and I don't look away this time, like other times when my nervousness takes over. We're completely fixated on each other until someone interrupts, asking if we're using the extra chair at our table.

"I really like you, Maggie," he blurts out.

"But …?" I mumble, already expecting the worst, waiting for that shoe-to-drop moment, the one that happens in a relationship when something goes wrong or isn't quite right.

"But what? There's nothing more to it—sometimes you think the worst," he says.

I laugh. "Sometimes?"

"When can I see you again?"

It's refreshing to hear that he doesn't assume he's staying the night. Besides, my spa appointment has already been booked for the morning, although the thought of him next to me makes me want him even more. I excuse myself, use the bathroom, and call the spa while in there, leaving it to fate. If they can move my appointment for later in the day, I'll invite him over.

On my way back, Ryan has his head in a book and messes with his shoelace with one hand as he reads. A child runs by and trips in front of him. Ryan hands the boy his toy, and when he notices me, reaches for my hand as he gets up from the chair.

As we walk out of the café, Ryan asks, "So, have you decided?"

"On what?" I ask back.

"When you're free again?"

I decide not to play games. "How about tonight? We can read our books to each other in bed."

CHAPTER 26

Ryan kisses me good-bye in the morning and after Chili gets a long walk, I catch up on a few emails, jump in the shower, and head out for my spa appointment. The parkway is moving at a fast pace considering it's drizzling. What is it about rain that usually sends drivers in a frenzy to make sure their brakes work?

I'm about fifteen minutes from the spa when the words *Tire Pressure Low* show up in small orange letters on my dashboard. There's plenty of time before my rescheduled appointment so I pull off at the next exit, where there's a service center on the opposite side. I know this exit well because it leads to Rachel's house, where I've been a million times for pizza, wine, and girl talk. The light turns green, and I zoom down the service road to the parking lot. It's filled to the brim and instead of double parking, I make my way to the side where cars and mechanics are lined up in their bays.

A mechanic turns around and grabs a towel to wipe his hands before walking toward my driver's side. He's early twenties with short blond hair and a nice tan that complements his light-blue shirt. I roll my window down and look up. His name is stitched on a patch and easy to remember since it's the same one as my neighbor's.

"Hey, Matt, something's going on with the tires. At least, that's what my dashboard says."

"Yes, ma'am," he answers. "Let me take a look." He waits for me to get out of the car and sits in the driver's seat.

"Have you tried turning it off and on?" he asks.

I nod and, when realizing that doesn't do the trick, he gets out to grab his tire gauge, the kind that Nate would always tell me to keep in the car for moments like these.

Matt puts the gauge into each tire, one by one, reading the results. He gets to the last one and stands up after checking it.

"They're all good, ma'am. Let me check the spare," he says and pops the trunk, pulls out my recycling bags, various toys for Chili, and an umbrella. He rolls the spare into the station to check it. I realize I've taken him away from his other job but he's so accommodating and nobody in the bay seems to mind. I'm hoping whatever he's doing inside, even if it's mixing a magic potion, will do the trick and take me on my way—and not take more of his time.

After a few minutes, he rolls the spare toward my car and puts it back into the trunk.

"So, what's the verdict?" I ask.

"It was low. Sometimes when the spare's off-balance, it will set off the warning."

He closes the trunk and starts the car. We wait, with my fingers crossed behind me, while the dashboard goes through its mental exercise. After a minute, all of the lights turn off except the one for the tires. Matt says we have two choices: leave the car with them to see what's going on or he can reset the light. I ask what he recommends and he's honest, which is so refreshing, not because he's a mechanic. Because he's human.

"Sometimes it gets glitchy. We could check for nails or holes," he says while wiping his hands with a towel before telling me that all tires check out, so they'd probably wind up resetting it anyway. "If you just want a reset, I need to finish up something inside first. It'll take about ten minutes. You can wait inside … there's coffee."

I'm not a coffee snob by any means but there's a cute little café two blocks down in a shopping plaza. I grab my purse from the car and walk over to the shop, thinking about calling Rachel to meet me there, even though there's not much time with my spa appointment within the hour.

After turning the corner, I stop to hide against the building, trying to erase who's up ahead of me. It's Rachel and Ryan, and they're dressed in gym gear, about to go into the café. He holds the door for her, and before they go inside, Rachel smiles and laughs at something he says.

This can't be for real. How do they know each other?

Maybe they're just friends? And if so, why wouldn't she tell me?

There's no figuring this one out. Except why is everyone lying to me?

I pull out my phone and call her. It rings several times before going to voicemail.

Thoughts of more betrayal flood my mind. Watching the cars speed by makes me nauseous. I'm about to vomit and lean against the building again before squatting and putting my head down.

"Miss, are you okay?"

I look up. An older gentleman with a gray plaid cap and oversized sunglasses stops to check on me.

"Yes, thank you, I'm fine." I take a few deep breaths to ease the dizziness.

A twenty-something woman sipping on coffee shows up a minute later and offers to walk me back over to the tire shop. I'm too embarrassed to tell them what's wrong, so I make up some lame excuse about not eating breakfast and my sugar dropping to an all-time low.

They relate and offer to grab me a muffin from the coffee shop. That's all it takes to get my act together. I stand up straight, thank them, and hightail it back to my car, hoping that Matt's done and I don't break down in front of him since he's nice and honest and calls me ma'am like his Southern mamma, or maybe his boss, taught him to do.

My car's taking up two spots and Matt's hanging out the door halfway while reading from the manual. He flips to the next page and, at the same time, fidgets with a knob that's poking out of the dashboard, turning it left, right, then left again. It's like a combination on a safe, hopefully, one that works to get me the hell away from here. After a few minutes of troubleshooting, Matt figures it out and the tire warning on the dashboard turns off.

"Hallelujah," I yell. "Thank you so much for taking care of it. I feel bad that it took you away from your other jobs."

"No worries, ma'am. Happy to help," he says and places the manual on the driver's seat.

I fish into my purse and pull out a twenty. He fights me for a moment, pushing it away, telling me it's not necessary. "Buy yourself some lunch," I say, almost sounding like my mom, who used to throw gas money on the table when she visited me at college.

"Thank you." He puts the twenty in his pocket. "It'll help. I'm saving up for an engagement ring."

"Exciting! Does she know?"

"Nope, I want to surprise her."

As if I'm a dear friend, he shares how they met in their high school history class, how they've never had a fight, and how her family invites him along to every family vacation. His exciting news warms my heart.

At the same time, I want to give him advice. Don't rush. Make sure she's the one, whatever that means. Make sure you have everything out of your system before getting married so you don't break her heart. Make sure it's not just physical chemistry, that you're compatible and have the same values.

Remember, Maggie, not every guy's like Nate, I tell myself.

And not everyone's like Ryan. Or Rachel.

My best friend's face looms back into my mind. Why didn't she tell me she knew Ryan? The smiling and laughing together. Are they sleeping together, too? If you can't trust your closest friends, who can you trust?

I check my watch and see there's ten minutes to spare for my appointment. There's no way I'm going to let Rachel and Ryan's betrayal, or the sick feeling in my stomach, stop me from making it.

Matt wishes me well, and I call the spa and explain the situation. They tell me not to worry, that there's plenty

154

of time since they had a cancellation after mine. I back out of the lot, wave good-bye to my super sweet mechanic, and leave the lying, caffeinated assholes in the dust.

Chapter 27

I'm tired of crying all the time, so instead, my steering wheel gets the brunt of my anger as I grip it so tightly my palms burn. At the traffic light, the lady in the lane next to me looks over in disbelief after I bang the top of the dashboard. She turns away quickly when I roll down the window and yell: "Take a picture, it'll last longer!"

It makes me laugh out loud because my grandma used to say it all the time to her nosy neighbors, the ones who didn't like us running around on the street in front of her house. The woman in the car spins her index finger around her ear, insinuating that I'm crazy. I yell once more, "Tell me something I don't already know," as she drives off. The guy behind me honks several times, as if he's choosing sides in our tirade.

The engine roars when my foot hits the pedal and as he overtakes to pass, the two of us start racing—at least in my mind, because I have to win at something, anything this week.

Rachel and Ryan looked so chipper as they practically skipped into the coffee shop. How could my best friend want to steal him from me? I replay the night Rachel and I met at the bar and how she said Ryan was cute. Did she slide her number to him when I wasn't looking? Or did they pass each other on the way into the restaurant?

It's ridiculous to fathom, but it can't be swept under the rug and forgotten about. When she texts to tell me to enjoy my massage, did she already know my new appointment time because Ryan told her? How convenient, how conniving—and how clueless could I be?

In fifteen minutes, I pull into the parking lot of Serenity & Wellness and an attendant greets me when she hears the bell ring out as the door opens. She asks for my name and walks me to the changing room, where I get undressed and slip on a robe and flip-flops before taking a seat in the lounge. A massage therapist named Susan, who's dressed in a light-pink tunic and matching pants, leads me to her room, and moments later, I'm lying on a massage bed in a room scented with lavender essential oil. Susan tells me to relax as she works her fingers into the hard knots in my shoulders and neck. "You work at a computer all day, don't you?" she asks.

I give a thumbs-up as an affirmative because I'm already tense enough and don't want to share what's on my mind—how everyone in my life seems to be a liar. That nobody can be trusted, even my best friend.

"Whether it's stress from the job or something in your personal life, I'm glad you made time to see me today," she says, while putting a drop of lavender oil under my nose.

"Follow the flow of your breath," she continues in a soft, lyrical voice as she presses her fingers down both sides of my shoulders.

Relax, Maggie, I tell myself, and listen to the sound of the ocean playing through the surround-sound speakers. Before long, the rhythmic ebb and flow of the waves soothe me.

Moments later, Susan asks me to turn over onto my back. She swivels away in her chair and, when she comes back, blots a tissue on the corner of my cheek. "A massage can have that effect," she says. "Let it out; it's good for you. Then breathe in. It'll help you relax."

It's amazing how listening to a stranger—someone you've never met—can do wonders and know what's right for you.

CHAPTER 28

I can't concentrate during our morning meeting at work. I give the wrong sales figures to my boss in the afternoon. A cyclist cusses me out for almost running into him on the way home.

It consumes me. Rachel and Ryan together, laughing about life, or maybe about me. How could she do this? Another day goes by and I stare at Rachel's text:

How was the massage?

I stir in the middle of the night, thinking of what to say.

I wake up in the morning, start typing, and hit delete a dozen times.

This happens for a few days until I finally respond with:

Been busy, massage was nice …

Because I'm clueless on what to say—and scared of what she'll say back.

Do I call her out? Pretend I didn't see them? Curl up into a ball in the corner of the kitchen with my two favorite companions: Chili and a bottle of wine? Or drive over the speed limit with my rock playlist, all loud and angry?

The funny part is, Rachel's always the one there for me, telling me that everything will be okay, and giving me a shoulder to cry on. Not this time. This time she seems to be messing with my head.

CHAPTER 29

I've been feeding Ryan a line that work's been driving me crazy, with no spare time. It gives me time to think things through. Besides, it's the first Saturday of the month—the following weekend after seeing the two betrayers together—so it's time for Chili to jump into the back as we make our way to Longwood.

George works every Saturday and sits behind the check-in desk, making sure nobody slips through the cracks without signing in. I usually tease him, asking if he needs my blood type and Social Security number. And when I do, he chuckles even though he's probably heard this a thousand times before. He makes everyone feel good and important, as long as you have your ID to prove your existence. I pass on the jokes this time because he looks tired and disheveled. He hasn't shaved, his expression lines look deeper, and his eyes, normally bright blue and clear, are cloudy.

"Is everything okay?" I ask.

"That bad, huh? You're not the first person to ask." He grins and leans over the desk to whisper. "I went out with my neighbors for happy hour last night and it turned into dancing and more drinking. I'm too old for this."

"You're never too old for that. Maybe you should've called in sick?" I say, trying to guess his age. His crow's-feet and thinning salt-and-pepper hair make it challenging. He could be anywhere from forty to fifty-five.

He shakes his head and hands me the sign-in sheet. "And miss seeing Chili? No way."

After scribbling my name, I make my way down the hall with Chili prancing by my side. Visiting Betty and Al puts a lot in perspective. They're so damn positive, and it's obvious that they still love each other deeply by the way they hold hands and kiss when they finish each other's sentences. It's so refreshing to see a couple be so affectionate after all these years.

Al waves to us while Betty snoozes in her chair. She's wearing a pastel-pink tracksuit and white tennis shoes. Her makeup is done to perfection with pink lipstick and rouge, matching her rose petal earrings.

Chili wags her tail and runs up to Al for a good petting. She places her muzzle onto Betty's thigh and waits. When Betty wakes up, she smiles and even though her teeth are stained and chipped in a few places, it's a beautiful sight that lights up the room. Betty bends down to pet Chili, and Al reaches over to do the same.

"Chili, you're back," Betty sings. "Al, you have any bacon for her?"

"Not today. Ate it all up. Sorry, Chili," he says while unwrapping a napkin. "I have something even better." Al tells her to sit and she waits obediently while staring at a cookie.

"Wait," I say quickly. "What kind?"

"Sugar," Al replies. "Don't worry, we had dogs. There's no chocolate in these."

Chili devours the first one and then gobbles up two more cookies before settling down in front of Betty's chair.

"So, how's the divorce going?"

"Al! Maybe she doesn't want to talk about it," Betty quips.

"It's okay, really. It's done. I'm officially divorced," I reply, tucking some hair behind my ear.

"Congratulations," Al says.

"That's right, dear," Betty adds. "It's time to move on. You're so young. See how life unfolds for you."

Not sure if it's the matter-of-fact advice Betty gives that makes me want to agree. Or if it's the two of them working as a team. There's something about listening to a couple who have been married this long and are decades older than me. There's respect as well as love and admiration. And you can't pretend or make that stuff up.

While Al pets Chili some more, Betty chats about the new escapades at the retirement home with enough juice to almost make me blush. Since she's a little hard of hearing, she tells me in a loud voice, almost yelling, which makes Al shush her, and naturally, makes Betty shush Al in return.

Supposedly a woman, who remains nameless due to privacy issues, has contracted a nasty STD, so she has to put a list of names together of fellow residents she's slept with in the last three months. Naturally, senior moments strike, and the woman can't remember everyone she's been involved with, which provides Betty and Al with plenty of commentary.

"Why only the past three months?" I ask.

Betty shrugs and Al chimes in. "Maybe the other ones have already kicked the bucket."

"From the STD?" Betty exclaims.

"No, silly, from old age!"

I laugh because it's impossible not to. I also want to slither down in my chair. Is this what happens when you get older? You have absolutely no filter? And you don't care who's listening? If so, I'd like to skip the next fifty years and be eighty right now. Why wait so long to be comfortable in your own skin instead of worrying about what people think?

Betty finishes her story with how many men wind up on the list—without sharing names, of course. She tells me about the apartment that has opened up next to them and then about the new exercise class that includes yoga and bladder-strengthening stances. She gets up, bends at the knees, and stretches her arms out in front to show me one of the moves. After catching her breath, Betty sits back down and asks me about my love life post-divorce because she thinks it's the best bet for moving on.

"I'd much rather hear more about you guys," I tell her.

"Look around, darling." She juts her arm out in a wave-like motion, which makes Chili leap up and pad toward her, tail wagging. Betty leans down and rubs Chili's back. "Napping. Doing crossword puzzles. Looking out the window. It's all very exciting!" she adds in a higher tone as Chili looks up at her.

"For Chili, it is," Al chimes in. "Come here, girl." He pats his hand a few times on the side of his leg.

Chili dashes over in an instant.

"Traitor," Betty jokes.

"Nah," Al says as he pets his furry friend, "she loves us equally, don't you?"

Chili's fixated on Al. She sits facing him, with her muzzle on his knee, looking up at him with her big, brown eyes.

"Did she tell you that?" Betty adds while admiring the two of them.

Betty and Al look at each other and reach for the other's hand at the same time.

Are they that in sync? And are they silently sharing a memory they had that nobody else in the world knows? It makes me think of Savannah and of Ryan. Will he think of me whenever he hears "Save a Prayer," even when he's with someone else? And if he smiles when it's playing, will he lie when asked what he's thinking about?

My chest feels tight when I think of him and, to keep my emotions in check, I bite the inside of my lip and turn away to look out the window. As the rain beats down, an elderly man from across the room gets up, walks over to the window, and pushes down on it to make sure it's secure.

"A penny for your thoughts, my dear," Betty says.

I turn back to face her and ask, "Is it possible to be unlucky in love?"

Betty shakes her head without having to think it through. "There's no such thing. I consider it lucky when you're able to come out of a relationship and grow from it. The other day on the news they were interviewing a marriage counselor. She said, 'When going through a breakup, you shouldn't look at your relationship as a failure. You should see it as a time for growth—a time to rediscover what you really want.' And I think she's right."

"That's great advice. But this time it's something different," I say and begin my story about meeting Ryan, before sharing the tire mishap along with the coffee shop discovery.

"How long ago was that?" Betty asks.

"Last weekend."

"And have you spoken to either one of them?" she continues.

"They've texted."

"Geez," Al chimes in and shakes his head. "Nobody talks anymore. All this texting."

"Ryan wants to see me. I told him I'm busy."

"You really think they're getting it on?" Al asks.

I shrug and feel nauseous when thinking about them together. "Whatever they're doing, they're great at hiding it from me since neither brought it up."

"Maggie, do you want my advice?" Betty asks. I nod and she continues. "They have no clue you saw them. They think everything is fine and they're not giving this a single thought. But it's eating you up inside." She pauses. "If you ask me, this is one of those things where you can't be on the fence. You need to ask Rachel what's going on or you need to let it go. You can't stay in limbo-land where it's bothering you. It's not good. You'll toss and turn, and it'll drive you crazy."

"I'm scared."

"Of what?" Al asks.

"Hearing the truth. What if they are having an af-fair? I'm so tired of getting hurt."

"Sweetheart," Betty says and puts her hand on mine. "Even if you don't talk to her, it won't be the last time you get hurt. That's the way life is. You have to figure out how to handle what life throws your way. It comes with the good and the bad. If you care about Rachel, say something. And if you don't care about your friendship, say something. Either way, you'll get an answer, and you'll have to decide whether you believe her or not."

"She's right," Al adds. "Like your husband, good riddance to her if she went behind your back. You don't need her as a friend. Sometimes we have friends our entire lives and they show their true colors when the time comes. It's in your control. You get to decide whether you want to keep them in your life or not."

What they say is true. I need to confront Rachel, but when and how?

"And don't wait too long," Betty adds as if she's reading my mind. "Because if you wait, you'll talk yourself out of it."

Betty's advice takes me back to when Nate cheated on me before we got married and how we should've broken up then. Instead, I chose to believe him—that it wouldn't happen again. I had been betrayed and didn't know how to handle the deceit except to wish it away and forgive him. Back then, nobody, not even Betty, would have been able to give me advice. Because I loved Nate and couldn't imagine my life without him.

"Don't forget," Betty adds, as I bend down to pet Chili. "You can always forgive. Betrayal is a horrible thing. Hear her out first, find out what's going on. You don't have to give up on your friendship. Maturity often shows up in ways that others would describe as weakness."

I take Betty and Al's words to heart. I've only known Ryan for a few months, but I've known Rachel since college. What we have is stronger, more solid, or at least that's what I thought.

I say good-bye to George on my way out, take a breath, and text Rachel.

> *Whatcha doing tonight? Wanna meet for dinner?*

Her response comes straight back.
Sure, you're being spontaneous!

> *Great, how about 7:30 at Beauregard's?*

I wait a few minutes before replying.

> *See you then.*

I make my way home and take Chili for a quick walk before getting ready to meet my so-called best friend.

CHAPTER 30

I snag a great parking space on the street in front of Beauregard's. It's Saturday night downtown and normally I'd call an Outro but today's an exception. Who knows how it'll go with Rachel, and I might need an easy escape instead of waiting curbside for my driver.

She waits at the booth by the entrance and smiles when she sees me. We hug because, even though I'm pissed, I don't want her to sense something's wrong. Building up the courage to say something distracts me when she taps my arm and tells me there's an hour's wait for a table.

The hostess puts our name on the list and we grab two seats at the bar next to an older couple sharing a bottle of champagne. He's wearing a gray-striped suit and she's in a navy dress with sequins on the cuffs. By the way they're dressed, it must be a special occasion or perhaps a night at the theatre. We make small talk and find out it's their fiftieth anniversary. They seem happy and carefree. They seem everything I'm not.

"Impressive, huh?" Rachel says.

The couple remind me of Betty and Al, except he seems a little bossier of the two, demanding they order the mussels in wine sauce instead of the clams casino that she wants.

"Wonder what keeps couples together so long?" Rachel says, leaning in so she's not too loud.

"I'm starting to think it's all about accepting character flaws and realizing nobody's perfect."

"Maggie, is that you?" she jokes while waving her hand in front of my face. "Doesn't sound like something you'd say."

"Putting things into perspective, there are some things you can't ignore," I say, sounding cryptic. "Like lying and cheating … and there are other things you might have to relax about, like leaving dishes in the sink, dirty socks lying around, or an annoying laugh."

"You're right," she adds and starts telling me about some of her ex-husband's habits that she now remembers as cute rather than irritating. And how being married once, and knowing what she wants from a partner, puts everything into perspective for her.

I'm about to snicker. I want to call her bluff and a liar now that the wine has started to do its job.

"Oh, how was the spa?" she wonders. "Can't believe I forgot all about it."

"Amazing. Especially after the morning I had." It begs her to ask for more details and helps me get ready to segue into the painful part. When I tell her about the tire, stopping to get it fixed, and sweet Matt who took care of everything, she frowns, which makes me wonder if she's calculating the close call.

"Geez, that's crazy. I'm glad he figured it out and you made it to the spa in time."

She changes the subject and tells me about her day. How she went to the farmers' market and ran errands, going on about how rainy weather brings out the crazies. She continues to look straight at me, like liars often do to prove their honesty. And even though it's dimly lit in the bar and her brown eyes don't show much expression, she's easy to see through. I've been lied to before—more than once—and now I know better.

My phone pings, and it's another text from Ryan.

> *Hey there, left you a message earlier. Hope everything's okay.*

I look without responding and place the phone face down.

"Is everything okay?" Rachel asks.

"It's Ryan."

"You can get back to him, I don't mind."

"You don't?" I say sarcastically. I'm still afraid to hear what she'll say, so I play mind games first to see who'll win. "Think I'm gonna break it off."

"What! You were so into him. What happened?"

I shrug and pick up my glass, downing half and wiping the side of my mouth as it goes down a little too fast. "Just not feeling it anymore."

"Doesn't make sense. You were feeling it a thousand times over."

Rachel has no clue she's digging. Not sure why she cares. I wind up telling Rachel that Ryan came on too strong. And that I'm just divorced and want to play the field. Truth is, I'm scared shitless to confront her, ignoring Betty's advice of getting it off my chest sooner rather than later so it doesn't fester.

The couple next to us say good-bye and we wish them another fifty years of marriage. They don't even think about the impossibility of that kind of longevity, and thank us while walking out hand in hand.

We sit in silence at the bar. It's uncomfortable and I'm trying to find subjects to talk about other than Ryan. How her job's going. What's new with her brother. Any upcoming vacation plans. How her sister and the new baby are doing. I'm pulling all kinds of conversation starters out of me to avoid the confrontation that brought me here.

Rachel can't let it go, which surprises me. She keeps digging, wondering how my mind could change so quickly. Affairs of the heart, I wind up saying, are complicated, fleeting, moody, all of the above. She's shocked to hear this nonchalant, almost apathetic approach to my love life. Finally, she lets go, saying that she's happy for me and my new life.

I'm chickening out; I know it. Every time Rachel looks my way, I see our friendship in front of me: someone who's been there for me when my grandparents died; when I got laid off and she called everyone under the sun to help me find a job; when I hit rock bottom during my separation. Can I forgive and forget as Betty said? Maybe it's in me, but all that's on my mind is Rachel and Ryan hiding their relationship.

The hostess comes over, ready to offer us the next table. She sees that we've already ordered at the bar and scoots away with the menus in hand. My friendship with Rachel may never be the same, whether she's confronted or not.

After downing my drink, I'm in no shape to bring it up tonight. My head starts to spin and I'm feeling dizzy. Rachel notices and convinces me to take an Outro and pick up my car in the morning. She orders us some coffee to help sober me up and pulls up my Outro app to call a ride for me.

My driver stops in front of Beauregard's, and Rachel waves good-bye as we take off. I want to kick myself for being a coward. *Next time, without the wine*, I mumble as my phone rings with a call from Ryan.

CHAPTER 31

Ryan's standing by my front door when the Outro drops me off. The lamppost shines brightly and he's leaning against the wall of my townhouse. He's in his usual summer attire—a fitted tee, baggy jeans, and flip-flops—and when he sees me get out of the car, he straightens up and fidgets with his keys as I walk toward him.

He took a chance showing up here, clearly not taking no for an answer. I told him on the phone there's nothing more to say—and that my mind's made up about not seeing him anymore. Maybe if I'd confronted Rachel, it would be easier to tell Ryan. She needs to know before anyone else.

I'm about to cry when he walks toward me because before seeing him with Rachel, I imagined so much more with him. And I'd fallen hard. He'd recently talked about another adventure for us, a weekend away to Chicago, one that we'd been talking about the other day. But it's not only the fun and adventure that draws me to him.

When I got married to Nate, there were so many items to check off on my list that don't matter. That so-called marriage material, like someone who's financially secure? It's a load of shit. What matters to me now: Someone I can trust. Someone who doesn't lie. Someone who only wants to be with me. Just me. Is that too much to ask?

"Maggie, what's going on?" he asks.

I ignore his question and pull the keys out of my purse. It's not like me to be passive-aggressive. I can't continue like this. Does he get the same story fed to Rachel earlier tonight? Do I lie to him and protect myself from hearing the truth?

"Ryan, like I said, it's me. Not sure what I was thinking. It's all going way too fast. You know, I just got divorced, right? You were taking a chance on someone whose head isn't on straight."

"Your head seems fine to me. And I don't care about the divorce. Hell, I wouldn't care if you were married. I like you and want to be with you."

"Really? You wouldn't care if I were married?"

He pauses and scratches his ankle. "Can we go inside and talk? The mosquitos are killing me." He brushes one away that flits around his head.

I unlock the front door, and we enter the house and walk to the kitchen.

Ryan opens up a bottle of red wine that he brought and pours us both a glass. He leans his elbows on the granite counter. "Maggie, I don't understand. We were having such a great time. It can't just be me who thinks that?"

"We were. And I like you, too, but it's not fair to you. I want to date other people."

He frowns and tilts his head as if he didn't hear me. "Was it something I said? Or did?"

I shake my head and keep going with the story, repeating the same thing. That I'm out of a divorce. That we're moving too fast. That my feelings are overwhelming me. We stare at each other but it's not like before, our moments of comfortable silence. This time, there's distance between us.

"Remember when you asked me about dating? And I told you that I can't date more than one person at a time?"

I nod and wait for him to continue.

"It's true. I can't, and I'd hate for you to be dating others because I want to spend more time getting to know you. And I thought you wanted the same thing. That's why it's so out of the blue to hear … look I'm having a hard time understanding, but I'd never want to get in the way."

How can I believe this liar? He doesn't want to see other people? Only one woman is enough? What a load of crap. The way he looked at Rachel. The way she laughed with him. There's no denying something's going on.

"Maybe I need time to figure some things out."

"Maybe," he says. "Or maybe you already have."

"Ryan, come on. Have you given any real thought to it? Even if I were ready, with your demanding job and travel, our relationship isn't sustainable."

He gives a tight smile, as if he's still confused. Chili comes into the kitchen with her tail wagging. She begs for a good ear scratching and Ryan gladly obliges. "Sustainable? What the hell does that even mean? Since when is our relationship part of an ecosystem? And by the way, I don't travel that much; it's a few times a year."

We stare at each other without saying a word. It's true. It's not sustainable. Not in the mindset I'm in.

Ryan leans over and puts both hands on the counter. He shakes his head and then laughs uncontrollably before giving me a serious look. "Sustainable? Seriously, Maggie. Did you see that on a greeting card somewhere? Wait. I can picture it now."

He grabs an envelope from my counter, pretending to open it and pull out a card. "Sorry, it's not you; it's not me, either. It's our relationship—it's just not sustainable. But folks, don't worry," he adds in his pretend sports announcer's voice, "this card will be fine—much better than our unsustainable relationship—because it uses recycled paper." He looks down and fidgets with the edge of the envelope before pushing it away.

We stand in silence and it's eating me up. What we had was going so well, and now his actions speak loud and clear. He could stand here day and night, saying there's nobody else out there for him. And even if he did, how could I believe him after seeing them together?

Ryan comes around to my side of the counter and brushes the hair back behind my ear. He touches my cheek softly and when he bends down to kiss me, I step back. "Wow," he whispers. "I must've done something shitty to you in a past life."

He picks up his keys and heads to the front door. Before leaving, he turns back around. "You know, when we first met, it felt right. Like we had a strong connection."

"As I said, it's all me."

He reaches for the handle and opens the door. "Yeah, okay, whatever. If you want to tell me what really happened, you have my number."

He closes the door behind him, and Chili follows me back into the kitchen. She darts out when I bang my hand on the counter in frustration and the glass slips and falls onto the floor, smashing into tiny shards as the wine seeps into the cracks of the hardwood. It'll smell like wine forever, even after every remnant has been soaked up with a sponge, and I'll remember its permanence. I've got to deal with my emotions and my mind races into a whirlwind.

I need to confront Rachel and forget about Ryan.

I need to confront them both and forget about both of them.

Or maybe I need to tuck it away and swear off dating—and friendships, for that matter—forever.

Trust is so complicated. All the advice out there tells you not to hold previous relationships as the guiding light for new ones, to not make a new guy feel like he's going to lie and cheat the same way the old guy did. How can it be so easy to flip a switch like that? To go from one relationship to another with open arms and see where it takes you? I tried moving on and look where it got me—sitting on the floor, picking up broken glass, losing myself again.

Chili comes back into the kitchen once the mess is gone. We sit on the floor, and she puts her muzzle on my leg and looks up at me.

"It's you and me, girl," I say and pet her belly. "Nate's gone. Ryan's gone. Maybe even Rachel will be gone. Fuck 'em all," I add in a more heated tone and she looks up at me. I pretend her look is one of agreement until realizing that I've simply stopped petting her. "You needy little thing," I say and laugh.

We're all needy and, if not, we become that way sooner or later. Chili lifts her head and barks that special bark, as if she's agreeing with me or telling me it's time to take her out. Whichever it is, thank goodness for Chili. And thank goodness for the distraction.

CHAPTER 32

It's early afternoon the following Tuesday with distraction playing its part again—in the worst way. Instead of writing the product brief that's due to Jillian Wednesday morning, I've got my browser open and ready. Being in a cubicle makes me wary, so I look around before starting my search.

How to catch someone in a lie?

It comes back with several results and from the first article, the author says to watch for nonverbal cues. What the hell does that mean? We're not all born detectives, so by nonverbal cues, does she mean they'll look away when they talk? Fold their arms? Ignore your questions by pretending not to hear them? Fake an impending bowel movement for a diversion? She doesn't elaborate or serve up anything helpful. I delete my question and enter a new one in the search bar.

How to catch someone cheating?

The results seem more straightforward and even provide pictures and steps, a sort of how-to for idiots like me. Put a tracking device on their car (too much work). Listen in on the landline (who still has one of those?). See who's texting by accessing their cell (easy if you know their password). Oooh, I like this one: Get a baby monitor and listen in. I'd never thought of that as a sneaky way to sabotage an affair. It probably wouldn't work in this instance—might've been great for my shitty marriage.

"Hey, whatcha doing?" Jillian asks behind me, making me jump in my chair and minimize the screen.

"Nothing, why?"

She smiles and hesitates for a moment before leaning against the cubicle wall. "Is there something you're not telling us?" she whispers and raises her brows.

I stare back and shrug, waiting for her to get to the point.

"Hello? The baby monitor? I knew something was up. Your skin is glowing, with a capital G."

It sounds so ridiculous that a woman would be recently divorced and pregnant. Jillian's young and doesn't think it through. Or maybe her sense of humor is wasted on me, and I'm the one who doesn't get it. "Oh, that. I've been invited to a baby shower and it's an item on their registry." Thinking on my feet these days comes easily, as if it's my new superpower.

Jillian nods. "I hope I didn't offend by mentioning it. You have a nice glow and it's the first thing that came to mind."

She's not joking, after all. She must feel sorry for me, either for being recently divorced, not being pregnant, not having children. Or maybe all three.

"It's my recent massage—or could be that it's hot as hell in here," I say and pick up a folder from my desk and start fanning all around me. "They can't seem to get the temperature right. It's either too hot or too cold."

"Like Goldilocks."

"Like what?"

"Goldilocks? The porridge? Hot or cold."

"Oh, right," I say and realize my mind is churning over Rachel and Ryan. How long has it been going on? Where have they been meeting? What about Rachel's new boyfriend? Maybe they're not exclusive.

"You okay?" Jillian asks.

"Actually, I'm not feeling that great. Think I'm gonna head out." I dash out of the cube with my bag thrown across my shoulder.

"Feel better," Jillian calls out. "Don't worry about the brief. I'll extend the due date."

***

It's almost three and Rachel gets off work soon. Sometimes she stays after to tutor, but it's a Tuesday and she usually has yoga unless she's switched up her schedule. I check Exhale's website and make my way through traffic to get there. Exhale, which offers yoga and meditation classes, sits in a strip mall between a grocery store and florist shop.

Rachel always tries to convince me to go. Yoga and meditation have never been my thing. My mind always races and gets clouded with my to-do list or what to prepare for dinner. In other words, it never slows down.

Women carrying their mats and wearing flattering yoga pants strut through the parking lot. It must be an advanced class for those who stand on their heads with ease and proudly post pics on social media. A few of them chat near the entrance, and I slouch down as a few more walk past my car. There's a tap on my passenger-side window and it startles me, making me grip the wheel. I look over and it's Rachel. So much for my investigative skills at work.

She jumps into the seat with her cute turquoise and pink yoga pants that match her tank top. "Hey there! Why didn't you tell me you were coming?"

"It was very last minute. Lots of people were MIA today for a meeting so I skipped out early."

"Totally awesome! You'll have a hard time doing yoga in that, though," she says and points to my red pantsuit. "Lucky for you, I've got an extra something in the car. Sit tight." She jumps out and sticks her head back in. "Actually, meet me by the door. Be there in a minute."

A few women with tight asses and perfect biceps smile at me on their way to the front. There's no way I'll survive this class, but I go along with it when Rachel passes me a gym bag and we go into the locker room to change.

We head to the back of the studio, one that's kept way too cold, and it makes me want to find the thermostat to bring it up a good ten degrees. Before long, the class starts chanting while I'm rubbing my arms trying to warm up. The instructor, a woman named Brooke, fiddles with her hair and waves at the only guy in the class. She tells us to breathe deeply and exhale before taking us into a stance that she calls a mountain pose. Within a few minutes, Rachel leans over.

"How's it going?"

"Is it too late to hit Dairy Queen instead?"

"Don't worry," Rachel whispers, "it gets easier the more you do it. There's a beginners' class on weekends. We can go next time if you want."

Brooke walks over when she hears us chatting and calmly refocuses me. As I'm in a downward-facing dog, which is making me light-headed, she fixes the position of my feet and says a few encouraging words to help me hold the pose longer.

Rachel doesn't realize that no type of yoga class—even beginners—is on my list. I'm here for a reason, on a mission to get information. The yoga ladies move into a new stretch and Rachel looks over when she turns her head to the right. She looks content, and the thought of Ryan races through my mind. How could she do this to me? To us?

"I need to pee," I whisper, and she nods.

I head out of the room and back into the changing area. With shaky hands, I open our locker and reach into Rachel's bag, pulling out her cell phone, and then make a mad dash to the stall. The phone is locked so I pull mine out and search, *how many tries to unlock a phone?* The first few results say the same thing: six tries.

First, I put in the year she was born: 1979.

Then, her street address: 2582.

No luck with two tries.

Maggie, think. What numbers would Rachel use?

Something simple? 1234.

Next up, the year she graduated college: 2002.

Those don't work either and with two more tries, my time is running out.

It dawns on me. My password is my year of birth, backward: 0891. My fifth try is hers: 9791.

It opens and takes me to the main screen. No pat on the back needed. Besides, this is no time to get confident. Sudden chatter in the bathroom makes me freeze on the spot. A few women mention their kids' teachers and the school's high expectations. Then they make small talk about annoying neighbors who keep them up late at night with their cocktail parties and loud music. They run the water, pull a paper towel from the dispenser, and continue chatting on the way out.

I look at my watch and see there's only fifteen minutes left for the class. The phone locks me out and my fingers do their handiwork to get me back in.

What am I doing? How could I be spying on my best friend, the one I'm supposed to trust more than anyone? Then Nate comes to mind and how he was supposed to be my best friend and look what happened?

Her texting bubble shows numbers in red, indicating a few unread messages. My finger taps on the icon without opening up the new texts. I scroll through the list and find Ryan's name a few rows down. It has that same grayed-out moon icon that Nate has next to Kira's name. I read the message on the first row without opening the entire conversation. It says: *the coffee shop by your place?*

My heart beats faster. With no extra time for sleuthing, I dash out of the stall, put the phone back in Rachel's bag, and make my way to the class. They're all seated with their legs crossed and eyes closed. I take my place, joining them in the quiet of the room.

Brooke whispers *Namaste* before the class repeats the word and starts moving about.

"So, what did you think?" Rachel asks as she rolls up her mat. "A little too hard?"

"Definitely. Both the moves and the meditation."

"It's a mindset, that's all. You'll get used to it," she says and takes a final stretch, bending over from the hips, and touching her hands to the floor.

We head to the bathroom, and my stomach churns. Will she notice her phone's been tampered with? I wait and watch as she grabs her bag, pulls out her phone, and checks for messages. She clicks to lock it and throws it back in her bag while searching for her keys.

"You ready for Dairy Queen?" she asks while we walk through the parking lot and to her car.

"You're joking, right?"

"No. Why do you think I exercise?" she says, throwing her bag on the passenger seat.

I pass, knowing I'm not in the right mindset for confronting her.

Rachel says we'll get ice cream another time and waves good-bye while speeding out of the parking lot.

Another time? Not so sure. Then again, putting myself in a sugar-induced coma might help ease the pain of betrayal. "Say hi to Ryan for me," I hiss, and of course, she's already gone. *I'm such a coward*, I think while sitting in my car, wondering about our friendship—and whether it can withstand betrayal and my lack of trust.

CHAPTER 33

Traffic's at a standstill on the way home from running errands. It's one of those rainy yet sunny days, and it's hard to tell which one is the culprit. Today, we can't blame the rain or the sun. A fire engine, some flashing lights, and a car with smoke coming from its hood justify the backup.

It's hard not to rubberneck during these moments and as the traffic creeps by, my phone pings with a text. It usually sits face down, so it doesn't bother me when driving, but ever since the Rachel and Ryan discovery, I've been distracted and forgetful. While waiting to inch up, I reach for the phone. The text doesn't show me a name, only a number. Right away, the message makes sense and gives it away.

Hey, Maggie, it's Drew, Just Drew

Remember me? From the conference?

How could I forget Just Drew, the one from the rooftop; the one who told me we had a connection; who never called or texted from four months ago? And yes, I've kept count. The driver behind me honks, and I catch up to the car in front of me to inch my way to the next exit.

Wonder what he wants? Is he having second thoughts? Or does he want to tell me something interesting about the conference? There's no way he's texting me to apologize. Guys don't do that when they've ghosted you. In all fairness, he didn't ghost me. He never said he'd contact me, even though he asked for my number.

The traffic clears up after we pass the accident. In ten minutes, I'm home, snagging a great space on my block in the process. My hawk-like abilities make me cheer out loud, because snagging a killer space is something to be forever proud of, like great parallel parking skills. I keep the car running and reach for my phone to see if Just Drew has sent a response to my text.

His follow-up says:

So sorry for not contacting you.

This makes me totally eat my words and at the same time wonder, why now? The rest of his text explains it.

Really liked u but…

Been involved with someone who got back with her ex while separated. Afraid that would happen again.

Been thinking about you. U divorced yet :-)?

His message catches me off guard yet doesn't surprise me. I probably wouldn't date for the same reason. When someone's separated, they're waiting for closure. Anything could happen. It could take years to get divorced. Or they could change their minds. Just Drew thinks and acts logically with his head, instead of his heart. That's good, right?

I contemplate whether or not to respond. At least now I know the reason for not texting. Even though interested, he didn't want to get involved with someone he considered still married. I get it. And appreciate it. He earns points for that, but why wait all these months? Why not check in with me after a few weeks? Or tell me the reason when we met?

Chili waits for me in the foyer, as always, wagging her tail and wiggling her butt. She presses her nose against the leash and it's her way of saying that she's ready for her walk. Sometimes she jumps in place to show her excitement and today she does it even more as she waits patiently.

Hey there, of course, I remember you!

And yes, I'm finally divorced.

I drop the phone in my pocket after texting back and take Chili out. I'm tempted to check, but my cell stays in its place because I'd be such a huge hypocrite. One of my biggest pet peeves is seeing people on phones while walking their dogs. Once a dog lunged at a teenager while the owner stood with his head stuck in his phone, and I couldn't help myself, so the f-bombs went flying. It came across as harsh but the last thing you need is an owner who shouldn't have a dog in the first place if emails and apps capture his attention more.

After our walk, we stop by the mailbox. Our usual routine. Chili sits quietly while I reach in and sort through the pile. Junk mail, bills, and newspapers get shuffled and at the bottom is an envelope with Ryan's name and address in the top-left corner. My heart pounds, and I'm scared to open the envelope. Not because I'm worried about what's inside—but what the after-effects will do to me. Will his words piss me off? Or turn me inside out and make me miss him?

Chili almost takes my shoulder off when she darts after a squirrel on our way to a nearby park bench. Our neighbor, Cynthia, walks by with her two pups and my first thought is that she has shitty timing. Or maybe it's me with the shitty timing. Either way, it's impossible to ignore Cynthia when she spots me.

Her small talk spills out and without pause. I continue to nod, struggling to get a word in edgewise, and my relief shows when her husband gets out of his car and joins the conversation. It allows me, for the first time since being divorced, to see how they interact with each other—or, rather, how Cynthia nags him to high heaven: David, did you pick up the light bulbs from Home Depot? Did you remember to take out the trash? Did you see the ant problem we're having in the kitchen? I'm surprised she didn't ask if he remembered to floss his teeth.

Finally, it's David who asks how I'm doing, maybe to be polite, or to change the subject. We talk about the movies we want to see, the books collecting dust on our nightstands, and the traffic that keeps getting worse. It makes me wonder if the two of us have more in common than he does with Cynthia.

After a few minutes, they go on their way, and I tear open the envelope with as much energy as the final divorce decree, dying to see what's in there, anxious at the same time to read what Ryan couldn't tell me in a text.

CHAPTER 34

Chili sits by my leg and puts her muzzle on my foot. It's a beautiful day, and normally the loud kids and bicyclists whizzing by on the path would distract me. Today, Ryan's letter takes all my attention, so we hang out on a park bench as I open the envelope and start reading.

> *Maggie,*
>
> *I know what you're thinking. Why won't he leave me alone and use the Find My Horse app to stay busy? Instead, I decided to download the I'm So Confused app, which doesn't seem to be helping.*
>
> *Were we getting too close? I used to be like that, when I'd had a bad breakup and didn't want to get hurt again. You say you want to date others. I don't believe that.*
>
> *I get it—you got burned along the way and you don't know what to believe. But I think about that night we met. Sitting at the bar, making paper airplanes. And how you said "yes" to Little Joe's when you're not the spontaneous type.*
>
> *What matters is that we had instant chemistry. This isn't complicated—or it shouldn't be. I*

imagine it must be hard to go through a divorce and pick up the tiny little pieces. You don't have to hide those feelings. You can tell me you're having a hard time trusting again. Believe me, I understand. I protected myself by breaking off relationships before getting burned.

The last relationship I had—the one before you that lasted six months—I fell hard, and she cheated on me. But I can't go into every relationship thinking I'll be cheated on. Not everyone is like this and it takes time to heal, I get it.

If that's not what's going on and you really want to see others, that's cool. No matter what happens, there are so many good memories! Especially our oyster shots and how you became competitive on the second one (go ahead, deny it 😅) And the Find My Horse app, which by the way, could be a best-seller—if only there were more horses!

I wish you the best and want you to be happy.
Ryan

A child knocks into the bench and startles Chili. Her parents apologize, pick up the girl's bike and head on down the path.

So many words in Ryan's letter hit me hard. At first, it's all the memories he mentions, but how could he say these things and be seeing Rachel? Did they end it and he's trying to hit rewind?

Even though we have this connection and think about the same things, like the same music, feel the same way, it doesn't matter. Not after seeing Rachel and him together. And what gets me is the specific words he uses. The same ones I've used—but never to him. Like picking up the tiny little pieces, about getting burned, and not knowing what to believe. I've never said them to Ryan, only to Rachel or while talking to myself at home, wondering how Nate could betray me. If Rachel's the only one who's heard me, it makes sense that they're seeing each other and talking about me.

I fold the letter, shove it into my pocket, and run back into the house with Chili. It's still driving me crazy and doesn't make sense. Why would Ryan write me a letter and be seeing my best friend? My head goes into overdrive as I reach for my phone to search for "signs my boyfriend's cheating with my best friend" and see Drew's reply after mine about being divorced.

> *Can u forgive me for not calling? Got spooked about you not being divorced yet. Would u consider meeting up?*

I respond back to Drew, telling him to pick a time and place and after that, text Rachel and ask her to meet me for dinner. Because it's time for me to get over my fear of confrontation and find out why she's lying to me.

CHAPTER 35

Rachel picks Little Joe's, and I go along with it even though that's where Ryan took me. He's probably taken her there by now, too. She isn't onto me yet and why we're meeting, and we grab a booth in the back corner.

She can tell something's going on because she keeps asking if I'm okay, that I don't seem like myself. Rachel has no clue it's about her. At first, a fib slips out easily—some lame excuse about work driving me to drink if we have to come up with one more promo to sell the newest celebrity line with a design that looks like it's done by a preschooler with a haphazard crayon set. Rachel believes me, and we laugh while coming up with stupid ways to sell the celebrity line. This buys me some time and I wait until the red wine kicks in to summon up some courage.

"You have to admit, you have a pretty cool job. You get to come up with fun promos," she says while folding the slice of pizza in half and taking a big bite.

"And you get to have summers off," I say, taking a sip of wine as I remind her that being a high school history teacher has its rewards like a long break, pretty decent hours, and better job security than my career choice.

"Beats the time I taught middle school, that's for sure. Must've been a fight every other day there. It was much tougher to get through to them, too."

I place my glass down on the table and stare at my pizza, counting the pepperoni covering the top. Rachel's been my best friend for so long. The thought of losing her scares me, but this can't go on. And I keep remembering what Betty told me: Don't wait too long or it'll eat away at you.

"Rachel, is there something you wanna tell me?" I finally blurt out.

"About what?"

"You know…"

"It's true. I've been holding out. I'm pregnant with triplets," she jokes.

"Funny. Who's the father?" I say defensively. The wine has kicked in, turning me into Miss Passive-Aggressive.

Rachel laughs and doesn't pick up on my snarky jab. "I didn't want to tell you … your celebrity promo guy, well, we've been having a thing for a while now." She picks up her phone and pretends to read a text. "Ooh, wait, he's asked me to be in an ad with him—on a bed—for his new line of sheets. This could get naughty."

I don't laugh, and she looks straight at me after putting her phone down, realizing the seriousness in my tone. "I'm sorry, didn't realize you were that stressed about work."

"It's not that," I say and play with the pen on the table. "You've been keeping something from me. I'm all grown up, you know. You can tell me what's going on."

"Okay," she says, and her voice rises with concern. A napkin flies off the table as a waiter walks by, and Rachel bends down to pick it up. "You're being cryptic. Not sure what you're talking about, nothing's going on."

"Don't lie to me. I can't take it anymore."

"You say you're all grown up but you're not acting like it—more like a teenager pissed off about something."

We stare at each other for an uncomfortable minute. Rachel breaks the tension with a smile. "I have no idea what you're talking about, Maggie. Seriously, I don't."

"I feel sorry for your new boyfriend. Although you probably don't care."

"Why would you feel sorry for him?" She plops her purse on the table. "Okay, what the hell is going on? Stop beating around the bush and tell me!"

"You and Ryan."

"What are you talking about?" she says and looks away when the waiter approaches to clear our table and, while he's there, she scribbles on the check and hands him the restaurant's copy.

He takes forever to tidy up and it gives me a chance to chicken out, but I've already come this far. My stomach churns as it always does when I'm emotionally fraught, and that's when she gets an earful about the day I saw them together. How the two of them went into the coffee shop, smiling and laughing.

"Maggie, it's not what you think."

"Oh my God!" I yell before realizing I need to bring it down a notch. "Why is it when anyone lies to me, that's what they say? Please. Give me a break." I pick up my purse and fly toward the front of the restaurant. The hostess holds the door for me, and I take off down the block. *Why didn't I drive this time for an easy escape?*

"Maggie," Rachel screams as she follows me. "Slow down, will you? Let me explain. I swear on my grandmother's grave I won't lie."

I stop and turn around. "You already have by not telling me."

"That's not true. Holding out isn't exactly lying."

"Seriously? What the—"

"Maggie, wait. Hear me out and then decide if you hate my guts." She waits for my nod. "Please don't be mad at me. I was only trying to help."

A few people dodge around us on the sidewalk as we stand down the block from Little Joe's. It starts to drizzle and we move underneath an awning of a jewelry store.

"I do know him." She sighs. "He's a friend of mine. We haven't been in touch for a long time."

"How long have you known him?"

"Since college."

It takes a minute to sink in. They've known each other since college? She's never mentioned him. "That doesn't make sense," I wind up saying. "How would I not know him?"

"Actually…" She pauses. "You do. Well, you know of him. He's Rob. My Rob, remember? The one I dated briefly, who graduated the year before you and I met."

Now she's really confusing me. What does Rob have to do with Ryan? "Yeah, I remember you talking about Rob. Is this a case of mistaken identity? Or are you trying to confuse me to change the subject?"

"You know me and my nicknames for guys. There was Lev, for Lucas Elliott Vaughn, remember? And Dan, for Dylan Aaron Nichols. I also had one for Ryan. It was Rob—which stood for Ryan Oliver Brennan."

It starts to pour and we move farther into the small alcove as the rain beats down around us.

This can't be happening. Ryan is Rob? And then I remember. The two of them did date, before my time, and she only mentioned him in passing. And then it hits me. "Shit! That means you've slept with him and never told me!"

I pull the phone out of my purse and call up the Outro app. A taxi driver stops in front of us, rolls down his window asking if we need a ride. Rachel waves him off.

"Maggie," she says and puts her hand on my arm. "It was so long ago."

"Come on, how does anyone go from being involved to just being friends? It's impossible."

"Easy," she says. "We went out a few times and he always made me laugh, but we didn't click. There was absolutely no chemistry. We both agreed that we'd be better off as friends. We didn't stay in touch that much after he graduated, and when he moved back—"

I cut off her rambling. "The thought of you sleeping together is totally weirding me out. That's a whole different thing. Why didn't you tell me you knew him when he sat down next to us that night at the bar?"

"Long story." She sighs before continuing slightly above a whisper as people pass us on the sidewalk. "You were going through such a hard time with Nate. You kept blaming yourself. He cheated on you that first time and you trusted him. It's like, what the hell? Does Nate need that much attention? And Ryan's such a nice guy. I wanted you to have a nice guy for a change."

Her eyes well up and her nose turns red. She pulls a tissue out of her pocket and keeps it handy. "The night I came over and you ripped that beautiful dress, I felt so bad for you. You were hurting so much, and honestly … that first month, you were walking around like a zombie. I was concerned and wanted to distract you." She pauses and folds her arms. "And I sort of did it to get back at Nate."

"Did what? You also did something to Nate?"

"No, not really, basically to spite him," she continues. "I knew Ryan was your type, so I asked him to come to the bar, like a blind date, to see if he could cheer you up. I asked him not to say we knew each other, because you wouldn't be down for it. Remember that one time after college when I tried to set you up?"

Relief sets in, knowing that nothing's going on between them, but it still doesn't sit right. "Why didn't you say anything? You could've figured out how to tell me, right? Instead of keeping it a secret."

I pause and look down, allowing myself to think things through, remembering how I told Rachel about Savannah and called it our river-walk rendezvous, the same term Ryan used after the fact.

"It all makes sense now! All the things he knew about me: Imagine Dragons, Duran Duran, my tattoo. Did you feed him stuff about me?"

She doesn't answer and looks away.

"Did you tell him I called Savannah our river-walk rendezvous?"

For once, she's speechless as she nods.

"You told him all that about me, so I'd think we had stuff in common … what the hell, Rachel? What if I'd fallen for him and he didn't like me?"

She leans back against the jewelry store's window. I can see she's trying to get out of it. "It doesn't matter. What matters is that he's crazy about you. Don't you think?"

"How can I be with someone where the relationship started with lies? All lies. This whole time he was doing you a favor by meeting with me, right?"

She doesn't answer.

"Right?" I yell, not caring who's watching.

"Only the first time. After that, it was all him." She continues, defensively, "Maggie, I did it to make the landing softer."

"The landing softer? What the hell does that mean?"

"I wanted to cushion the blow from Nate. For you to get distracted by a cute guy. Because I didn't want you to grieve too long over your divorce. And you're right. Who knows if there was another affair? Maybe that was the fifth time. And then there was Drew, and you getting upset that he didn't call."

"Don't change the subject," I say calmly, even though I'm about to explode. "At least you could've told me afterward that you set us up. But not saying anything and feeding him stuff about me so I'd think it's for real? When were you going to tell me?"

"I was planning to, then…"

"Then what?" I ask.

Rachel doesn't answer so I ask her again, firmly this time.

"I don't know. When you told me you wanted to see other people and not Ryan, I was surprised at first, then kind of relieved. Because then you'd never have to know."

My face feels flushed and my head starts pounding. "That might be the shittiest thing a best friend could ever say."

"I'm sorry. I should have never gotten involved. My intentions were good, though."

"Soften the landing, my ass. You made it worse," I say and storm off while texting Drew to see if he can push our date up to tonight. If anyone can help cushion the blow, he can.

CHAPTER 36

As I continue down the block, I cancel my Outro and walk into Hannigan's, a local Irish pub three blocks down from Little Joe's. The bartender pours me a beer, and I take a seat and wait for Drew to arrive. He's still Just Drew to me, simply because it makes me laugh and that's my medicine right now. Laughter and libations: two things that will make me feel better, even if temporarily.

Drew texts me that he's on his way and tells me his drink of choice. The bartender fixes a Bulleit whiskey straight up and places it next to me. Condensation forms on the outside of the glass and I draw a smiley face with my finger.

"Hey there," Drew says, and I get up from the barstool to give him a big hug. It's been several months since seeing him, and it could be the beer talking, but damn if he doesn't look good. His sideburns are longer, and the sun seems to have kissed the tips of his dirty-blond hair. He's wearing a blue and burgundy plaid button-down and tan skinny jeans tucked into black lace-up boots.

"Love your dress. Makes your eyes stand out," he says.

"Thanks. Someone once told me plum does that. Love your boots, by the way."

"I live in boots all year-round."

"Even at the beach?" I joke.

"Yep. I have a pair that matches every Speedo." He grimaces. "Oh shit, could you imagine?"

I'm about to laugh and stop myself, realizing he might be one of the few who'd look good in Speedos, boots, and nothing else.

We both sit down and he stirs his drink. "Thanks for ordering. It's exactly how I like it." He takes a sip, puts the glass down on the counter, and grins. "So…"

"So," I say and smile back.

"I'm really glad you texted me. Again, sorry for not getting in touch after we met. Can't help but get cold feet about dating a married woman."

I'm getting tipsy from the beer and about to flirt my ass off, in spite of Rachel and Ryan.

"It's okay, I totally get it," I tell Drew. "It's hard, the whole dating thing."

"On paper, you were still married. And my heart doesn't know the difference."

His response sounds romantic. It also sounds like he's been hurt. To him, being separated still means you're not available.

"I should've explained instead of being an ass."

"Let's forget about it and—"

"No, let me explain," he interrupts as he finishes off the last of his whiskey. "I dated a woman a couple of years ago who was separated and fell for her. Three months in, she dumped me and said she and her husband were reconciling."

"Sounds like she broke your heart."

"You could say that," he says, gazing at me.

It's silent for a minute before I change the subject and ask if he's been trotting around the globe, doing his keynotes.

He stretches and puts his arms on the sides of the barstool. "A couple here and there. I've cut back some to finish my book, then I might pick it up again when it's published."

"That's cool. What's it about?"

"You'll think it's crazy or boring, not sure which."

"Try me."

"It's called *The Business of Lying*. It's about whether it's okay to lie to protect your brand and company."

Interesting, I think and wonder about lying in our personal lives—because we've all done it. When is it okay to lie? Should we do it to protect ourselves, or others? And who's to say if it's right or wrong? "Love the title," I wind up saying.

"Thanks. I'm about halfway done with the draft. Need to get it to my publisher by the end of the year."

He pulls out a card from his pocket and hands it to me. With dimensions a little smaller than a bookmark, the front has a picture of him sitting on the front steps of a brick townhouse. His name and website are listed underneath.

"How'd you come up with the book idea?" I ask, looking at the card and flipping it over to the back.

"I already have a podcast with the same name. Been doing it for a few years now. It's a lot of work but I love it. Businesspeople call in anonymously, so they can talk freely."

"How's it different from lying in your personal life?" I continue, wondering how quickly he can think on his feet, while making a mental note to check out his podcast.

He takes a swig of whiskey and looks down as if he's thinking. "That's a great question. It's completely different when you're dealing with emotions. There shouldn't be feelings involved when dealing with business. It's a lot more black and white."

"Some might disagree with you."

"Yeah, it's a pretty controversial subject. Some say you need empathy when you're in business, that you'll be more successful."

"Who knows," I say. "Maybe that'll help sell more books. People like stories about professional growth. And it's different from anything I've ever heard of."

"We'll have to wait and see. Anyway, enough about me. Speaking of emotions, are you doing okay since the divorce?"

It's sweet of Drew to ask about my life and of course, it's my turn to lie, to tell him everything's great and I'm loving my single life and empty nest even though the kids weren't mine or with us every day. Having Chili has certainly helped ease the emptiness at home.

Drew listens and asks questions, and like I remember from the rooftop at the conference, isn't self-absorbed. Then it's my turn to ask more about him and make another mental note to do a search later to see what, if anything, is bogus.

"It's kind of interesting that you're doing a book on lying but couldn't tell me the truth—that you didn't want to date a woman who's separated," I say, putting air quotes around the last part, instantly regretting the words because it sounds defensive.

"I'm sorry. And you're right. That's a whole other judgment call."

"What is?" I ask.

"Whether sparing the truth is bad or considered lying so someone doesn't get hurt."

Drew's words sink in and make me think about what Rachel and Ryan did, wondering how it would've been different if they'd told me the truth from the start. "Sometimes not saying anything is worse."

"Fair enough. I'm a wimp," he admits and winks, making me blush and look away.

***

"So," he says after we've sat for an hour talking about everything from travel to our jobs and families.

"You like saying 'so,' don't you?"

"It's my segue when I have a hard time asking or saying something."

"Don't worry, I can take it."

"Okay." He pauses and then rubs his hands together. "Do you want another drink or maybe you'd like to invite me up to your room?"

"My room?" I pause. "What are we? Teenagers hoping our parents won't catch us?"

"Hmmm, that's kinda naughty," he says, and at that moment all I can think about is Ryan.

But Ryan needs to get out of my head and what better way to make him disappear than by being with another guy. Drew comes in closer, and I let him kiss me. It's nice. Like the-guy's-had-a-lot-of-practice nice. He's taking it slowly, playing almost, stopping close to my lips before starting up again. I'm trying desperately to forget Ryan and there's one easy way.

"So," I tease. "I don't have whiskey, but there's plenty of wine at my place."

He grins and hands the bartender a credit card. We leave Hannigan's and call an Outro back to my place.

When I open the door to the hallway and Chili sees me, she wags her tail, all excited for her late-night walk. Drew joins me in taking her out and grabs the leash from me when Chili nudges up to his leg. She doesn't growl or bark once, which tells me she likes him right away.

On our walk, I share stories about elaborate Christmas decorations in the neighborhood every year and we admire the full moon until we reach my house again.

He kisses me in the hallway and we kick off our shoes. Instead of heading to the kitchen to have some wine that baited him, Drew follows me upstairs. Chili looks at me with her big brown eyes, and I close the door before she makes her way into the bedroom. *Being intimate with someone is becoming easier*, I think before we take our clothes off and get under the covers.

***

I wake up the next morning with Drew kissing my ear. He moves the blanket away that's nestled between us and makes his way down my neck and to my shoulder.

"You're so beautiful," he says. "Last night was nice. Thanks for inviting me over, even though we never got to the wine part."

"Wine, sex, what's the difference?" I joke and throw off the covers. "I need to pee and brush my teeth."

Drew laughs and reaches for my arm, pulling me close for another kiss. "You're so romantic."

"So much so that Hollywood called. They want me to star in a remake of *When Harry Met Sally*." I grab my phone on the way to the bathroom and take a long look in the mirror, overthinking what I've done.

Why would I sleep with Drew when I'm still crazy about Ryan? On top of it, I feel so guilty. Did I use Drew to get back at Ryan?

My phone pings with a text from Rachel.

> *Maggie, I'm sorry. U have every right to be pissed.*

> *I was trying to help. Hated seeing u miserable after Nate. Call me.*

Rachel's trying all she can to make up and make me understand. Would she still feel this way if she knew about my lackluster spying to check her phone? Then my anger takes over. It's one thing to set someone up on a blind date and not mention it. It's another to feed information about them and hope it won't last so you don't have to say anything.

Why's everyone trying to orchestrate my life? Can't they stop thinking they know what's best for me?

I pick up my phone and swipe. Her message gets read once more and goes unanswered. Ryan's day-old message sits under Rachel's. He's still texting me. Even after sending the letter. And he's still on my mind, with our connection consuming me. Just Drew should be enough for me. He's lying in my bed right now, waiting for me to return.

Miss you, I text to Ryan without thinking and instantly regret it. I've broken my rule of contacting him. Love, lust, or whatever you call it, gets the better of me. My willpower is shot to hell.

Then three dots appear.

Miss u 2. Can we talk?

My heart pounds as I reread his message several times.

Now's not a good time. Call you later?

Ten minutes pass and my bed is empty. Drew's gone, along with his clothes. I throw on some sweatpants and walk to the landing at the top of the stairs. Chili looks up and barks as she sits patiently by the front door.

"Hey there, should I run out and get us some coffee? Or take Chili out?" Drew asks from the first-floor hallway.

I dash down the stairs and plant a kiss on his cheek. "Thanks, I'm sure she'd love that. I'll make us some coffee in the meantime."

He wins me over in an instant with his thoughtfulness. You'd think that, along with his good looks, it would be enough. More than enough. But you can't help the way passion makes your heart skip a beat, and in a second my mind wanders to Ryan's letter and what he says in it.

I think about that night we met. Sitting at the bar, making paper airplanes.

Me, too, Ryan …

Drew heads out and plays with Chili in the front yard. While watching them run around, I think about Drew. I really like him. But it needs to be more. It has to be. I want to be crazy about him, where my heart beats faster when he's in the room. When he smiles. When he puts his hand on my leg. When he kisses me. When he says I'm beautiful.

It's only the second time I've seen him, though. Maybe he'll grow on me. I want him to grow on me. But Ryan keeps getting in the way.

CHAPTER 37

The next evening, the doorbell rings and Chili goes berserk. I already know who's there without looking out the peephole and peek out anyway to be cautious. Ryan's standing by the door with a bottle of wine and chocolate, like he did the last time.

Not sure why he thinks it's going to be like old times. Well, actually, I do know—from the text exchange where we both said how we missed each other.

Maybe we should have met in public instead. I'm regretting so many moves lately, like inviting him over, but I'm not thinking straight these days, not since that day at the DMV.

I open the door and he steps into my foyer. Chili warms up quickly and rolls over onto her back. Ryan bends down, holding the wine and chocolates in one arm, and gives her a good belly rub. She has an upside-down smile and when her teeth show, it makes us laugh.

Ryan gets up and walks to the kitchen, placing the bottle on my counter. Before either of us says a word, he comes in close for a hug. I don't pull away but my embrace isn't like before. I'm cautious because my heart still aches.

"I'm glad you texted me. Please don't be mad at Rachel," he says before breaking away.

I sit on the stool by the kitchen counter and wait for him to open the wine.

It's an uncomfortable silence until he continues. "We both feel like crap. Look, be mad at me. You guys have been friends for a long time. She meant well … can't you see that?"

A snicker comes out because it takes less effort than crying. "She practically gave you my résumé, highlighted with bullets. Was I on a job interview? And do you interview all your dates the same way?"

He pours some wine into our glasses and hands me one. "Just because she told me what you liked doesn't mean I didn't already have the same interests."

"Oh, come on, what about when we were in Savannah? In that store? Did you go in advance and pay her to play Duran Duran?"

Ryan laughs and wipes away the wine that stains the top of his lip. "That's insane. Rachel told me you liked them, but I had no idea you'd always wanted to dance to that song." He sighs. "Look, that was as real as it gets."

"Do you have any idea how many times I've fallen asleep thinking about that moment? It's completely ruined." I start crying. I can't help it, and when Ryan comes closer, he gets pushed away. "Why'd you even have to say anything? Why'd you have to tell me you liked Imagine Dragons, or mention the tattoo, or take me away on a romantic trip? Why?"

He comes closer and puts his hand on mine. This time I don't push him away. "Maggie, you realize all those things don't matter. What we have is real. It's a connection. We would've had it whether I'd mentioned them or not."

Maybe it's true and I want to agree, but there's no giving in on my part. Because giving in means accepting what Ryan did to get my attention. Yes, the attention and being with him helped get my mind off Nate, but the deceit outweighs the outcome. It outweighs the ability to trust him and know what's real or not.

"Maggie, I'm not sure what else I can say to convince you," he adds and bends down to pet Chili.

"There's nothing more to say, Ryan."

My furry companion is looking up at him and their eyes meet. She's in love with him, too.

"Will you do something for me?" He smiles and his chipped tooth makes an appearance. "Can you at least destroy the horrible karaoke video from Savannah? The thought of me singing in public—"

"You know you loved it." I pull out my phone and send him one of the shorter videos, along with a few photos. "Here, for when you're bored and having nothing to watch."

He reaches into his pocket, and I lean over as he opens up the message. At the top by my name, it says Maggie MIA.

"What the hell?" My voice startles Chili. She looks up and runs out to the foyer with her tail between her legs. "Maggie MIA? Like I'm missing in action? Or only when you want me to be around?"

"No, not at all!"

"Then what is it?" I fold my arms and glare at him. "My middle name isn't Mia. Neither is my last."

He leans his palms on the counter. "It stands for Miami."

It puzzles me for a moment and then registers. "Like the abbreviation for an airport?"

He doesn't deny it or look away. What we have must be so casual that he can't even take a second to put my last name in—yet has time to put in the location—as if he has another Maggie or two in some other town and uses an airport code to keep track of it.

"Is there a Maggie LAX or maybe Maggie ATL? Or both?"

"Of course not! When we first met, I didn't know your last name, so I put MIA for Miami, so I'd remember your number. I would've just put your first name, but my sister's name is Maggie. Didn't want to confuse the two."

He pauses and runs his hand through his hair. "I'm pretty sure I told you; I have a sister named Maggie. She lives in Colorado, remember? I also have a friend named Maggie." He starts to sound defensive. "It's a pretty popular name. Don't you think you're being a little too hard on me?"

My phone pings and a text lights up from Drew. It's sitting upright on the counter and catches our attention. We both look at the message. It's hard not to.

> *Hey, beautiful! Had a great time with you*
> *last night.*

Ryan pretends not to see the message. And he can't hide his disappointment. "I think I should go," he says.

"Ryan," I whisper.

He turns around on his way toward the door.

I imagine what he thinks will come out of my mouth. That I'm sorry he saw that text. That whatever happened last night meant nothing. Or that I'll pretend not to know who's texting me. It's none of that. "Thanks for telling me how you feel. I wanted you to come over because I needed closure. Sorry, I just can't be in a relationship based on a lie. I had that before. Not anymore, or ever again. It's more than I can handle."

"I'm sorry, too," he says and opens the front door. "Seriously, though, was it really all that bad that I didn't tell you? Do you really think I'd want to date someone I wasn't interested in?"

"Honestly, it's more about me and my trust issues."

"Trust issues, with me? Because I didn't put your last name in my contacts? You can't keep holding onto the past and what's happened with other relationships."

"Easier said than done. And it's more than that."

"Whatever." He picks up his keys from the front table and opens the door. "We all take chances and make choices, Maggie. That's what life's all about."

"We can definitely agree on that. Take care of yourself," I say and lock up behind him before sliding down behind the door. Chili shuffles over and lies down next to me. She's more than my companion lately. She's my pillow. My shoulder to cry on. My everything.

CHAPTER 38

When I arrive at Longwood to visit Betty and Al, there's an ambulance out front. They take out the stretcher and wheel it through the front door, making me nervous while wondering if something has happened to my two favorite residents. George sees me and says not to worry, that it's Victor, a long-time resident, who's passed away. Someone I don't know. He was a recluse, remaining in his room most days. It makes me sad for the loss and the calls they'll need to make to his family … if he has anyone left behind.

The sunroom's busier than usual and when everyone sees Chili, they brighten up and smile. Chili notices too, and when several residents call out her name, she perks up and prances around, letting them pet her. My two favorite residents make their way through the room slowly; they're running late today. Sometimes that happens when Al takes a longer-than-usual nap. They're holding hands as they approach and find two chairs near the window. Betty's colorful as always with a bright-purple tracksuit, light-pink sneakers, and a baseball cap that matches and covers her rose-colored curls.

"Look who we have here," Al says and pets Chili behind her ear. He knows the perfect spot and Chili responds by licking his hand. "Must smell the chicken soup I had for lunch."

Al reaches in his pocket, then tells Chili to sit, lie down, and roll over. Chili does all with ease and not with the least bit of stubbornness. She gets back up after Al says, "Good girl," and gets two biscuits for a job well done.

Coming here never gets old. The residents' outlook on life is more inspiring than some of the twenty-somethings who work with me daily. Sometimes when my coworkers start complaining about the little stuff, I want to grab them by the arm, throw them in my car, and drive them to Longwood for a visit. Al and James, the guy in the corner who likes to dance in his chair, could tell them war stories of how hard it was growing up. It would put their daily dose of quasi-drama on ice and make them realize that maybe it's not half as bad as it seems.

"Al and I are taking a vacation in a few months," Betty says, arranging herself, so she's more upright in the chair.

"Where you going?"

"Well, that's the problem. We can't decide. He wants to go to the Bahamas, and I'm voting for San Francisco."

"Why don't you flip a coin?"

"Nah, of course, we're going to San Francisco. Because," he adds and puts his hand on Betty's, "my beautiful wife wants to see the Pacific Ocean."

"You're trying to butter me up so you can have my dessert after dinner," Betty teases.

"You got me. I'm a sucker for sweets and pretty women."

You'd think Betty would be jealous, but she smiles and pats Al's hand in response. "So, my dear," she says and looks my way. "Tell me something new. How's your job?"

"Job's the same," I say and fill her in on some new drama about our interns and the projects they're working on.

"And did you talk to Rachel about what happened?" Betty asks.

They listen intently when I fill them in and even when Chili nudges them for a rub, they don't look away. I leave out the part about Rachel sleeping with Ryan during college because, to me, that's the least of it. When Al tries to interrupt, Betty keeps her hand on his and pats it anytime he's about to talk.

"That's quite the story, my dear," Betty says. She probably wants to say more, and my intuition proves me right. "Sounds as if you like this Ryan guy."

"I do. Well, I did," I say and pause. "What's a relationship based on a lie? There's no way moving past that."

Betty and Al love giving advice and have plenty to give with their eighty-some years of experiences. "Forget about Ryan for a minute," Betty says. "Let's talk about Rachel, because you have such a long friendship. To me, the most important part of a relationship is trust. Although sometimes you have to fib a little to protect people or make them feel better."

"Come on—" Al says.

"Goodness gracious, let me finish!" Betty continues, "For example, I'd never tell a friend if a certain style didn't look good on her, but I'd sure as heck tell her if her zipper was down or a button was undone on her blouse."

"I'd hope so! But how can you compare these with what Rachel did?" I add.

"Don't be so hard on her," Betty says. "Rachel had the best intentions. So what? You met a guy you liked. Be happy you had feelings that many never have."

I contemplate what she says. Betty's probably right, but am I mature enough to admit it?

She continues, "You want to blame her for making you feel happy? That's so funny."

"Listen to my wife. She's always right."

Betty leans toward Al. "Buttering me up again for my cake?"

He leans closer and stops short. It takes them a few extra seconds to find their lips. Once they do, Al plants a long kiss on his wife and they stay close for a moment, gazing at each other.

Laughter. Admiration. Respect. Al and Betty have it all and so when someone like that gives you advice or says something so meaningful, you take notice. Maybe she's right. Why should I blame Rachel for wanting me to get over Nate and move on? On second thought, I could've done that myself, eventually, without anyone's help.

"What about Ryan?" I ask Betty, keen to hear her advice.

"Now that's a different story. I'd never give advice about love. Only you can decide. Remember that a relationship can't be based on attraction alone and how they act when times are good. It's got to be deeper than that."

Al nods and reminisces about the time they met and how Betty was seeing a handsome guy who worked in the next department over.

"I had quite the competition. He was dapper, with his nice suits and colorful ties."

"He was," Betty admits. "Turned out to be a complete bore, though!"

Chili barks and runs to the window. I get up to investigate and sure enough, she sees a squirrel stop in its tracks on the branch of a tree outside. Chili stares the squirrel down until it climbs up the tree. I pet my companion, and she looks up at me as if she's smiling.

"One more treat before we go?" I say and her tail starts wagging fast. She looks at me, then over at Al. Chili knows who has the best treats. She runs over and sits in front of him. Al reaches into his pocket and takes out a biscuit wrapped in a napkin. He breaks it into four pieces.

"Chili, it's your lucky day," I say, smiling while she gets spoiled.

As we walk to the door, Al calls out. "Remember what I always say?"

"What's that?" I say back even though I already know.

"Life is long. Make it matter."

I nod in agreement, and Chili stays by my side as we walk through the hallway. We wave good-bye to George, who's talking to a nurse, and walk outside the front entrance to my car. Chili jumps in the back and I start reversing then stop and put it in park, fumbling for my phone in my bottomless purse on the passenger seat. It rings twice before Rachel picks up.

"Hey," I say. "If you're not busy right now, can I stop by?"

CHAPTER 39

Rachel opens the door with a half-smile until she sees Chili standing beside me and then breaks into a full-on grin. Having Chili along helps both of us feel calmer. She bends down and pets her behind both ears while she makes baby talk. They've known each other since the day I picked her out at the adoption event, when Chili was hiding in the corner.

We go inside, and Rachel pulls out Chili's bed that she keeps for her visits. Chili spins around a few times and plops down before putting part of her body on the bed as her paws and muzzle pour out on the ceramic floor.

"Want some wine?"

"Sure," I say, my body tensing up.

She grabs two glasses from the shelf and starts opening a bottle. "You wanna grab the crackers?"

I reach into the pantry for the snacks and then pull a plate from the kitchen cabinet. I know where everything is in this house, been here a thousand times for catching up or for celebrations. Never like this, though. Never tense. It's hard to imagine knowing someone this long and never even having a disagreement. That's why her deception stings so deep.

Rachel fixes her headband and stands against the counter, watching me put the crackers on the plate. Her nerves get the better of the situation and she starts rambling a mile a minute. "What I did was purely out of love. You're right, I shouldn't have given Ryan all those details about you. And I should've told you about us."

"You guys sleeping together feels weird to me, but it was so long ago. It's the keeping stuff from me—and the feeding stuff to him—that's upsetting."

"Yeah, I feel shitty for getting involved. It should've happened on its own."

I look away when Chili growls at a UPS truck that pulls up outside. "It made me think you felt sorry for me and that's the last thing I need. Well, that and not knowing what's real and what's not between Ryan and me."

"I'm sorry," she says and fiddles with the cheese and crackers, lining them up like dominos.

"I know you meant well. And honestly, I don't want to be mad at you."

Rachel comes closer and wipes away a tear from her cheek. We hug for several minutes and, as I feel the stress drain away from my tight shoulders, Betty's words stay close. She's right. How can I be mad at my best friend, who was trying to help? For wanting me to be happy? And how could my imagination take over and assume the worst? To make me take her phone and snoop?

"Thank you," Rachel says. "It would kill me if you didn't forgive me." She reaches in the cabinet for dog snacks and hands one to Chili after she sits in front of her. "What about Ryan?"

"I don't see how it can work. After Nate, I can't be in a relationship based on a lie."

"So you're able to forgive me, but not him?"

Rachel makes a good point. Is it a double standard because she's been in my life longer? The length of knowing someone shouldn't be the determining factor. As I look back, though, the decision is easy: She's been my rock for so many years, for so many reasons. In the middle of the night. When I've cried in my car. Through thick and thin.

"You're like my sister. Can't break the bond," I say and then blurt out that I met up with Drew.

She raises her eyebrows, waiting for me to continue but doesn't seem that surprised.

"I needed to take my mind off Ryan. Out of the blue, he contacted me. Said he got spooked, didn't want to date a woman who was still officially married."

"At least he's being honest."

"True. Would've been nice if he'd told me when we met instead of waiting and making me wonder this whole time."

"Don't hold it against him," Rachel says as she pets Chili.

"I'm not. It's just…"

"Just what?"

"Hard to explain. He's not Ryan. I don't feel the same connection."

"Look, I get it. If you're not feeling it, you're not feeling it. Maybe you should give him a chance?" Rachel says. "It can grow. Sometimes that crazy passion fades and then what do you have?"

I shrug. "Odd that you'd say that. Isn't that what happened with you and Ryan?"

Rachel looks up at the light, waiting to gather her thoughts. "Not exactly. He also felt the same way, that we didn't have chemistry."

I lean my elbows on the counter and take a deep breath. "It's hard. Whenever I'm with Drew, I'm still thinking about Ryan. Can't get him out of my head. It's probably because it was such a whirlwind. Rachel," I say and pause before adding, "am I that kind of person?"

"What kind?"

"The kind who always needs a guy around. It's like I can't be alone."

"You know, as far back as I can remember, you've had a guy in your life. Honestly, what's so bad about that? Could be a helluva lot worse." Rachel hesitates before continuing, "Can I tell you something?"

My heart beats faster while waiting, not knowing what she'll say next.

"Ryan texted me, asking if you hooked up with some other guy. I'm guessing that was Drew?"

I nod and tell her more about what happened when Ryan came over. And how, at the time, I didn't care that he was hurting because I was hurting, too. Being with Drew helped me mask some of the pain.

"There's no manual on how to deal with our emotions," she says, "and there's nobody telling you who you should or shouldn't see. Well, as long as I don't get involved, which was stupid."

"What did you wind up telling him?"

"That I didn't know, and then he texted…" She picks up her phone and scrolls to find his message to read aloud:

Trying to set Maggie up was a bad idea.

We should have left it to fate. Cuz I really did like her.

What he says sinks in—but I want to hear his words once more. At least the last part. "Can you read it to me again?"

"Here," she says and hands me her phone.

I'm about to click on the text icon when a new text pops up. It's from Nate and stops me. All it says is:

Did it work?

I pretend to read Ryan's text while thinking about what Nate's text means.

Maybe she had a problem with something in her house? Unlikely. Nate's an accountant who never has time to fix anything, and he isn't handy at all. Besides, Rachel calls on her neighbor who owns a home contracting business when she needs a repair.

Maybe she had a tax question. That's a possibility.

I hand the phone back over and tell her matter-of-factly that there's a text from Nate. She checks the message, and puts the phone down without saying a word.

I can't help myself because she didn't tell me they'd stayed in touch. "Did it work?" I ask.

"What?"

"Nate's text. What does he mean by did it work?" I ask and start tapping my fingers on the kitchen counter. I'm on the defensive these days, not knowing what to think or trust.

She takes the phone from me and looks at the message. "So, you're reading all my texts now?"

We stare at each other. She knows I'm not letting up.

"You want me to be honest, right?" she finally says.

"Oh my God, yes! I want you to be honest! And please, don't say, 'It's not what you think' because I'll go bananas!"

"I wasn't gonna say that. He asked me if I'd convince you to meet with him. He's not completely over you."

"Why can't everyone let me live my life without getting involved?"

"I'm trying," she says. "And I told him to move on."

"I've been way too nice. Text him that we talked, and I agree to meet. Tell him I'll be in touch."

Rachel tries fishing for more details then shrugs. "Sounds cryptic, then again, it's not like I have much to say, considering the whole Ryan situation."

Chili trots over to the counter when she sees me grab the leash.

"Nate needs to hear it straight from me and face reality," I say as Chili follows me to the hallway. "Before meeting with him, there's someone else on my list."

CHAPTER 40

Thoughts about hearing the truth—and telling it—turn me into an insomniac every night for a week. Everyone wants to hear the truth. At least that's what we tell ourselves. But when we hear the truth, we're often not ready for it—and sometimes that's the reason our family and friends hide stuff.

And there are other reasons. They don't want us to get hurt. They want to protect us. They're scared. And that's why, if you ask me, a stranger is more likely to be honest than somebody close.

When anyone tells the truth, they take a chance—like those who deceive us. Betrayers risk everything without realizing it because they don't think about getting caught. Like Nate with that woman. He certainly didn't think about me when he met her or planned their day trip. He followed his emotions, his heart, or whatever body part you want to blame. And for the life of me, I still can't let it go.

It eats at me, and my imagination takes hold again. How many times did they meet? How many times has he done this without me knowing? Did he do this to his ex-wife, Heather? Does Heather still think about what happened, too, whatever it was? It's strange to imagine we might have something in common.

When I find myself distracted at work, missing a deadline, and rushing in late for meetings, I text Heather a few days later. She agrees to meet with me. After all, there aren't any hard feelings. We've been around each other plenty at talent shows and soccer games for the kids. This is the first time I've asked her to meet with me one-on-one.

I'm already sitting at a table in my neighborhood coffee shop when Heather walks in. She's wearing a base-ball jersey, jeans, and red Converse that match her tee. She's changed her hair from dark blonde to auburn and into a layered bob, making her look ten years younger, as if she's in her early thirties.

She walks over, sits down, and we make small talk about the traffic, the library renovation, the hipsters moving into the neighborhoods, and some of the houses that have been bulldozed to build modern ones that look out of place next to the art deco buildings. She's pleasant with me, always has been, but cuts to the chase after a few minutes.

"So, what did you want to meet about?"

Hesitation sets in, because even though she seems direct, I'm not sure how she'll react—or whether she'll want to talk about it. I play with my spoon, flipping one over between my fingers. "I guess we could've spoken over the phone. I don't know…"

Her voice changes, lower and softer, with more of a concerned tone. "Maggie, what's going on? Now I'm getting worried."

The waitress interrupts us and takes the rest of our order after placing two cappuccinos on the table. Heather grabs a sugar package from the container and shakes it before ripping the end off. I'm buying some time while she stirs with the spoon and places it down on her napkin.

Every time a woman comes in with short blonde hair, I imagine it's the other woman and my mind goes into overdrive again. I take a deep breath and ask, "Not to get into your dirty laundry—but would you be willing to share why you and Nate broke up?"

She looks surprised. "Why does it matter now? You're divorced and hopefully moving on with your life. That's at least what I tried to do. Living in the past and dwelling, it's never a good thing."

Regretting coming here, I quickly apologize and tell her that she's right.

She looks at her phone when a text appears before putting it in her purse. "Nate never told you why we broke up? Interesting …"

I tell her we talked about it, and Nate would change the subject when my pushing for more details annoyed him. She nods and takes a bite of her croissant. "I don't blame him for saying that—because, no doubt, he feels guilty. He kept using yet another lame excuse that he was working late. You know, always saying that it was tax season and he was knee-deep in returns."

I roll my eyes. "Yep, knee-deep. Sounds like the same line he fed me."

"What he was really knee-deep into," she says and leans in to whisper, "was getting blow jobs in his office."

I'm taken aback by her directness that lacks bitterness. It's more matter-of-fact than anything. "You caught him?"

She nods. "Looking back, there were definite red flags that I ignored. One day I went over to bring him dinner since he'd always complained about working late. Let's just say he was taking a break when I stopped by."

Her story makes me imagine the scene and how she must have felt showing up there. "Sounds like he couldn't pretend it was an emotional affair like with me?"

"Oh, don't worry," she adds and lets out a laugh or more like a scoff, making me feel like we've been in this together. "That was the excuse he used before. Telling me I was overreacting and that nothing was going on."

A snicker comes out, almost matching hers in intensity, because it sounds like the same old story. A neighbor gets my attention when she waves at me near the front counter. I wave back and look next to me, making sure there aren't any extra seats nearby. This isn't time for socializing. It's strictly ex-wives comparing notes.

"Just curious," I ask. "Did he try to get you to take him back?"

"Oh yeah, a few times." She explains the whole story and it sounds all too familiar. How he told her over and over again that it meant nothing, how he showed up at the house and her office and in front of her favorite coffee shop. He begged and swore it would never happen again. Until it did—and that's when she threw him out.

"Geez, no wonder he didn't want to talk about it."

Heather nods and takes a sip of her cappuccino. It's obvious she can't stand him and has no emotional ties, other than being bound by the kids. "Is that what happened to you?" she asks.

"More or less. Like you, it took more than once to realize it. The first time was right before we got married, and I was an idiot for not leaving then."

"You're not an idiot. Same thing happened to me—we were in love and overlooked stuff. You wanted to think he'd change. Obviously, he didn't. Don't think twice about him or what happened."

I tell her that I've been trying to move on, that he's the one stuck on reconciling. She quickly reminds me that he'll never change, and it's most likely that he's scared to be alone.

"Maggie, nip it in the bud. I bet that woman has already dumped him. He'll keep trying with you until he meets someone else who will put up with his bullshit. Don't fall for it."

I nod in agreement. Heather doesn't say it to protect me or to be mean. She almost tells me out of solidarity. We finish our meal and walk out together.

She waves good-bye and drives off as her words ring true with advice that needs to be taken seriously. *Nip it in the bud, Maggie. Or he'll keep trying.*

Before leaving, I text Nate to meet me on Saturday.

CHAPTER 41

Nate and I decide on Marty's Café and since they have a cool playground next door, he brings Emily and Max along—because I've asked. He thinks we're meeting to discuss our relationship. He thinks I'm going to hear him out and try to understand his side of the story. To maybe give him another chance.

The warm, sunny day calls for shades and they come in handy to hide my expressions—or lack of them. It has been more than six months and the kids haven't changed much, except Max is taller and has lost some of his baby fat. I'd still recognize him if he walked down the street. Another six months, or a year from now—I'm not so sure and it kills me.

Emily and Max run around, flying through monkey bars and mazes as we sit on benches around a wooden picnic table under the sunshine. Emily, quick on her feet, runs away and giggles as three toddlers chase her around a large wooden ship. They giggle back when she calls out "Try and catch me!" She's still a little bossy, and mostly funny, and I realize in a few short minutes how much I've missed them.

"Thanks for meeting me," Nate says. His aviator glasses fog up after he takes a sip of coffee. He puts the cup on the bench and lifts his glasses up and places them onto his baseball cap.

I continue watching the kids. "They're growing up so fast. How are they doing?"

"Great. Emily is getting straight As in everything and Max is getting a straight A in the only subject he likes—recess."

"That's not what I meant. How are they doing, emotionally? Are they okay?"

"They seem okay, you know? They don't spend that much time with me. Heather tells me they're fine."

His answer sounds rehearsed, as if it comes from a textbook that he's read a thousand times. "What about you?" he asks. "How are you?"

I look toward the playground and watch the kids chase each other. They keep me in my happy place. "No complaints. I'm at a point in my life where I'm accepting things as they are."

"Sounds a bit depressing." Nate reaches into a bag and pulls out a muffin. The sound startles me when he crunches up the paper into a ball and throws it. The bag ricochets off the edge of a trash can. Nate gets up to retrieve it and put it into the bin.

"Sounds realistic to me," I say when he comes back to sit down. "You can't change people, so why try?"

As we watch the kids, he shrugs. "I don't know. You shouldn't throw in the towel. Don't you think we can all change and grow?"

When I ask Nate to elaborate, he hesitates before sharing that he's been reading a lot lately and reflecting. "I'm trying to understand more about myself," he adds. "And why I acted that way."

I want to tell him it's a load of crap and that he enjoys the attention because I discovered it firsthand by uncovering his texts and photos. It doesn't matter anymore because what I'm about to tell him is the story he'll most likely remember.

"What if I promise to always be honest and open up to you," he says and brushes against my arm. "Is it really too late to give me another chance?"

His touch makes me flinch and want to move farther away. I'm already on the edge of the bench and there's nowhere to go.

"How could you possibly want one?" I ask and watch a cute toddler with wild curls chase Emily and Max around.

"Because I still love you? And miss you? Honestly, I'm relieved you decided to meet me, considering."

"You'll change your tune once I tell you something you don't know."

By the grin on his face, he thinks we're about to shoot the shit. "I'm not afraid of a little secret … or two."

I laugh, not only at the comment but the way he makes it sound like it's a tease, some kind of foreplay to arouse me. Instead, since I'm no longer attracted to him, it repels me. It's amazing how easily the switch can flip. One day, you can be so into someone and, the next, disgust takes over. Disgust has limits too, because, yes, I'm sharing a bench and a conversation for the greater good, to finally have closure and peace of mind.

Max jumps over a wall and brings me a few rocks he finds in the sand. I grab a handful and plant a kiss on his cheek as he rubs it off and runs back over to pick up some more rocks. Emily, on the other hand, has become popular with a few toddlers who follow her around like she's a princess. She seems to be loving the adoration.

"The kids miss you," Nate says again. It seems to be his go-to line, as if to induce guilt. He's probably being honest and the feeling is mutual about Emily and Max, but it's not a good enough reason to spend your life with someone. Just because of the kids.

"I miss them, too," I say instead of arguing with him about the times he didn't want to put them on the phone with me.

He reaches for my arm again. This time I pull away.

"There's something you need to hear. I know you wanted Rachel to help us get back together, and she told you—"

"That was wrong of me."

"Nate, let me finish!"

He squirms in his seat and then places his arm on the back of the bench as I continue in a calmer voice. "The reason I couldn't give you another chance is because an emotional affair isn't good for a marriage."

"Look, I fucked up," he says before looking around, trying to keep his voice low. "How many times do I have to tell you? Nothing happened this second time. I swear. We spent some time together. We talked about our lives. That's it. I didn't think it through, obviously."

How can he sit here and tell me this? And, even worse, how can he tell me he's a changed man? It's hard for me to hold it together and not scream "liar" to his face. I stay calm and say, "Believe it or not, this isn't about you."

He hesitates, taking a breath as I cut in.

"Let's say you didn't have sex with that woman ..."

His face flushes red. "I didn't …"

I put my hand up to stop him from talking. "Regardless, an emotional affair is something so much deeper, because when you trust someone on an emotional level, you start developing feelings even if you weren't physically into them at first. And that almost always leads to more intimacy." I pause for emphasis because the last part is what matters. "I'm telling you all this because maybe I know firsthand."

Nate tilts his head, as if he's letting my words sink in. "What do you mean, maybe you know?"

"It starts with talking, being friends at first. Like you said, sharing ups and downs, life experiences, and before you know it, you're—"

"When?" he interrupts. His voice comes out louder than expected and makes me jump.

"Maybe last year after we dropped the kids off at summer camp."

"Maybe last year? Is this some kind of sick joke?"

There's silence and then he laughs. He gets up and walks toward the playground and stands there for several minutes, hands on his hips, watching the kids.

I've caught him off guard because he never expected me to drop this emotional bomb. And he knows he can't lose his temper around the children. Yes, it's all part of my plan. I need the kids to be here as a barometer for peace. A restaurant wouldn't have worked because they would've been at the table listening in. That's why we're at Marty's with its great coffee, fun playground, and beautiful day, so we could be outside.

Nate walks back and he's grinning. This is the first time in the years we've known each other that I'm not able to read him. He sits down, not as close this time, and looks away. We stay in silence and the atmosphere is tense and uncomfortable.

I try to make small talk to get rid of the awkwardness. "How's work going?" I add.

He ignores the question, so I pick up my cup and sip some lukewarm coffee, trying to find something to do with my shaky hands.

And then he finally turns to me and with distaste says, "I can't believe you threw me out, considering what you did. What a hypocrite."

I catch my breath. "You're right, I am. But it doesn't change anything." I don't apologize, because I'm not sorry for what I've said. Not in the least. Besides, there's no emotion left, and it's not worth the energy.

"I'm not sure if I want to hear the details or leave it right here," he says, attempting eye contact, as if he wants to know.

"We should leave it right here. It won't help or make a difference. That's why it was never going to work this second time around. Honestly, it would've been better if we'd split up back then, but I figured—"

"Figured what? That you'd get back at me by fucking someone else? A revenge of sorts?"

"Look, I'm not the one shuffling women around like songs on a playlist. After being mortified at the DMV, it confirmed you can't be trusted. I wanted to end our relationship before it got really ugly, before the fighting and the horrible resentment. I wanted us to remain human and not stoop to something low."

"Do you realize how hard this is to process? You had an affair to get back at me!"

This time, I'm the one who laughs. "Nate, you know the one thing I've finally realized after everything?" This time, I'm the one who checks that the kids aren't nearby before continuing. "You're so self-absorbed. I didn't do anything to get back at you for the first time you pulled this. I just know an emotional affair can lead to something more intimate, and don't make me paint the picture for you."

"Well, so you know," he says, and I can feel he's about to hit below the belt, "the other woman and me … we connected on a spiritual level. It was deep—something I never felt with you. We could talk for hours. But I wasn't as attracted to her, like I am to you."

"Attraction grows, Nate. So does love. Don't try to fool yourself. Or me."

"Max, Emily!" he calls out. "Time to go." A minute goes by and they ignore him. Nate stands up and puts his hands on his hips. "Now!"

The kids run toward us, and I stand up as they approach.

"Dad, ten more minutes?" asks Emily, flashing her big brown eyes as she tilts her head to one side, which makes me want to laugh at her ploy.

"Come on, Dad, please," shouts Max, as he holds another handful of rocks in his filthy palms.

Nate's not having any of it. "No!" he shouts, his face screwed into a grimace.

I walk forward and hug the kids as Max pulls away because he knows a kiss is about to come his way.

Nate doesn't say a word to me. They leave, and Emily looks back and waves. She doesn't smile; she thinks she's in trouble because her dad's walking ahead at record speed. I watch them drive off in their black SUV and one thing's for sure: I'll probably never see the kids again and it makes my anxiety go through the roof. Imagine having kids you love one day—even if it's part-time—and the next day they're gone. Suddenly, I feel unbearably lonely … single, childless, alone with only my crazy thoughts for company.

CHAPTER 42

Images of the kids consume me, especially the way Emily looked back at me as she waved good-bye. I'll miss the kids terribly. It's also more about the unknown. What will happen to them? Where will they end up? Will they be happy? Will Nate's two divorces affect them, making them insecure, or unable to trust people and have relationships of their own? It eats at me, the fact that Nate and I have affected their future lives.

With barely four hours of sleep, I wake up with my shoulders tense and tight. I try to push away feelings about the kids, knowing that it's not me who controls their future, but it is me who controls my thoughts. I have to remember: I'm the one who kicked Nate out. The one who wanted the divorce. The one who wanted him out of my life.

I could have stayed and become a victim of self-denial; to look the other way; hold onto our pretend-beautiful life with the kids, the dog, the nice house. To do that, I'd have to trade authentic feelings of happiness for deeply held resentment.

Back to work the following Monday and the crazy fifty-hour weeks start to eat at me. Getting ready for holiday promotions and long, cross-country flights to meet with new merchandisers zaps my energy. Trips to New York, Atlanta, back to New York and home again over the past two months rack up the frequent-flyer miles and deepen my dark circles.

I know what to expect this time of year. And in the past, to make up for it, I'd take a Monday or two off from work, turning it into a long weekend to recharge. This year, a year full of change, needs more than a recharge. It needs a reset. For my mind. For all my new decisions.

And there's more going on at work, making me exhausted: The newest celebrity line not living up to expectations, based on bad reviews. My boss breathing down my neck for less-than-stellar sales figures on the dorm line we should've never bought. Hiring recent grads who want high salaries with remote work and getting it, which makes me think, *Damn, why didn't I ask for that?*

My job usually never overwhelms me, but feeling overworked makes me snap at our new intern when she bumps into me and spills coffee. After apologizing for my tone, I dash off to the bathroom to dab my jacket with water and look at my reflection. Black liner around my eyes has smudged, making me look haggard.

I walk back to my cube, realizing how much I need to get away. To put my toes in the sand. To hear the waves crash. Feel the salt on my skin, and on my lips, when a cute bartender hands me a second margarita way before noon. Even though it's everything Miami has to offer, I want to go somewhere else, somewhere far away where nobody knows me or about my life.

My cube, even with its small space, has character and will help me decide. On the wall, black-and-white photos of Miami's art deco scene line one side and a world map, in full color, takes up the other.

I look at the map and try to remember all the state capitals without help to keep my memory fresh. It has been on the wall since day one and I tell my coworkers it's there to remind us where all our merchandise comes from. Really, it's there to remind me of all the places I've never been—to daydream when there's a moment to spare. And when my coworkers walk into my cube while I'm daydreaming, they get to hear about our newly minted partnership with a company in Wisconsin that sells dorm-room sets or about the beach line from a retired travel agent from Southern California. But today isn't about business. It's about my reset button.

I make up a game and the rules that go with it. Wherever my finger lands on the map is where my vacation takes me. I get three tries—no more, no less. I close my eyes and get started, feeling around the map with my hand.

First up: Toronto. Great city. Too cold this time of year and as a Floridian, I'm used to warm weather. It's an easy pass. Next.

Second try: the middle of the Atlantic Ocean. That would be a sink-or-swim situation, and not the best for accommodations unless you're a mermaid. Next.

My last try lands on Pittsburg. Never been. Heard it's a great place. Ryan's from there and the last thing I need is to think even more about him. Next.

That's right. There's a next. It's my game and nobody's playing against me, so I decide to break the rules—or, rather, make up new ones—giving myself one more try.

It has to be a place I've never been.

And it has to be warm.

Jillian swings by and startles me. "Marketing's telling me your creative brief doesn't have enough meat." She plops down in a chair next to me and starts biting her nails, something she always does when stressed. "They need more info to start the ad campaign. They don't even care about the deadline. And you know what'll happen? I'll get blamed when the shit hits the fan."

She calms down then hands me a printout and waits, allowing me time to read through it.

"It's two pages with full info about the line and our competitors. What more do they need?"

"For starters," Jillian says, "they have no clue what tweens are." She puts air quotes around "tweens" when she says it, and then gets up to look at one of my Miami photographs. "And, to be honest, neither do I."

I feel a flash of irritation. "Really? Okay, my bad, I should've defined it." Then my sarcasm rears its ugly head, because I'm tired, cranky, and in need of some time off. "You know, there's something called a dictionary."

My browser's already open and it allows me to cut and paste the definition of tween into the creative brief, along with more details about the demographics. Jillian, in the meantime, downloads a dictionary app onto her phone and seems to have beaten me to the punch. "Ahh," she says. "It's a preteen, ages nine to twelve. They're gonna love this new line! Shit, I love this new line!"

I smile, thinking about Jillian's sudden enthusiasm. "Let me read through the brief, make sure it's all set. I'll email it back over to you in a few."

"Sounds good," she says and gets up. "What were you doing with the map? Looked like you were playing pin the tail on the donkey, without the donkey. And the tail."

"Trying to plan a vacation."

"With your eyes closed?"

"Yeah, with my eyes closed."

She shrugs and stares at the map. "Okay, do your thing. I'll let the team know the updated brief is on its way."

I wait for her to leave before going back to my game and its changed-up rules.

It has to be a place I've never been.

And it has to be warm.

This time, not only do I break the rules, I cheat, keeping one eye open slightly to choose the location.

San Juan, Puerto Rico, where have you been all my life? We're going to become best friends very soon.

Chapter 43

My boarding pass and hotel confirmation sit on the dresser. Chili barks for her walk and then gets distracted when she finds a tennis ball in the corner of my bedroom. She pushes it back and forth toward me, and I ignore her while trying to decide what to pack. I'm only going to Puerto Rico for a few days, and the amount of stuff needed for a beach vacation would make even the best packer a little frenzied.

The mess on my bed makes my head spin. It's covered with bikinis and one-pieces, cover-ups and sundresses, two sweaters, various sunscreens and bug sprays, three hats and even more shoes. Stuff for when it's hot, when it's cold, when it's hot and cold at the same time, when the mosquitos try to devour me, when the sun overstays its welcome.

I go to the closet and pull out my new magenta carry-on bag, remembering the plaid luggage that Nate took with him, the one we used for our honeymoon. Good riddance to that baggage—to Nate, and all that came with him.

I should be grateful for all that he brought into my life and move past the resentment. It's easier said than done because I'm stuck trying to figure out what's next in my life and the freedom surrounding it. It's liberating to know freedom awaits—even though its exactness leaves me wondering—with the scene playing out in my head: a kind of freedom that comes with driving with every window open—or the top down—with nowhere to go.

It's crazy to think that a sense of freedom is how this all started—with Nate driving with the top down. What if we'd never bought that convertible? What if my license had never expired? What if he'd paid the ticket? I'm doing it again to myself: reliving memories that should be stowed away and forgotten. My phone pings and snaps me out of it. My heart races when a text from Ryan shows up.

Hey … is all it says.

The three dots flash as if he's continuing to type and then a minute later, they disappear before a short video pops up, followed by his next text:

Can you guess my whereabouts?

The short video shows a riverfront, a few boats, and people walking on a cobblestone street. There's no curiosity building on this one; I know exactly where he is.

I sit on the bed and throw the tennis ball back and forth to Chili while thinking it through. He told Rachel it wasn't a good idea to set us up, so what does he want? And why is he torturing me with a video of Savannah?

I pick up the phone and watch the video three more times. Make that five. *Don't do this to me, Ryan. Don't bait me with memories.* It's hard to ignore the message and, before long, another one comes in.

Have you checked your mail lately?

My heart beats faster again. I drop the phone and run downstairs and dash out to the postbox as if my life depends on it. Bills and junk mail line the box and I throw them on the ground to sort. Within the mix is an envelope with Ryan's address in the top-left corner. I rip it open and there's a card inside. It has a picture of a puppy on the front.

Inside it says: *Nothing is Pawfect. I miss you.*

Normally, I'd make fun of something so cheesy but then I read Ryan's handwritten note.

> *Maggie,*
>
> *You're right. It's hard to be with someone where the relationship starts off with a lie (although to me, it was more like truth being withheld). But nothing is perfect. I'm not perfect. So what if Rachel fed me stuff? All of that doesn't matter because I can't snap my fingers and forget our connection. There have been many times I've wanted to reach out, send you funny memes, and see how you're doing but held back.*
>
> *Whatever happens, I'll never forget the time we spent together,*
> *Ryan*

"Maggie, are you okay?" one of my neighbors says as she passes.

I don't realize that I'm sitting on the street with my legs folded, wiping away tears, and making up a story about having a bad day at work. She helps me up, asks me over for a cup of tea. I decline and head back home as Chili greets me at the door and we both sit in the hallway. I read the letter again and can't get through it without tearing up more. Chili can feel my sadness and reaches up to lick my face.

The letter makes me think. My head is all over the place. Ryan must seriously care about me to go to all this trouble. Then something inside strikes a nerve, making me tighten my shoulders. I take a deep breath and feel how uncomfortable the thoughts rest within my screwed-up mind. It's something I haven't acknowledged: Maybe I am worthy of someone who truly cares about me. Someone who has the same values. For that to happen, though, I need to recognize my own worth.

Chili follows me up the stairs. I pick up the phone and reread the message.

Have you checked your mail lately?

The chemistry we have still consumes me so much it hurts. But I need closure so the hurt becomes less over time.

> *Read your letter, it was really nice, and I'll never forget our time together either. TBH, not sure if we should stay in touch. We both need to move on.*

I wait several minutes for a response before getting up to finish packing. Nothing pings back, and Chili follows me downstairs. She wags her tail and jumps in place when we get to the front hallway. We go outside, take in a breath of fresh air, and we head off on a long walk as some neighbors pass us, stopping to pet Chili.

This has been my neighborhood for four years now. Sometimes I think about making a clean break, selling the house, and moving somewhere for a fresh start. For what purpose? To make it easier to forget by being in denial or not having reminders? That's never a good solution, and I'm again realizing how much a vacation is needed.

After our walk, Chili jumps in the back of my car and we head over to Rachel's, where she's looking after Chili during my trip. Realizing I'm running late, there's not much time for chit-chat. Chili heads to her bed in Rachel's kitchen, and I blow kisses to both of them before making my way out the door and to the airport for my flight to San Juan.

CHAPTER 44

The deck stirs with families and hip-hop blasts from the speakers by the pool. I throw my bag on a barstool and order a margarita. There's a tanned twenty-something couple sitting next to me, and we strike up a conversation about the beautiful weather and how much they love Puerto Rico. I tell them it's my first time and they insist on giving me a list of places to go for sightseeing and nightlife.

My phone rings with an unrecognizable number and I ignore it, going back to chatting with the couple and the bartender, who also weighs in on his favorite spots. He makes a few drinks and hands me a colorful one with lemon slices and strawberries floating between the ice.

"On the house," he says. "Just make sure you try at least one of those places." He points to the scribbled list on the napkin.

I thank him and reach for my phone to take a picture before the ink smudges from the humidity. There are a few texts, a couple from Rachel and Drew, and one from the front desk letting me know my room is ready. I swivel around in my chair and watch a family play pool volley-ball. They're having fun and their laughter is contagious.

It makes me reminisce about vacations with Emily and Max while missing those moments.

Hitting replay in my head only makes it harder. Looking forward to the future is what's needed even though it's not that easy. At thirty-eight, I'm youngish, I think. There's always time for my own family when the time comes, I convince myself.

The couple sitting nearby says good-bye as they walk back to the pool, hand in hand. I gather my belongings and follow suit, making my way to the lobby to pick up the key. It's almost unbearably loud with men in suits gathered at the circular bar and moms chasing after their rambunctious kids.

The attendant at the front desk welcomes me to San Juan and takes my driver's license. She looks at my ID and fiddles with her keyboard for a minute. "Miss Simmons, we've given you a complimentary upgrade," she says.

"Wow, thank you. It's my lucky day. What's the catch?"

"No catch. Between you and me," she says and leans in. "We're running low on rooms with two beds. A family of four needed a room with an extra one, so we didn't think you'd mind." She pushes a few more buttons on her keyboard and opens a drawer to pull out a small gray envelope. "How many keys would you like?"

"Two, please."

After explaining the services and amenities, she hands me the envelope and a brochure and wishes me a fantastic stay. I make my way to the elevator and the colorful wall photos of Old San Juan remind me of the hotel in Florida, the one I drove to months ago, the one where I couldn't stay. My mind was in a bad state then. Not being able to stay in a hotel because the room number matched the date of my wedding anniversary. Interesting how that turn of events allowed me to take control and decide my own destiny, to make me strong enough to tell Nate he'd be the one leaving the house, not me.

The elevator opens to my floor and my room key taps against the sensor, allowing the light to glow. Green for go, and it's the perfect prelude for what's to come after being blessed with an upgrade.

Splashes of turquoise and yellow accent the walls, with black-and-white photos of city scenes making the room feel more modern and city-like than an expected beach vibe. Pillows with the same colors take over the bed. On the right, a separate room includes a full-size bar, huge entertainment center, and a sofa that looks out toward the balcony. I sit on the loveseat, put my feet on the coffee table, and take in the view before getting up to head to the balcony. In front of me, lush palm trees block a partial ocean view.

On the balcony next to mine, two cute guys smile and nod as if we've already met. One of them passes the other a joint, and they don't seem to care that it's in front of me. We're close enough that they could lean over and offer me some, and before long, that's what happens. I contemplate for a split second, whether to take the joint from strangers, then decide, *What the heck?* I haven't smoked since college. And something about their smile, their relaxed pose, makes me trust them.

I take a hit and the guy with dirty-blond hair encourages me to take one more before passing it back. My head feels as if it's expanding and starts to tingle. Before long, we're telling each other our life stories and laughing at the littlest things. They're brothers from England who own a moving and storage business and love Puerto Rico, having been twice this year to take a break from the bleak weather.

As they mention their endless rainy days, clouds forming in the distance tell us a storm might be brewing. We quickly dismiss the notion and chat for a few more minutes. I go back inside, slip into my bathing suit and throw sunscreen, a hat, and a book into my beach bag.

There's a knock and, when my paranoia kicks in, the peephole comes in handy. When I open the door, Drew's smiling. He leans down for a kiss and presses a bottle of champagne against my arm, making me jump. I'm taking Rachel's advice and giving Drew a chance and, besides, it's still so hard for me to travel alone.

"Holy shit, Maggie, this is amazing," he says while taking in the room. "You did good." He walks toward me and pushes my ponytail back in place. "I love when you wear your hair back while it's growing out. You have such a pretty face."

"Trying to get in my pants, huh?"

"More like you out of that bikini," he says and runs his hand along my face and down my neck.

I pull back when his touch begins to tickle. The joint has kicked in even more, making me overly chatty while Drew grabs two glasses and pops the champagne. We toast to Puerto Rico and decide where we'll go first: the pool or the beach.

Drew changes into his swimsuit, and we make our way through the lobby. A guy with aviator sunglasses and a striped tank makes our decision easy. We choose the beach after he mentions there's nothing better than putting your toes in the sand, hearing the waves crash, feeling the salt on your skin.

Before making our way there, we stop at the poolside bar to grab a couple of beers, spilling them a little along the way, and finishing half by the time we get to our lounge chairs. The attendant brings an oversized umbrella and, before setting it up, hands us a drink and snack menu. When on vacation, anything goes—even the extra consumption of alcohol, calories, and small talk with strangers.

Drew lays the towels on both chairs, then takes off his shirt. He asks me to put sunscreen on his back and this is the first time I've seen his skin under the sun. It's perfect, not one blemish, just a scattering of freckles across his shoulders. No scars, no faded lines from stitches, no signs of a brave or clumsy childhood. He's lean and muscular and doesn't seem to work hard to stay that way. He eats what he wants, when he wants—and stays fit because he doesn't like to call it exercise.

After a few moments, Drew gets antsy and we walk on the beach, hand in hand. He tries to throw me in the water a couple of times, and I run ahead, laughing, until he catches up.

"Don't you dare," I threaten while running backward.

"Come on, it's not cold. Watch." He runs into the ocean and dives under a wave. I worry for a split second and then he pops up and runs his hands through his hair to push it away from his forehead. The water, mixed with the sunscreen, makes his body glisten and there's not much that would make him look any better except a slight tan and a tattoo in the right spot.

I dip my feet into the ocean and the temperature stings me.

Drew runs out and wraps his body around mine. "See, it's not cold at all!"

I scream and jump back to get away. "You're crazy!"

"No, a little tipsy."

"On one beer?"

"Don't forget the champagne. And an empty stomach."

Drew reaches for my hand, and we turn around to head back to our chairs. As we get closer, he lets go and wraps his arm around my shoulder. "You know, Maggie, I could get used to this."

"Used to what?"

He stops to pull me close. "I could get used to being with you."

My silence doesn't seem to faze him. "The keynote opportunities are great and all, but I'm tired of the travel. I want to stay put, amp up the podcast, and work on more books. And maybe do local consulting on the side?"

He says it as a question, almost like he's asking if it's okay to stay put with me, not in general. It catches me off guard, and it makes me fumble. I want to reciprocate, to say that he should stay put. "That's so nice, thank you," winds up coming out, making me sound like such an ass, a coldhearted one who doesn't give a crap.

It's not true. I do care, about us and about him. The question is: how much?

Getting used to it means consistency, stability, having someone around. I've had that and where did it get me? A divorce. An ex-husband who wouldn't let go. A life that makes me keep wondering what's next.

I want to eat my words, or at least apologize. But saying sorry would magnify them. We walk up and sit back down on our lounge chairs and order some lunch. He reaches for his hat and covers his face to block the sun.

"Drew, there's some stuff I haven't shared with you about my ex-husband."

He moves his cap away and looks at me before sitting up. "You know, you don't have to. Maybe some things are better left unsaid."

"This I really want to share."

And there, on the beach, between bites of a sandwich and sips of my mimosa, I open up and tell him about the DMV photo, what Nate did, and how he lied to me.

"That took some balls."

"What did?" I ask.

"To leave. It was brave."

His response takes me by surprise. Nobody has ever called me brave before, and his compliment empowers me to want to tell him more while waiting for the courage to kick in.

The waitress comes by and we ask for another round of mimosas. She writes down our order and takes away the plates and empty glasses.

When she returns with our drinks, I chug mine down and start fidgeting with the edge of my beach towel. "Drew, there's more to the story. And I'm not sure how you'll feel about it. Because I lied, too. To my ex-husband."

CHAPTER 45

The alcohol has kicked in and Drew listens as my story unfolds. He pulls the sunscreen out of his bag and doesn't say anything. Is he buying time to choose his words carefully or to decide how he feels about it?

I try to figure him out and hope he doesn't judge me. He's still quiet. It's obvious his moral standards are higher than mine. After all, he's the one who didn't contact me after the conference because of my impending divorce. He asks me to reapply the sunscreen to his shoulders, and we both stand up and face away from the direction of the wind.

"It wasn't easy to tell him," I say instead of waiting for his response.

"I understand why you did it. You needed closure."

Relief sets in. "Thank you for understanding. I know it wasn't the best. And it was hard for me to open up to you. I don't like talking about my ex but felt you needed to hear the truth. Especially since we're a thing."

He turns around and smiles as he presses his body against mine. "Oh, yeah, we're a thing?" he teases and puts his arms around my waist. "People still say that? What are we, seventy-five?"

His words remind me of Al and the bittersweet advice he always shares with me to make life matter.

"So, you don't think I did the wrong thing by lying to my ex?" I ask.

"Honestly, it's not my business to judge. It takes a lot to open up—and I'm glad you told me." Drew keeps his gaze on me and even when he's squinting, his blue eyes show their warmth. "In fact," he says and sits on the edge of his lounge chair, "I'm a bit embarrassed to tell you something."

I perk up, sitting higher as he continues.

"While listening to your story, it sparked an idea. A business one."

His response intrigues me. How could lying to Nate do that? And what does it have to do with business?

"Not sure if you'll be up for it. Hear me out?"

At first, he's a little hesitant because he never shares business ideas with family and friends; he says they're likely to talk him out of it. Since I've sparked the idea or part of the creation of it, he's breaking his rule. I'm his inspiration, so he says, and he wants to make sure I'm okay with it.

"Are you mad?" he asks after telling me about an idea for a podcast that sounds a bit far-fetched.

"No, why?" I say, not sure if being his inspiration should flatter me.

"I'm feeling like shit now," he says, "for using something so personal and turning it into something business-related."

"I don't see it that way at all. And I'd rather you be honest with me about what's going on in that head of yours."

"You mean all the crazy business ideas that keep me up at night?"

"Better than other stuff keeping you up."

He walks over and bends down to kiss me. "I'd like you to keep me up."

"We can arrange that. Are you free tonight?" I tease.

Manny, the activities director, skips by wearing an endless tan, turquoise shorts, and a matching visor. He calls out for a game of beach volleyball and the kids around us race over to help him set up the net. They bounce the ball around and kick up sand, annoying the two older couples sitting close by. Manny's still looking for a few more players and waves us over to join the fun. We wave back and tell him maybe next time, and he pretends he can't hear us.

"I bet Manny gets all the cougars. What do you think?" Drew says as he waves back at him.

"I think he gets anyone and everyone, no matter what age."

"Even Maggie Simmons?" he teases.

"Oh yeah, for sure. Especially after volleyball when he's all sticky."

As we watch them play a set, Drew reaches over for my hand. Our palms get sweaty and he rearranges his hand in mine. "Thanks again for inviting me here," he says before adding, "Are you sure you're not upset about my idea for the podcast? It's totally cool if we don't. I'll forget the whole thing."

"No, it's fine. Let's do it. My life with Nate, the affair, all of it—it's a thing of the past. And I can talk about it now without being upset."

"I'm glad it's behind you—and thanks for telling me; I'm sure it wasn't easy." He pauses before asking me if there's anything else.

"Nope, nothing," I say and it's true.

Chapter 46

We leave Puerto Rico behind, and I settle back into work with its endless emails, looming deadlines, and weekly sales reports due on Friday. Thoughts about Drew conflict me all week. We get along well and there's definitely an attraction, but are my feelings being clouded because I need a distraction from Ryan? Is Drew the one for me? Or should there even be one right now?

By the time Saturday rolls around, I realize it's time for my monthly visit to Longwood. Chili hops into the back and we head over, grabbing a spot a few rows back by the main entrance. The automatic doors open and George smiles when we approach the front desk. It isn't his usual smile. I've been visiting long enough to know the difference.

"What's wrong?" I ask and sign the visitors' log.

He shuffles some paperwork and puts his pen down. "Nothing. Why? Nice tan, by the way."

It feels like he's changing the subject. I go along with it, hoping that he's making small talk and there's no meaning behind it. He bends over the desk and waves a biscuit at Chili. She wags her tail and jumps in place a few times, but she knows better, to put her bottom down and sit calmly before getting a treat. George greets his coworkers who pass by and makes Chili wait. She's patient now and keeps her gaze on George as he comes around and hands her two treats. She gobbles them down in record time.

I fix Chili's leash and pick my bag off the floor. One of the magazines for Betty falls out and Chili sniffs at it, hoping that more treats or crumbs found their way in between the pages.

"Maggie," George says. "It's only Al today."

"I could feel it. What happened?"

George stands up and grabs a napkin to wipe his hands. "Betty had to have heart surgery. Don't worry, she's gonna be okay." He continues, "Al has been out of sorts the last few days. You know, they're practically inseparable."

"I know."

"He'll be really happy to see you and Chili."

"Mostly Chili." I smile and bend down to let her kiss me.

"Not true. You didn't hear it from me," George says in a playful tone, as if it's a rumor, "he talks about you a lot. Maybe you can try to cheer him up some."

I nod and tell George that we'll do our best. Chili leads me down the hall and to the sunroom. The skylights work overtime to warm up the hallway a little too much. It's unusually hot inside and she starts to pant.

Residents come and go, and I always hope they're napping in their rooms or outside for a walk. Mostly they disappear and never come back. New faces take their places and their conversations involve one of three subjects: their grandkids who never visit, how their knees hurt, or their cholesterol medicine is giving them aches and pains. The next minute, they forget it all and pull out old family photos.

Betty and Al are different. They rarely talk about their ailments and they've only mentioned grandkids once—that they never had any. Al gets up from the table and walks toward the window to look out. He turns around and lights up when he sees Chili.

"There's my beautiful girl."

I let go of her leash, and she runs toward Al and stops short. She knows not to jump and to be gentle. He reaches for the chair and sits down to be at the same level with his favorite furry companion.

"Chili, don't tell your mom," he whispers, "I saved the bacon today."

"You know I heard that, right?" I pull a chair up next to Al's and sit down. Pretending that George hasn't filled me in, I ask, "Where's your beautiful wife today?"

"Recuperating after a bypass. You know," he pauses, "you get to a certain age where you think you're out of the woods."

He gets distracted and rubs Chili behind the ear. "You're such a good girl, yes, you are! Aging isn't for sissies, Chili. That's right, it's not." He sings the words in a cute, whimsical voice that makes her tail wag.

Al tries to hide his concern, so I recite some silly jokes that Emily used to tell me and show him cute pet videos on my phone. His body shakes with laughter, and he takes the phone from me to continue watching while I fish into my bag and pull out a present for him. He puts the phone down on the table and takes the T-shirt, a turquoise one with a tropical Puerto Rico scene with sand, sun, and palm trees.

"You shouldn't have," he says and throws it over his red flannel button-down shirt.

"That's a good look." I chuckle and place a coffee mug on the table that says *Life's a Beach* on one side and *This Belongs to Betty* on the other. "For when your beautiful wife comes home."

"So, tell me about your trip to Puerto Rico," he says, and after listening, adds, "Okay, let me get this straight. You like Ryan but invited Drew."

"When did I say I like Ryan?"

Al smiles and nods. "That's the story and we're sticking to it." He looks at me and we get into this staring contest, as if he's trying to figure me out. Neither of us breaks away. In my head, I'm comparing Ryan to Drew, to Nate, and to all the other guys who came before.

"You know, Maggie," he says and then pauses for a moment as if to gather his thoughts. "We have one son and he's married. I love his wife to the moon and back, but it's not the same as having a daughter. She has her parents, and Betty and I rarely see them. I actually see you a lot more than her. So, I know you don't want it, but I'm going to advise you as if you were our own daughter."

He gets my attention and it makes me miss my mom. I make a mental note to visit Seattle, where she and her boyfriend moved last year.

"This is what I'd tell her," he says as I cling to every word. "Live in the moment, but if you live in the moment all the time, and you don't think about your future, you may not realize what you need in the long run. Because often what feels good right now is not going to make you happy five years or even a year from now."

"Al, I don't get it. Is this about my love life?"

"Maybe. Maybe not," he adds. "Take it any way you like."

"So, what are you saying? That I should follow my head and not my heart?"

"Neither." He pulls another piece of bacon from his pocket. Chili sits very still and licks her lips, waiting for the treat. Al breaks it up into a few pieces and hands it to her, bit by bit.

"Then what?"

He pets Chili then stops to look up at me. He lifts his glasses up. "You should never follow your head or your heart. You should follow your gut."

"Really? Never realized there was another choice." I get up to look out the window. It's a beautiful day, without a cloud in sight.

"Al, let's go."

Chili's ears move back and she jumps in place. She loves hearing *Let's go* because, to her, an adventure always awaits.

He peers at me. "What are you talking about?"

"You said I should follow my gut. And it's telling me we should get in the car and drive."

Al stands up slowly, resting his hand on the arm of the chair. "I don't know, Maggie. Not sure if I should leave while Betty's in the hospital."

"She's in good hands. Besides, we won't be long, and I think you need a little road trip."

"Where are we going?"

"It's a surprise. You should probably grab your sunglasses. And bring a jacket in case."

CHAPTER 47

We walk to the lobby and tell George we'll be back in a couple of hours. When we get to my car, Al opens the passenger-side door and Chili jumps into the back. She takes her seated position because she already knows we won't go anywhere until she settles down.

This is the first time Al's been out with me. He wipes dog hair off the seat, gets in, and buckles up. I've since traded in my car so the crumbs left behind by Emily and Max after eating their snacks are long gone. I still remember it, though, as if tiny remnants of the past are a reminder that the kids aren't in my life anymore.

"Woo-hoo, Mario Andretti, watch out!" Al says once I get on the highway and floor it. He reaches for the handle when we go around a curve to merge into the next lane. Even though he's holding on tight, it doesn't make me slow down. It makes me want to go faster so he has that edge-of-the-seat feeling, even though he's in his eighties. Or maybe it's because he's in his eighties and life is long, as he always says, and we have to make it matter. And what matters right now is to give Al a change of scenery.

"Didn't you have a convertible before or am I dreaming?" he says, remembering the numerous photos I've shown of Chili in the back with the top down.

"No, you're not dreaming. Traded it in recently," I say.

"When you traded in that ex-husband of yours?" He chuckles and it's what I wanted to add, but held back. At least Al can say what I'm thinking.

"Hated how my hair ended up in knots," I fib. "It would take hours on end to comb through the tangles."

"If you spend too much time combing, this is what happens." He takes his hat off to show me his bald spot. "I'm the perfect candidate for a convertible."

Al puts his cap back on, rolls the window down further, and leans closer to the door. I take the exit and we cross over the Intracoastal Waterway. Traffic is building up, so we swing down a side street instead of inching down Collins Avenue. I turn left a couple of miles up and catch someone pulling out from a parallel parking spot.

"South Beach?"

"Where'd you think I was taking you?"

"I don't know," he says and gets distracted when a few women walk ahead in their bikinis. "To the mall, where us old farts go to walk?"

"Would you rather go there? We can get some pretzels and lemonade between our laps around the stores."

"Heck no. I haven't been to South Beach in decades. Heard it's changed a lot." He gets out, with Chili following behind him. She comes over to my side when she's called and sits until her leash gets fastened.

"It's pretty much the same," I say as we pass bars, drag queens wearing their glitter and makeup, and restaurant hostesses tempting us with menus. Tourists huddle in front of a restaurant that was Gianni Versace's former house and we overhear stories about his life and watch as a couple takes a selfie with the property in the background. We offer to take some pictures for them before crossing the street and head toward the beach. Chili heels by my side and Al pets her head when she looks up.

"You lucked out in the dog department," he says. "Such a good girl. I think she's aching to get that leash off."

I look at my watch and realize it's already pushing five. "We could go to Bark Beach, where she can run free."

Al agrees and we head back into the car and over to the park's entrance. After hopping out and walking toward the beach, Al leans on a palm tree, takes off his shoes and socks, and wraps his jacket around his waist.

I remove Chili's leash as we approach the beach. Chili knows the drill. When she hears me snap my fingers, she takes off and makes a mad dash to the ocean until I nervously call her back when she goes too far.

"Look at her. She was itching for that freedom," Al says.

"Aren't we all?"

"What are you trying to run away from?"

"I'm not trying to run away from anything," I snap, realizing how defensive it sounds. "I'm saying we'd all like to be free and more spontaneous."

"Follow your gut, and you can be."

"Wait a second. Back at Longwood, you said to be careful about living in the moment."

"I did. It's tricky, knowing when to live in the moment or when to think things through. That's why life's so damn hard sometimes." He pauses and watches Chili run back toward us.

She stops along the way to play with a white poodle and gets distracted when a wave crashes nearby. "Betty isn't the love of my life," Al blurts out. "I've always been in love with a girl named Liz."

Something about the way he says it saddens me. It sounds as if he's thought about her every moment since.

"I saw her on the bus every day to and from work," Al adds and continues, saying it was the same bus that Betty rode but a few years earlier. In his head, she was like Elizabeth Taylor. She'd often catch him looking at her above his newspaper. She had beautiful skin and the prettiest smile. Even to this day, anytime he sees someone with jet-black hair, fair skin, and light eyes, he thinks of her.

"What happened?" I ask.

He looks at me and fixes his cap. "Where do I start?"

Not wanting to push, I don't say another word. We walk in silence, watching Chili run around while several pet owners call out for their dogs to come back. In the distance, surfers try to stay on their boards as waves crash on and around them.

"I was shy as hell when I was younger," Al continues. "I know, I know, hard to believe!"

He bends down to pet Chili when she runs up and around us before taking off again, throwing up sand with her back legs in the process. "I admired Liz from afar, too chicken to approach until one day I got up the courage and sat next to her. We started up a conversation and hit it off. Funny part is, her name was actually Liz, just like

Liz Taylor. And next thing you know, we couldn't keep our hands off each other."

"Ooh," I say, elbowing him lightly.

"Well, we were discreet in public. Behind closed doors it was something else. Couldn't go to bed or wake up without thinking about her. Liz was on my mind all the time." Al pauses, as if he's playing out every detail in his head. "She was so beautiful. A petite little thing, always having to stand on her tiptoes to kiss me. I fell madly in love but never told her."

"And?" I ask. Part of me wants to know what became of her, hoping nothing tragic happened.

"We'd been dating for about six months. Then one day, out of the blue, she called it off; said her parents would only let her marry someone Jewish. When I kept pushing, she told me they were fixing her up with a young dentist who had just joined their synagogue."

"She couldn't say no or stand up to her parents?"

"Even worse. She hadn't even told them about me. I was a secret the entire time."

"That must've hurt, being blindsided like that."

Al nods and continues his story, telling me that, a few months after breaking up, he's walking down Broadway and sees Liz in a restaurant, sitting by a window. He stops and watches her. At first, he thinks she's waiting for someone. A few minutes later, she reaches into her bag and pulls out a book.

"From the moment she started reading, I knew she was alone. She was too polite to read while with someone. Or even while waiting."

"Did you talk to her?"

He shakes his head and frowns. "That's the part I regret the most and always think about. I told myself if I ever saw her again, I'd profess my love no matter where or when. I did nothing that day, kept walking down Broadway, stopping a few times to get up the courage, but didn't go back. And I never saw her again."

"So you don't know what happened to her?"

"No. Don't even know if she ever married the guy." Al stops, leans against a lifeguard stand, and wipes the sweat from his brow. "Don't get me wrong; I love Betty more than anything—and it feels like betrayal to even talk about this. Betty's my best friend. But I often think about Liz. I wonder if she ever had kids, where she ended up, whether she was happy. And if she's still alive."

"Maybe it's best to have that memory of her, with nothing to mess it up. And you never know, maybe she thought about you all this time, too."

Al smiles and fixes his cap. "Maybe, maybe not. If I'd followed my gut, I would have gone in to talk to her," he adds. "The point is, Maggie, you need to follow your gut. Don't overthink things because when you do, you might miss opportunities that come your way. And no, I'm not just talking about your love life. It's about life in general."

Chili startles me when she bumps into Al and practically knocks him over. She's having the time of her life, without a care in the world. Two dogs chase behind her and when they get a little too rambunctious, Chili growls at them for being annoying.

After hearing Al's confession, I take his guidance to heart. He's right. Life is tricky, complicated. Life is a balancing act filled with different paths and journeys. One wrong move—whether through words or actions—can torment us. If we knew how to balance all the stuff thrown our way, we wouldn't have to give or take advice. We'd have it all figured out.

We walk back to the car and drive away, saying good-bye to the dogs, the impending sunset, the sound of the waves crashing. I pull into Longwood's circular driveway and drop Al off at the front entrance. Before getting out, he gives me a pensive look, one that doesn't cross his face often.

"Don't worry," I say, reading his mind. "Not a word about Liz from me." I hand him some magazines to give to Betty when she gets back home. "Give your sweetheart a big hug for me."

He leans back to pet Chili and, as he walks toward the building, waves good-bye with the magazines in the air. As we drive off, the Killers come up again on my playlist and I'm reminded of Nate—his indifference, the infidelity, the pain, the laughter, the fun, and the madness. They're all memories, the good and the bad, all wrapped into one giant heap. I remember our last time together at the playground when he heard my news about the affair. I'm not proud of my words or actions. It's for a greater good, necessary and only fair to both of us so we can move on. And so he can let go.

Then Al's words of wisdom haunt me again. Follow your gut, he says, not your head or heart. But I can't follow my gut until I tell someone the truth.

CHAPTER 48

From what Nate tells me, I'm a hypocrite, a title nobody should be proud of. Why do I bring it up? Because I'm tempted to text Ryan, even though it's wrong. By texting, I'm afraid of falling back into the way things were and strengthening our tie. But he deserves the truth, the real reason we can't see each other, not some bullshit one about me wanting to date around now that I'm officially divorced. Texting is out of the question and seeing him in person will make me reminisce and think about our times together, making it hard to move forward.

Several notepads and pens sit in the bottom drawer of my nightstand. They're for when insomnia strikes or when an idea about a new sales strategy comes to me in the middle of the night, not for writing to ex-boyfriends or lovers. This time around, that's its purpose. I pull out the pad with light-blue paper and start the letter.

Ryan,

I'll never forget the day you showed up in front of my house after I told you not to come over. You in your T-shirt, faded jeans, and flip-flops. Nobody wears them better. But that wasn't what got me that night. It was how you knew me so well!

You called me out for saying that you didn't believe I wanted to date other guys now that I was officially divorced. Remember? I hate to say it, you were right. It is bullshit.

I'm a firm believer that relationships won't work when they're based on a lie. Learned my lesson the hard way with my ex-husband. Not anymore. Not ever. My rule is firm and unwavering. No matter how you look at it, that's how our relationship started. And it's a form of betrayal.

The night we danced is etched in my memory. I try to block out how you knew I loved "Save a Prayer" without me knowing and used it, among other things, to make me feel closer to you. Go ahead, deny it all you want. Say again we would've still ended up together because we have great chemistry. And I'd agree with you—we do have great chemistry.

But chemistry can only take you so far. It's only part of a relationship and all relationships have to be based on trust. And yes, I'm dealing with some trust issues because of my divorce. And that's making me realize, a little too late, that I shouldn't have started dating while separated. It was too much too soon, and I didn't have time to fully process my emotions and figure out what's best for me.

The fact that you hid those things from me isn't the only reason I could no longer see you. It's what you said to me more than once: that you wouldn't care if I were married; you would have still dated me. When I asked if you were joking, you said no, because you can't help who you fall for, whether the person's married, separated, or single. I have a problem with that because there's something as important as chemistry and trust— and that's values. To me, it's not a matter of being right or wrong. It's a matter of being on the same page.

You might be wondering why I'm writing when I told you in my last text not to contact me. You're probably thinking I'm a hypocrite! If so, it wouldn't be the first time someone has said that. To be honest, writing gives me closure and will help me heal. And you deserved to know the real reason. I'll never forget you, and only want you to be happy.

~Maggie

I rummage through my drawer to find a stamp and head out to the mailbox.

Paul, our mailman, picks up his bins and places them into his vehicle. He looks over and waits when he sees me waving as I make a mad dash to get there before he leaves. "You almost missed me."

I catch my breath and hand him the letter. "There's always tomorrow."

"Actually, I'm retiring. Today's my last day."

"Really? You look so young."

"You're too kind. Been forty years in the job. Me and the wife are taking the RV cross-country."

"Sounds fun."

"Not really," he says and pauses as if to choose his words wisely. "That's always been her dream. What's that saying?"

"Life's too short?" I ask.

"No, the other one. Happy wife, happy life."

Part of me feels envious of Paul's wife, someone I don't even know, someone who's cherished and knows how it feels to be a priority because her husband puts her first.

We shake hands and say good-bye. "Send me a post-card," I say, and as he drives off, I have second thoughts and start running for the truck while screaming Paul's name. The truck's lights turn red and when it stops, he pushes the window to the side.

"Miss me already?" he teases and leans out the window.

"Of course, and I wanted you to see my sprinting abilities." I catch my breath once again before adding, "Can I have my letter back?"

He leans forward and puts a hand on the steering wheel. "In all my years, I've never had that request."

"Sorry for being such a pain. Long story," I say as he stands up, puts on his glasses, and bends over to reach into the bin. He hands me the letter and sits back in the driver's seat.

"Thanks," I say and look down at the envelope. Sending the letter won't help. Ryan doesn't need the door kept open to communicate. It only confuses things. Besides, he doesn't need to know that he's still in my heart, even if he can't be in my life.

Paul waves good-bye, this time for good, and I walk back to my house. From a distance, it's hard to make out the kid who's hanging out on my doorstep. He's wearing a gray hoodie and a backpack sits next to him. His head is down and buried in a phone, but I'll never forget that mop of wavy hair as he pulls the hoodie down, and when he looks up, his crooked grin is the same as before.

"Hey there," I say with a big smile. I want to ask if everything's okay and instead, try to hide my excitement at seeing him.

"Hey," Max says back and walks toward me.

CHAPTER 49

Max grabs my keys and runs to escape from my hug. He unlocks the front door and Chili dashes out and into Max's arms. They chase each other on the front lawn and, after a few minutes, tucker out and plop down under a palm tree. In the warm sun, Chili puts her head on Max's lap, and he pets her belly until she falls asleep. I pull out my phone and take a few pictures and realize nothing has changed: the same-old Max moves his head to the side on purpose to mess up a seemingly great photo.

"Come on, one for me, please?"

Chili opens one eye and looks my way at the same time as Max.

"Wouldn't hurt for you to smile, you know."

I stand there and wait. "Okay, fine, don't smile, see if I care," I add, and it seems to do the trick and my phone clicks away with a half a dozen pictures to choose from.

I'm surprised he's shown up and wonder why, and wait for the right moment to ask. My next-door neighbors wave as they get out of their car and chat with Max while getting groceries from the trunk. They mention how big he's gotten and want to know about his favorite subject, all the boring, nondescript questions everyone asks kids these days. Max, the more polite one out of the two kids, pretends to show interest and answers questions thrown his way.

Chili barks as if she knows we're trying to finish up the conversation, and we say our good-byes and head inside. Max still knows the drill and takes his shoes off in the hallway. It's a Wednesday, which means it's his day with Heather, so it doesn't make sense.

"Do your parents know you're here?"

He shakes his head and bolts to the kitchen. The cabinet doors slam from one to the other as Max rummages his way through most of them. "Where's the cereal?" he calls out.

"Sorry, didn't expect you, so it's mostly stuff you don't like. We could order a pizza if you wanna stay for dinner." I grab the hummus and carrots from the fridge and lay them out on the counter. "There might be some pretzels in there, in the back behind the pasta."

Max stands on his toes to look and spots the bag. He pulls them out and, standing by the counter, starts dipping into the hummus, one by one. It gives me time to choose a photo of Chili and him to send to Nate. I attach it with the message:

Look who showed up on my doorstep.

Before long, Max finishes off half the bag of pretzels and licks the hummus container. He gets up and stares inside the fridge, looking for more food.

"When was the last time you ate, last Thursday?" I joke.

"Pretty much."

"So, what's going on?"

He shrugs, closes the fridge, and pulls his phone out. This is the first time I've seen him since Marty's Café, and he hasn't shown up at my place since the separation. For a split second, I feel bad about making Nate leave, then snap myself out of it quickly. Sometimes it takes effort to remind myself that Nate's bad choices may not define him, although they've created his new circumstances.

My phone pings with a message from Nate.

> *WTH? He's supposed to be at school. Emily's there too?*

I picture Emily's freckled face and wish she were here.

> *Nope, just Max.*

> *Be there in 30 minutes*

Max chomps through one last pretzel and looks over at me.

> *Can you give us a little longer?* I text back.

My heart races. Will Nate be reasonable when he comes over for the first time since he moved out?

> *Okay. See you in an hour.*

Max asks if he can watch some TV and when the pizza arrives, we make our way to the living room and I turn on the Disney Channel. We sink into the sofa and Chili finds a spot on the floor between us. During a commercial, I pause the show, ready to find out what's happening.

"Max, is something going on at home?"

He remains silent, and I don't want to push it. He bites his lip, something he's always done when nervous.

"Let me guess, you wanted Chili to help you with your math homework," I add, poking him in the ribs.

When Chili hears her name, she comes trotting in with her tail held high and stops in front of Max. She's also silent because she doesn't need to make a sound. She's a therapy dog for everyone who needs it—for Al, Max, even me.

"I miss Chili," he winds up saying. "Dad won't let us get a dog."

He grabs the blanket on the back of the sofa and pulls it over him. "Emily wanted a cat. Emily always gets what she wants."

Max is clearly feeling neglected. Nate must be either too busy with work or his love life. It's no longer my business what he does with the kids. When one shows up at my house unannounced, though, it's a different story.

"I bet if you guys take good care of the cat, your dad might consider getting a dog. It takes a bit more responsibility."

Max doesn't answer and sits with his arms folded as he looks down.

I lean over and nudge his arm. "Tell you what. You can come over anytime to see Chili, how's that? Anytime, okay?"

He nods, and Chili starts growling as soon as she hears the doorbell. She runs out with her tail between her leg and ears up. I look through the peephole before opening the door and see Nate standing with his keys in one hand, work bag in the other. It's obvious he's come straight from the office by the way he's dressed in his gray slacks, light-blue button-down shirt, and black wind-breaker.

"Where is he?"

"Nice to see you, too," I say, and he walks into the entryway and past me toward the living room. He's obviously still upset with me for what happened at the park, and I can't blame him.

"Hey, buddy, ready to go?"

Max keeps watching TV and doesn't look over. An excited Chili doesn't get any attention from Nate, so she makes her way back to Max and sits in front of the sofa. Max slides down to the floor and sits next to Chili to play with her tail and rub her back.

Nate turns to me and twirls his keys. "Can we talk?"

I follow him to the kitchen and add water into the kettle before lighting the stove.

"I'm not here to shoot the shit over tea," he says, pointing to the kettle.

"Okay," I whisper and look at him. "Maybe I'm the one who'd like some. No doubt, you weren't thinking about me. You weren't thinking of me at all during our marriage, so what's new?" I hit below the belt for no good reason, and anytime he's near me now, anxiety builds up.

"Maggie, let's not go there. I'm here to get Max, that's it. And besides, you have some nerve." He pauses for a minute and continues. "Since you brought it up, I've been thinking about it. How could you do it?"

"How could you?" I snap back.

He shakes his head. "I've told you a thousand times. Nothing happened. You chose not to believe me."

"How could I believe you when you literally screwed me over the first time?"

"Look, I'm not here to regurgitate. Just saying you have some nerve giving me crap after what you did."

"Do you want to know the reason I told you?"

Nate's silence confuses me, making me unsure if he wants me to continue. After a moment, he nods.

"You kept wanting to get me back. We were both lying to each other—or keeping stuff from each other."

"I'm not sure what's worse," he contemplates.

"Seems like you're pretty damn good at both."

He leans back on the counter and folds his arms. "What you did is just as bad."

"Spare me. You never would've confessed. I'm the one who confronted you."

Nate laughs. He laughs hard, like the time at the park when he heard the news the first time around. "You're joking, right? You think confessing excuses your behavior? When you think you've heard it all—"

"I never said that. You're reading into it."

"Whatever," he scoffs. "I'm glad you told me. Makes me realize that you're not the one for me. Maybe you never were."

I bite my tongue. I bite it so hard because there are so many ways to hit below the belt on that one. Instead, we change the subject and talk about Max and what's going on at home. Nate tells me that Heather is traveling more for work and wants him to step up a bit and have the kids more often. Seems like Nate's working when they're there and isn't giving them attention, causing tension between the kids and with him and the ex.

I offer to have the kids, or at least Max once a week, and of course, he doesn't go for that, even though Max enjoys being here and hanging out with Chili and me. He's convinced I'm not a good influence, whatever that means, and we leave it there because, with good timing, the whistle from the kettle distracts me.

"You sure you don't want any tea?" I ask.

He shakes his head and leaves the kitchen. Chili chases a ball that bumps up against a barstool and Max giggles as he chases behind her.

"Time to say good-bye," Nate says to Max.

"Aww, come on, Dad. Five minutes."

"No, let's go. Your sister's waiting for us. I'll talk to your mom about visiting Maggie. How's that sound?"

Max smiles as he puts his shoes on and when I ask for a hug, he stands with his arms hanging to the side while I wrap mine around him.

"Be good," I say. "Actually, don't be good. Be you."

Max opens the door and dashes out to the car. He waves before hopping in.

"Thanks," Nate says and before he leaves adds, "Let's not do this again, the whole blaming game. My behavior wasn't commendable, neither was yours. Maybe something was missing from our marriage."

"You're right. Let's not do this again," I say and close up behind him without recognizing or agreeing about the failure of our marriage. Something was missing. At this point, it doesn't matter. Being nostalgic for something that didn't exist or existed for the wrong reasons no longer paralyzes me.

It's the first time in a long time that I don't want to slink down to the floor with Chili on one side and a bottle of wine on the other. And even if I did, there wouldn't be time for it. Drew's coming over soon, and my nerves get the best of me as I think about sharing my story— and my lie—on his podcast with possibly thousands listening in.

CHAPTER 50

Chili goes berserk when there's a knock on the door, as she does every time. You'd think she'd be used to his knock by now but her "it's a stranger" mode kicks in until she sees the friendly face. Drew bends down to give Chili a good scratch behind the ear. He picks up the duffel bag and throws it across his shoulder.

"We've got a choice of two rooms," I say after a kiss. "Let me show you what I'm thinking."

"I'm sure either will be great."

I take him to the office in the back and then show him the spare bedroom upstairs.

"Let's use this one," he says. "It's perfect. It'll be quieter."

Drew sets up his equipment, and Chili sits and watches him go back and forth, plugging cords in and setting up the mics. He asks me to grab an extra chair and places them side by side in front of the desk, then goes through the motions of how he'll record and master it before putting the episode on his channel.

"Here," he says and pulls out one of the chairs. "Let me know if that's comfortable."

I wiggle around and get up to add a pillow to the back. "There, that's better."

For about ten minutes, we record a few test runs and he says it sounds perfect. Drew checks our connection and makes sure his headphones sit just right.

"Are you ready?"

"I guess," I say nervously.

"You'll be great. Remember, nobody will have a clue who you are. Say anything that comes to mind. Just be yourself and make sure you talk into the mic normally or we'll get some distortion. I'll do a little intro first. Then wait for me to introduce you," Drew says as he puts introduce in air quotes.

"Got it," I add and salute him.

He uses his fingers to countdown from five to one and right away gets focused. "Hey, everyone, Drew Stafford here. Some of you might know me from my other podcast, *The Business of Lying*, which is now in its fifth season. Welcome to the very first episode of *Love the Way They Lie*, my new podcast devoted to getting all that bothersome stuff off your chest."

Drew pauses for a second and winks at me before continuing. "*The Business of Lying* is all about lying in the business world—and if it's okay to lie to protect your brand and company. For *Love the Way They Lie*, we're getting personal, so to speak.

"Here's how it works: What are your stories? What have you lied about? Do you want listeners to tell you whether the lie you've told is acceptable or forgivable? Don't worry. Everyone remains anonymous—even those who give us feedback—so you can tell us your darkest, deepest lies and not feel judged by someone you know. Anyways, let's get this started. I'm excited to have my first guest. Let's call her Julie. She's a nurse from

Philadelphia. Julie, thanks for joining us." Drew looks at me and reaches for my hand.

"Thanks. Great being here."

"Julie, are you ready to share your lie?"

I pretend to be Julie, take a deep breath, and exhale. I'm about to begin but to tell the lie, I have to tell the story that led to it. How I was married to a cheater who'd cheated before. I change Nate's name and all the other details about how the truth came out, especially the part about the picture at the DMV.

"First of all," Drew chimes in. "I'm so sorry you had to go through that. Divorce is really hard. And now, so we get this straight for our listeners: What's your lie? The fact that you had an affair and kept it from your ex-husband?"

"Nope."

Drew picks up on my nervousness. He reaches for my hand again and I continue.

"I lied about having an affair. I never had one. Made it all up so he'd leave me alone. He wouldn't stop even after the divorce. Kept showing up…more than once. I wanted to tell him something that would make him hate me, really hate me. If I'm honest—for a change—I wanted to hurt him for what he did to me."

"Ahhh, gotcha. You never had an affair."

"That's right. I thought I could get past his betrayal. I wanted to move on and be mature. Obviously I couldn't."

"Okay, listeners, you got that? So now we need to hear from you: Was it acceptable for Julie to tell her ex-husband about a fictional affair so he'd stop bothering her—and also to hurt him? Head over to LoveTheWayTheyLie.com and let us know. Click on Julie from Philadelphia and cast your vote. Once you click, you'll have thirty-two seconds to decide and it'll prompt you when you have ten seconds left."

He pauses for a moment. "Why only thirty-two seconds? Because I don't want you to overthink it. Go with what you feel is right. It was also my age when I made a big decision: to leave my full-time job and start my consulting business, which led to my books and podcasts. And I've never looked back. Okay, enough about me. While we're waiting, let's hear from a few of our sponsors."

Drew presses the mute button on his computer and looks my way. "You did great!" he says and kisses my cheek.

"You know why I like you, right?" I blurt out at the stupidest time.

"Because of my huge—"

"Heart."

"I swear I was gonna say that!" he teases.

"Right," I tease back and continue. "Because you were honest with me about why you didn't reach out to me."

"I leave all the lying to my guests." He winks and comes in for another kiss, then stops when he realizes that it's time to get back to the podcast.

He puts his finger to his lips, motioning to be quiet. "Hey, guys, we're back. Thanks so much, Julie, for sharing your story with us."

"Sounds weird to say 'my pleasure' but it was."

Drew pauses for a second and pets Chili, who puts her head on his leg. "For our next episode, we'll have a waiter from Sacramento joining us to share his lie. He was in quite the pickle and had a big decision to make. You definitely don't want to miss it. In the meantime, visit LoveTheWayTheyLie.com, where we'll share Julie's results and where you can ask her questions in the comments section. We'll keep the voting and comments open for one month following the episode."

He taps my knee for the final cue and we both say in unison, "And remember, if you tell us that you've never lied in your life, you'd be lying."

Drew hits stop and double-checks that it's no longer recording. He stretches and, a moment later, gets up and starts pulling the cords out and wrapping them up. "So," he says with a cheeky smile. "What did you think?"

"You want the truth?"

He laughs and nods. I'm about to tell him when Chili gets in the middle and we spend a few minutes giving her some attention.

"It's great," I say. "Pretty sure you'll be doing a gazillion episodes."

"Why? Because people love to lie?"

"No, but people love getting stuff off their chest. And listeners can be honest because they don't know anyone personally—and being anonymous is huge." I lean back in the chair. "Just Drew, you're pretty brilliant."

"Thanks for giving me a second chance."

I want to tell him that it isn't a second chance; second chances are when you screw up. It's what I mistakenly give to untrustworthy people like Nate.

Drew leans over the desk and picks up his phone to choose a song from his playlist. It's one I've never heard before, and the lyrics haunt me.

"That's beautiful. Who is it?"

"Tame Impala. I discovered them on a trip to LA. Loved them ever since."

The lyrics play out and they're making me choke up. Drew notices and reaches for my hand. We lean against the edge of the desk and continue to listen. When it ends, I ask to hear it again.

The song unfolds a second time and makes me wonder about the person he's singing about. And I can't help but think of Ryan. The time we danced to Duran Duran. About the night we kissed in the hotel hallway. When we compared paper airplanes. How he looked at me while singing karaoke. Every moment that he made my heart beat faster.

I want to push away the memories. It's hard to let go: the chemistry we had so quickly; the passion we felt; the way my body warmed to his touch. It makes me linger too long. I finally stay in the moment with Drew, because he's a person I can trust. It's a moment that nobody has connived or planned. It's a moment that's as pure as it gets.

The song ends, and Drew looks at me and smiles. We kiss, but I'm not feeling it, not this time anyway, not like the first night or when we were in Puerto Rico. Is it because it's the first time I'm completely sober? Or because Ryan keeps haunting me?

The words from my letter to him mess with my head, making me second-guess everything. How much should chemistry play in a relationship? What about trust and values? Should they be more important? Should I have given myself a break from dating to heal after my divorce?

"It's too much, too soon," I blurt out after we kiss.

"Okay," Drew says hesitantly. He moves his bag to the floor and sits on the ottoman. "I don't get it. You seemed fine a minute ago." He looks away and snickers. "Maybe I should've picked a different song."

My head's spinning with so many mixed emotions about making the right decision. "It's not that. I'm just not ready for a relationship."

"That's such bullshit. People only say that when they're not with the right person."

I want to get up and hug him, to tell him it's not true. But I'd be lying—to him and to myself—because Al's words still eat at me: that we need to follow our gut. "Honestly, not sure what I want." I look away, feeling his anger—and my shitty timing—as they weigh on me. "It's happening too fast. I think I need to be alone and work on myself. And I don't want to hurt you."

He sighs and starts packing up what's left of his gear. "It's not about hurting me. It's about being honest. I get the feeling you're keeping something from me—like there's more to the story you told me about your ex."

Chili jumps up when Drew puts the bag over his shoulder and walks out of the room.

I follow them downstairs.

"You know," he says when he gets to the foyer, "maybe I shouldn't have waited for you to get divorced after all."

"Why do you say that?"

"It would've given us more time to get to know each other while being cautious during your separation." He bends down to pet Chili. "Maybe we rushed into it by waiting? It's as if you signed the divorce papers and we said 'Okay, let's go!'"

"Like sprinting without a solid warm-up?"

"Pretty much," he says and leans against the railing by the stairs.

"Yeah, that was me a few months ago, the sprinter." I finally open up. "You weren't the first guy I dated after splitting with my ex. And I'm not over him yet. That's the part I didn't tell you. And that's it, I swear."

Drew puts down his bag and sits on the stairs. He waits in silence, thinking there's more. When we stare at each other for a few seconds, he continues. "Thanks for sharing. Can I ask why you broke up?"

"Turns out we have different values."

He nods. "I get it. Maybe he was your rebound?"

I pause to think it through, because I'm not even sure. "At the time, I thought jumping into something new would help me heal from the pain of my marriage ending. All it did was distract me. It was a Band-Aid."

"So which is it?"

"What do you mean?" I ask.

"Are you ending it with me because you need to heal from your marriage? Or do you need to get over the guy?"

Drew's such a nice guy. He doesn't deserve to be hurt—he deserves the truth. Our lives aren't a damn podcast where we can have people help us decide what's right or wrong. "Both," I wind up saying as my voice cracks.

Drew gets up and comes close. He puts his arms around me, and after a short moment, lets go and picks up his keys from the table.

"If you ever need to talk, I'm here. I mean it."

His words show me his maturity, a trait I still need to work on. And they make sense. Maybe more than anything, even more than chemistry or even values and trust, it's timing that overrides everything.

We hug good-bye and after he leaves, Chili looks up and follows me to the kitchen. On the counter, there's a bottle of my favorite red wine, the kind that has been a crutch and hanging around a little too much lately. I pick up the bottle, place it in the pantry, and reach for the tea that sits next to a can of chicken noodle soup.

It's not Chili's dinner time yet, but my furry companion deserves a special treat for being there for me all these months. After making my tea, I hold up the can and Chili starts wagging her tail and jumping in place. She follows me over to the counter and watches me open up the soup and dump it into her bowl.

"Sit," I demand. At first, she's too excited to listen.

When she finally calms down, I place her bowl on the kitchen floor and, while drinking my tea, watch her gobble up the soup.

A toddler running around outside, wild and carefree with a contagious laugh, catches my attention. It makes me want to jump in the car and drive with the windows down and nowhere to go—with the freedom and peace not felt in a while, a combination I've been dreaming of, the kind that works hand-in-hand.

"Chili, let's go."

She follows me to the hallway with as much enthusiasm as a few minutes ago while she gobbled up her treat. This time, I don't make her sit. I don't even put the leash on.

She trails me out to the car and jumps in the back before we take off and down our street. When we hit a red light, I put on my 90s playlist and floor it when we get on the highway. All four windows are down and, in the back, Chili has her head out with her ears flapping in the wind, making it matter as if her life depends on it.

EPILOGUE

If you tell us that you've never lied in your life, you'd be lying.
–Anonymous

Hello and welcome to Love The Way They Lie, a website that's devoted to a podcast featuring the same great name. Launched in 2019 by keynote speaker and best-selling author Drew Stafford, the *Love the Way They Lie* podcast offers a way for our guests to get stuff off their chests anonymously and without judgment from the people they know. In each episode, a guest shares their story and lets listeners decide if the lie that's told is acceptable or forgivable.

Thanks for visiting—and don't forget to subscribe to the podcast where all the action (and lying!) happens.

Episode One:
Julie from Philadelphia

In our first episode, Julie shared a secret that involved her ex-husband. Haven't listened yet? Don't worry, it's available—just don't read below until you've listened to the episode because, you know, spoiler alert!

For those who've already listened: Was Julie's lie acceptable or forgivable?

Votes are trickling in and there's still time to cast yours. So far, more than 3,000 people have voted. We'll share the final results one month after the episode airs.

Any questions for Julie? Add them below, where we'll keep it all anonymous!

CL489: Hey Julie, thanks for sharing your story. I was on the fence about how to vote and my time ran out! I have a question: Would you consider giving your ex-husband a second chance?

JULIE: I think you mean third chance! There's no way. I'm not going back on my word—or back to our old pretend-bullshit life. Sounds like I'm bitter, I know. That's not the case. I just don't want to live in denial and act as if nothing happened—he betrayed me twice, at least that I know of.

SU225: Do you think you got involved too soon with someone new after leaving your husband?

JULIE: Probably. Not sure if I was ready, maybe, trying to fill a void, or perhaps, I should have waited longer. Who knows? Living with what-ifs was my old life. I'm trying to live in the moment—although doing this podcast probably hasn't helped! Thanks for your question!

TI792: Do you think people end up with the wrong person? Do you have any regrets getting married?

JULIE: I have absolutely no regrets! I loved my ex-husband and got married for the right reasons. Not sure if people end up with the wrong person. It's not for me to answer, because it's so individual. Maybe we're supposed to be with more than one person in our lifetime? Because not one person can fulfill all our needs. Maybe there's room to love more than one or more than once. And maybe that's another podcast idea for Drew 😌.

JE133: Hey Julie, I'm one who believes that your lie was acceptable and forgivable. To me, it seems you lied to get him out of your life, and to protect yourself and set boundaries. I think it was okay.

JULIE: Thanks for your vote of confidence. Maybe you're right. I think there's a huge difference. I didn't cheat; he did. Although, I did intentionally lie to hurt someone, and that's not cool. I was willing for him to think I was a hypocrite and a cheater so he'd move on and forget about me. Is that so terrible?

DT844: Come on, seriously?! You didn't think he'd do it again after cheating on you the first time? Instead of voting whether your lie is acceptable, we should be voting on whether you were a fool to stay.

JULIE: I also thought I was a fool to stay—didn't realize it until the second time it happened. But guess what? It's not that easy. When you're in love with someone, you want to believe they'll change. Have you ever been in that situation? Would you have really left?

BE563: Hey Julie, I've had some shitty luck with ex-girlfriends, and it's hard for me to get involved. I think everyone's always gonna be like my exes, so I keep things casual! That said, I still voted that your lie was unacceptable and unforgivable. Two wrongs don't make a right. You should've ghosted him and moved on.

JULIE: Thanks for your honesty. I'm not a fan of ghosting, especially if it's someone I've known and loved for years. I felt like I had to nip it in the bud, or he would've kept at it. So not sure what's worse: being an ass for ghosting or being an ass for making him think I was a cheater. In the long run, I guess it shouldn't matter. What matters is that I can live with my decision. And living with our decisions is what should matter to all of us.

AN AUTHOR'S NOTE

Thank you for reading *Love the Way They Lie*. I'm so grateful you picked my novel when there are thousands of other choices! You probably already know this but, just in case, word of mouth is an author's best friend. If you liked my story, please spread the word. And if you have the time, I'd be grateful if you left a review. It really helps readers decide what to read next.

ACKNOWLEDGMENTS

I always say I'm a late bloomer, but it's still hard to believe this is my third novel and that it has taken me this long to get here. After my second book, I wasn't sure if I had another one in me. Then, one day, an idea hit me while driving (as many book ideas do). And this one stuck. The idea was: When is a lie acceptable and/or forgivable?

I took this idea, developed the story and characters, wrote the first draft, and worked on it a lot more. Two years later, here we are. None of this would have been possible if it weren't for some amazing people in my life. I've always said that, to me, being a writer isn't a lonely profession. And that's mainly due to the love and support from those close to me—and those from the book world near and far.

And, now, it's time to thank:

Libby Tripp Cox, Jennifer Schulman, and Jill Yager for sticking by me and saying an enthusiastic "yes" when I asked if you'd be my advance readers again. Your valuable feedback on yet another one of my novels helped so much. I'll never forget the messages—through voicemail, email, or sticky notes—left for me when you finished reading.

Sherron Mayes, my editor extraordinaire from The Editing Den, for your incredibly detailed story analysis as well as the individual edits and examples on how to improve my writing. Your critical eye for storytelling and character development blew me away, and I'm lucky to have worked with you. And Faith Williams, who also proofread my second novel, for making sure everything looked great toward the end.

Christine Chirichella, Elyse Cooper, Beth Falk, Rosalie A. Lacorazza, and Natasha Moussavi Lewis for your continuous support and sharing of my book news. And family, friends, and colleagues for cheering me on and asking when my next novel is coming out.

Authors Edwin Fontánez, Allison Winn Scott, and Rochelle Weinstein for great advice and support. And, Edwin, thank you for reminding me during a much-needed phone call the real reason why I do this.

Christina Huber for also being one of my advance readers and always being excited about my work. You've been there since my debut novel released in 2017, and I'll never forget this. Thank you, also, to the countless book bloggers and bookstagrammers who've read and mentioned my books and who've supported the writing community as a whole.

Jeffrey Malone for making me laugh (a lot!), listening to my book ideas, appreciating my crazy imagination, and making it such an easy choice to give it a go again. In case you're wondering, I'm still not a fan of a certain cymbal, but to make it up to you, I'll make sure a character in one of my future novels is.

Marla Greif for also being one of my advance readers and offering juicy bits to consider adding while we chatted on the phone for hours. Most important, for your love, loyalty, and friendship over the past three decades. It can't be put into words (even though I'm a writer!) how lucky I am that you're in my life.

Sasha for your creativity, talent, and insight. You may not remember but, back in 2019, we were sitting in my car and I told you about a pivotal moment from the book I was about to start writing. You said, "It would never happen that way," and then explained to me why it wasn't realistic. I'm so glad I took your advice! And I'm so lucky to be your mom.

And for my parents, whom I miss every day. Your chilled-out and strong-willed personalities live on in me, allowing me to "go with the flow" while remaining determined. These traits are exactly what's needed in the writing and publishing world.

About the Author

Linda Smolkin always wanted to be a writer—ever since she saw her first TV commercial and wondered how to pen those clever ads. She got her degree in journalism and became a copywriter. Linda landed a job at an ad agency where she worked for several years before joining the nonprofit world. She is the author of a few novels and writes about family, friendship, and moral dilemmas. When not in front of the computer, Linda's behind the drums, escaping into her pretend rock-star world. For more information, visit her website at lindasmolkin.com.

ALSO BY LINDA SMOLKIN

Among the Branded

The Secret We Lost